THE TREASURE OF PARAGON BOOK 4

# THE DRAGON OF SEDONA

*USA TODAY* BESTSELLING AUTHOR
# GENEVIEVE JACK

**Dear Reader,**

Love is the truest magic and the most fulfilling fantasy. Thank you for coming along on this journey as I share the tale of the Treasure of Paragon, nine exiled royal dragon shifters destined to find love and their way home.

There are three things you can expect from a Genevieve Jack novel: magic will play a key role, unexpected twists are the norm, and love will conquer all.

## *The Treasure of Paragon Reading Order*

The Dragon of New Orleans, Book 1

Windy City Dragon, Book 2,

Manhattan Dragon, Book 3

The Dragon of Sedona, Book 4

The Dragon of Cecil Court, Book 5

Highland Dragon, Book 6

Hidden Dragon, Book 7

The Dragons of Paragon, Book 8

The Last Dragon, Book 9

Keep in touch to stay in the know about new releases, sales, and giveaways.

Join my VIP reader group
Sign up for my newsletter

Now, let's spread our wings (or at least our pages) and escape together!

*Genevieve Jack*

# PROLOGUE

*October 1699*
*Appalachian Forest, North America*

"Run, Maiara, run!" Her father shoved her along the path, tugging their horse's reins behind him. The weary beast could move no faster, laden down as she was with pelts and supplies. Prickling fear raised the hair on Maiara's nape, and she desperately tried to incite the animal to move, joining her father in his efforts, but the mare dug in her hooves. The headstrong beast won the battle of wills.

Maiara's moccasins slipped on the slick mud, flinging her to the forest floor. She broke her fall with her bare hands, the earthy scent of decaying leaves filling her nose. Above them, her hawk circled, the bird's shrill screams a warning as their pursuer closed in. Crushing pain throbbed within her rib cage, more from her pounding heart than from the fall.

She couldn't think about the pain. Not now. With a single-minded focus, Maiara scrambled to her feet and clutched her father's arm. "Leave her!" She pried the reins from his hands despite his protests.

An arrow whizzed past her ear and lodged in the tree behind her. Her father's blue eyes widened over his ruddy cheeks. Finally he saw reason. Abandoning the mare, he grasped her hand. His was large, burly, and pale. Hers was small, dark, and smooth. There was comfort in that hand. Trust. He'd saved her life before.

"Run," he commanded. She did.

They weaved among the trees, the monster haunting the edge of her vision. At first the thing appeared to be a man in the image of a warrior from the Mohawk tribe, bald except for a roach of black hair decorated with porcupine quills, bones, and feathers. War paint striped his cheeks. Despite the bracing chill, he wore only his breechcloth and a pendant, an orb the size of a human eye that winked at her as it pulsed a soft blue light at the base of his throat.

The monster might have looked like a man, but if what followed Maiara and her father had ever been human, he was no longer. Now he was a *wendigo*, a demon sent from the netherworld to rid this land of her kind, a relentless shadow, disappearing when the sun was high, only to stretch toward her again. He would not rest until every one of her people was dead. The blue wink of the stone around his neck turned her blood to ice. Whatever that was, it was unnatural, perhaps a remnant of the evil curse that had made him.

Another arrow flew and she ducked, narrowly avoiding its barb. The *wendigo* stopped at the place their mare blocked the path and roared. Its eyes glowed as red as burning coals, and its mouth opened wide enough to swallow her entire head. All illusion of its humanity melted with that bone-chilling roar.

Now the mare moved, tried to gallop away, but the *wendigo* snared its haunches with a set of razor-sharp claws that sprang from its hands. In a flurry of flashing teeth, the hell spawn tore through the pony, ignoring its equine shrieks. Blood sprayed. Maiara pressed her hand to her mouth as the scent of death reached her, and her stomach threatened to spill its contents. She averted her eyes, but the crunch of bones echoed through the woods long after the horse's squeals abated.

Maiara strained to put more space between them and the demon. She gripped her father's arm tighter and forced him forward. They both knew the meal wouldn't be enough for the *wendigo*. The savage beast had an insatiable appetite.

"You must protect yourself." Her father stumbled. He could not keep up with the pace of their run. She used every muscle in her diminutive frame to help him to his feet. "It's the only way." He was pleading with her now as if she were a petulant child.

Another arrow, another roar. As she'd feared, the creature had already resumed its hunt. It would never quit. Never stop. Not until Maiara was dead.

"Now, Maiara. Go!"

The demon's gaping maw drooled only yards behind them. Her father's gray hair was slick with sweat. Through a throat raw from panting, she rasped, "No! Try harder."

His feet gained purchase and they were off again. "How did it find us?" he muttered, more to himself than to her. They were fools to think the *wendigo* wouldn't pursue them, not after everything. He stopped short, clawed at his chest as if it hurt. "Maiara! You must leave me."

"I won't," she screamed, shaking her head. She would not abandon her last living family.

"You have no choice." He squeezed her hand again. Her father had raised her. Her father had saved her. He'd always been wise, and now the truth in his gaze cut straight to her heart. "Don't let your mother's death be in vain."

Above them, her hawk cried out another warning, this one sharper than the last. She heard the bowstring snap, the whoosh of the arrow. Her father's eyes widened, and in a final burst of speed, he shifted in front of her. The arrow, meant for her, landed in his back. He collapsed against her. Her scream was silenced by a sharp bite of pain. The tip of the arrow that had passed through her father's body pierced her chest.

Trembling, she thrust with all her might, tearing the arrowhead from her flesh and allowing her father's dying body to fall from her arms. A sob caught in her throat.

"Go," he whispered. His eyes turned unblinking toward the heavens.

Too late now. Too late. She raced down the path, breathless, thighs burning. Blood from the wound in her chest blossomed like a rose on the front of her deerskin tunic. The *wendigo* closed in at alarming speed.

She had no choice and no reason now to stay behind. At a full run, she scanned the trees, extending her arms. Desperate prayers to the Great Spirit tumbled from her lips. With a last glance toward her faithful hawk above, she did what she had to do.

She escaped.

# CHAPTER ONE

2018
*Sedona, Arizona*

Alexander felt like Wile E. Coyote, only instead of blowing himself up trying to kill the Road Runner, his efforts to free himself from the purgatory he suffered were repeatedly thwarted by a different sort of bird.

His personal vexation was a red-tailed hawk hundreds of years past its natural expiration date yet far too stubborn to die. Unlike the cartoon Road Runner, the hawk made no attempt to run from him with a resounding *meep, meep!* and leave him in its dust.

On the contrary, this bird rarely left his side. Despite his many attempts to separate himself from the winged creature, it remained an obsessive, magical pain in the ass.

"You're not going to stop me this time, Nyx," he said, meeting the hawk's intelligent amber eyes. Ironic that she resisted so thoroughly when his motivation revolved around her. The two of them were cogs in a never-ending wheel of pain. He only wished to throw a wrench in the gears and save them both.

He called the bird Nyx after the Greek goddess of the night. Red-tailed hawks weren't nocturnal animals, but this one had ushered darkness into his life. The kind of darkness that lived on the inside of a man that no amount of desert sun could ever reach.

At one time, the bird had belonged to his mate, Maiara. She'd called the hawk Nikan, the Potawatomi word for "my friend." The two had been inseparable until the night Maiara was brutally murdered. After her death, after her body was burned, the hawk attached to him like a tick burrowing for blood, presumably bound to him by the grief they shared.

He refused to call her Nikan after that. She was no friend of his. She was a ghost. A demon. She was Nyx, the night, and her darkness had been with him ever since.

A stab of longing cut through him. Thanks to Nyx, not a day passed he didn't think of Maiara. The bird was a constant reminder of his loss.

"You have to let me do this," he pleaded with her. He wasn't beyond begging. Anything to end this horror-go-round of an existence.

The early-morning sun was blinding as he scanned the horizon from the top of one of the massive red mesas Sedona was known for. In his hand, he gripped a roll of thin, sharp wire. In his mind, he held an appetite for death. No, that wasn't entirely true. It wasn't that he wanted his life to end, just the pain.

For a dragon, losing a mate was like having a thin layer of skin scraped from their body. Everything was painful, stinging, astringent. His body and soul were raw nerves, left with no protection against the elements, no shelter from the burning sun. He hurt. Everywhere.

With a deep breath, he took in the beauty of his surroundings one final time. The landscape's signature red color, courtesy of iron oxide that veined like blood through the stone, provided a sharp contrast to the cerulean sky. The topography was roughly as dry and coarse as the surface of Mars, yet brimming with life, the occasional grouping of desert trees or cactus growing from the stone. Survival in the bleakest of circumstances.

There'd been a time he'd found its mystique comforting. Not anymore. A clear indication the time had come to end this madness.

"You don't want to go on like this, do you?" He stared at Nyx as if to will an answer from her. She let out a shrill cry that let him know exactly what she thought of his plan. "I will never understand you. This has to be as much a nightmare for you as it is for me. Whatever Maiara did to you to make you immortal has bound you to me. Never able to live as a wild bird. Never able to mate with your own kind."

He shoved his hands in the pockets of his jacket. "Have you ever stopped to think that if I died, perhaps you could be free? Truly free."

She flapped her wings and leaped to his arm, her talons digging into the black leather. Not that her grip was a threat to his dragon skin anyway. He might have looked human with his wings tucked away, but he was far tougher and healed much faster than any man. The hawk rubbed its head against his bearded cheek, its soft russet feathers ruffling at the contact. She brushed her beak against his nose.

As he stared at her, he saw his reflection in her tawny

eyes. By the Mountain, he looked like shit. Even in silhouette, he could tell he badly needed a haircut and to trim his beard, and he knew the rest of him wasn't any better. He was emaciated and likely smelled of liquor and self-loathing.

He gently nudged her back onto the branch of the juniper tree. "That's enough. Wait there. This will be over soon."

It was hard to kill a dragon. Technically, he was immortal. Poison wouldn't work. Walking in front of a semitruck wouldn't work. If alcohol could've done him in, he'd already be dead. By the Mountain, he bought tequila by the case. It would be easier to run his motorcycle off a bridge, but a fall for a dragon wasn't much of a threat. Dragons couldn't drown or burn to death.

There was only one foolproof way to kill a dragon: decapitation. He checked that the wire was properly fastened around the base of the tree and placed the noose around his neck, then backed up to get a running start.

This was going to hurt.

Glancing toward Nyx, he was relieved to find her gone. Maybe his lecture had gotten through to her after all. She'd left him. It was a sign.

He ran for the edge.

Three steps from the brink, Nyx flew straight up, sheering the side of the cliff. He cried out. Her wings fluttered against his cheeks and talons scraped his neck. Unable to stop his momentum, his feet slipped out from under him and he became a baseball player sliding into home, only the plate was open air beyond the cliff's edge. His dragon's wings tried to punch out but got caught in his leather jacket, store-bought—not part of the specially designed wardrobe his oread had made him to accommodate his extra appendages. *Fuck.* For a second he seemed to hang in the bright blue sky, Nyx with his noose in her claws hovering over him.

"You mangy-feathered, slimy-beaked, bit—" He dropped like a stone.

His back collided with the gravel in front of his motorcycle. *Oww.* Immortal or not, it hurt when bones broke. Perfectly still, he stared at the hawk as she banked and circled down toward him, her cries echoing off the cliffs.

"I really hate you," he whispered. It came out as a squeak. He worked to pull breath into his aching lungs as a sickening slurp indicated his bones were already healing. Not too much damage then. Slowly he raised a hand and ran his fingers through his hair. The back of his head was sore, but there wasn't any blood. He was fine. Depressingly whole.

The crunch of wheels on gravel turned his head. A minivan had pulled off the highway and parked next to his bike, and a tall white man wearing dark socks and sandals was climbing out of the driver's seat.

"Hey, are you all right?" The man hurried to him and leaned over Alexander, the floppy brim of his hat casting shade over his face and blocking his view of Nyx.

"I'm fine."

"What are you doing lying on the side of the road?"

He glanced toward his bike. "I'm, uh, just resting."

"Buddy, this is not the place. Someone could run you over."

He cleared his throat. If only that would be enough to do him in. "Hmm. Right. I'll be on my way then." He allowed the man to help him up and gave his neck a good crack.

"Hey... Hey! Are you that guy? You know, that guy who

paints the desert scenes with the bird." The man turned to the van and yelled, "Honey, it's that guy!"

Alexander groaned. Oh dear goddess, please open the earth and swallow him down to hell pronto. This was the last thing he needed today.

A woman in a Minnie Mouse T-shirt, jean shorts, and a green visor hopped down from the passenger seat of the minivan.

"My word, it is him. Alexander! We just bought one of your paintings. You're so talented."

"Thanks," he mumbled. "I really have to go."

"Oh wait, can we get a picture?"

"I, uh..."

The woman had already pulled one of his paintings from the back of the van. He recognized it—a piece he'd done a few years ago of Nyx, the red rock, and the blue sky. It was a money piece. It meant nothing to him; he'd just painted it for the money. It was the Thomas Kinkade of his work, beautiful and meaningless.

She held it in front of his chest, her husband holding the other end of the canvas, and then popped her arm out to take a selfie. He did not smile.

"One, two, three...," she prompted.

The glare from the cheesy grins on either side of him was almost blinding. Out of sheer guilt, he popped the corner of his closed lips a quarter of an inch. A series of clicks later, she slid her phone back into her pocket.

"Thank you! What a special moment," she squealed.

She loaded the painting into the van, and the two waved their goodbyes. He watched them drive away from the seat of his motorcycle.

Once they were gone, Nyx landed on the handlebars of

his Harley-Davidson and cooed her apologies. He glared at the bird. "So that's how it's going to be? No way out?"

She chirped and lifted into the clear blue sky.

He revved the engine. "What a fucking Monday."

# CHAPTER TWO

S edona, for all intents and purposes, was a desert, consisting of red rock, dry weather, and plenty of sun. Technically, the area got about sixteen inches of rain a year, an amount that earned it the label of semiarid, not a desert, if you were a stickler for the details. Still, for an average of 278 days per year, Sedona's rocky terrain baked beneath cheery golden rays without a hint of a raindrop.

This was a land of spiritual awakenings, of rejuvenation, home to an untold number of energy vortexes—intersections of natural, electromagnetic earth energy that humans here said had transformational properties. People came from all over the world to meditate, reflect, and heal here. And he'd witnessed their triumph hundreds of times.

*If only it worked on dragons.*

Alexander loved the heat and the rust-colored terrain as much as his dark heart could love anything—it reminded him of the volcanic environment of Paragon, the realm where he was born—but he was still waiting for that healing to kick in.

Before Maiara, before everything was ruined, he'd grown up in a palace among his siblings, a middle son of whom the royal family had relatively few expectations. And so as an introspective and creative child, he'd taught himself to sketch and paint. Art in all its forms had been his escape from the boredom that accompanied his privileged circumstances.

All that was over now. It was a million years ago, lost in the wreckage of his memories. His art did not hold the same joy or provide the escape it once had. Hell, if it did, if he had one way to lose himself, life might be tolerable.

He passed the sign at the entrance to the Church of New Horizons and cut the engine to his Harley. If his landlord didn't hear the bike, he might make it inside without another awkward conversation about taking part in the classes at the retreat. He'd rented a room there for years but never partook in the spiritual hikes, meditation, or yoga. Actually, he thought the whole lot of it was bullshit. But the owner and landlord, determined to save his tormented soul, had never given up on trying to convince him to participate.

Nyx, who'd been flying above him for most of the ride home, landed on his shoulder and rubbed her cheek against his. "Yeah, yeah. I forgive you. I don't understand you, but I forgive you."

Silently Alexander walked his bike up the drive and parked it in his spot in the small lot, then crept around the side of the stucco walls of the southwestern-style building. He breathed a sigh of relief when he set foot on the stairs to his second-floor apartment until the sound of sandals on gravel preceded a cheery, "Hello, friend!"

Alexander closed his eyes and pivoted slowly to face the owner of New Horizons and his landlord, Master Gu. As

THE DRAGON OF SEDONA

usual, the man wore loose-fitting black pants, a long-sleeved red tunic that tied at the waist, and a silver braid that ran down the center of his back. One clouded eye stared unseeing into the beyond while the other looked straight into him.

His appearance gave him a stereotypical master of martial arts vibe, but the truth was David Gu wasn't a master of anything. New Horizons was his invention, not an established religion, and until fifteen years ago, the guy had been a car salesman in Detroit. Somehow though, he'd established this retreat house and regularly filled it with people willing to pay top dollar for guided meditation, yoga, and learning how to harness the healing energy of the Sedona vortexes.

"Good morning," Alexander said flatly.

"Your aura is muddled today," Gu said, his brow dipping. "You need meditation and acupuncture to open your chakras and purify your qi energy."

Alexander removed his sunglasses and gave the man a steady look in his good eye. He wondered what had tipped him off to his foul mood. Perhaps the rocks embedded in the back of his leather jacket. He tucked his glasses into his inner pocket. "My aura is top notch, my friend, and my qi is flowing like the piss of an incontinent badger. I think your aura reader is on the fritz today."

Master Gu shook his head. "My aura reader is operational. Your bird, for example, has a beautiful spring green aura as she always does. Yours, on the other hand, is usually blue, and today it is dark gray and muddy."

"My bird has an aura?" Alexander laughed. The guy was wackier than a two-headed javelina.

"Oh yes, a strong one. She's the first, you know."

"The first what?"

"Bird with its own aura. Normally, birds have a collective energy. All the same. Bright blue and white like the sky. Your bird is different."

Alexander cast Nyx a sideways glance. She bonked his cheek with her beak. This bird was different all right. Immortal. Bound to him by a mystical force he didn't understand, like two moons orbiting each other as they gradually drifted into the sun. Different was an understatement. Try tragic.

"Your aura just got darker," Master Gu said with a tone of warning. "Staying like this is inviting misfortune into your life! The soul longs for balance. No one can endure spiritual pain forever. You must allow me to purify your qi before it is too late. I insist. I will do it for free."

Rubbing the throbbing ache that had begun over his right eye, Alexander cleared his throat and found what remained of his patience. "Wow, you *must* be serious. I've never known you to offer a freebie to anyone."

"I am worried about the darkness in you, Alexander."

He nodded. "Bah. Who could have darkness in a wonderland like this?" He gestured to the postcard views surrounding New Horizons.

Gu stared at him, unblinking, which unnerved the hell out of him.

"I'll think about it," Alexander murmured despite his better judgment.

A smile warmed the older man's face and he bowed. "As you wish. Don't say I didn't warn you if you wait and things go terribly wrong. The universe has a way of working these things out if you don't deal with them yourself." The man shuffled off toward the meditation center, gravel crunching under his sandals.

"For the love of the Mountain," he muttered to Nyx, rolling his eyes as he bound up the stairs. "I need a damned drink."

He reached the second floor and slid his key into the lock to his apartment. The one-room flat was perfect for him. Small, quiet, and with enough extra room to serve as an art studio. He pushed open the door.

And a man the size of a bull slammed into him. His head slapped the floor to the sound of Nyx's screams.

THE FIRST THING ALEXANDER NOTICED WHEN HE regained consciousness was the absence of Nyx on his shoulder. A twinge of dread shot through him, and he forced his eyes open and searched for her in a panic. He struggled against restraints that bound his wrists. If anyone had hurt her...

A dark, hulking figure stepped into his field of vision. Dark hair, dark eyes that always seemed to reflect fire even when there was none, and a physique expertly trained to inflict maximum damage. Alexander tugged harder against his bindings. "Gabriel."

"Calm down, brother. We need to talk. It's important."

He blinked slowly, then swallowed past the rage in his throat. "Are you real?"

"Of course I'm real. What else would I be?"

He glanced away. Reality wasn't always an easy thing for Alexander to ground himself in lately, and considering he'd smacked his head hard that morning, it seemed reasonable to check. Still, the familiar smoky scent that filled the room was definitely Gabriel's. His brother was there, and that nugget of truth burned in his craw more than the smoke.

When their mother had cast them into this world, she'd insisted they settle in separate lands. Any extended amount of time in the same area would produce a concentrated magical signature their murderous uncle might use to find them and kill them, the same way he'd killed their older brother. It was why Alexander had settled so far from his siblings and eventually lost touch with most of them.

As many questions as he had about why his brother was there, his first priority was his pet. "What have you done with Nyx?"

"Who?"

"My hawk." He growled, low and threatening. Threats were all he could make. Alexander had spent his childhood as an unwilling participant in Gabriel's training regime; he'd only ever won a fight against the dragon once, and even then, there had been extenuating circumstances. On a good day, Gabriel could easily kick his ass. It had been a long time between good days for Alexander and even longer since he'd had a good meal. On the other hand, judging by the sheer size of his warrior brother, Gabriel had maintained his peak physical condition. That didn't mean Alexander planned to cooperate. Hell, no. There were more ways to win a battle than brute strength.

Gabriel's dark eyebrows snapped together over the bridge of his nose. "The hawk is there with my *wife*." He pointed toward a dark-haired and obviously pregnant woman standing by the window. Nyx was happily perched on her arm. Odd. He couldn't remember the hawk ever intentionally acknowledging, let alone fraternizing with, another person other than he or Maiara.

Seeing her so comfortable with the woman caused a

strange uneasy feeling in his chest. He made a kissing sound to call her to him, but she stayed where she was. Damn bird. Couldn't get rid of her most of the time and now she was all chummy with his brother's... *wife?*

Alexander's head snapped up. "Wife? Did you say wife? You're married?"

"And mated," Gabriel said. A slight smile softened the harsh lines of his mouth. "This is Raven."

Well, that was that. This had to be real. Alexander could never imagine a woman who would put up with his brother, let alone marry him. Raven was round bellied but otherwise reedy, with long hair the color of polished ebony, Mediterranean features, and light eyes that held wisdom beyond her years. An old soul. She smelled strange, unlike anything he'd ever encountered before. He took a deeper sniff. What was she? Not simply human, that was for sure.

She rubbed a circle over her beach-ball-size belly. "Nice to meet you. I apologize for the way my husband said hello. He thought you'd run if he didn't knock you down and tie you up like an animal." She gave Gabriel a disapproving look.

"He was right," Alexander admitted. "If I'd seen him coming, he'd never have found me. Anyway, we're *supposed* to stay apart, or hasn't he told you?"

"She knows. And that's why I'm here. I have news, brother. News that changes everything." Gabriel dragged the other hard wooden chair out from the table and took a seat across from him. "Our forced separation is officially over."

A chill crawled evenly along Alexander's vertebra and made his scalp itch. He could not have heard his brother right. "What are you talking about?"

"We do not have to stay apart anymore. In fact, it would

be an extremely bad idea for us to do so. Everything we were told when we left Paragon was a lie."

As Alexander tried to process the revelation Gabriel had just shared—was it true or was this some kind of a trick? —he heard footsteps and turned his head to find Raven moving for the door, the hawk still on her arm. "I'll update the others while you two chat."

Alexander tensed. "You can't take Nyx with you." He growled. "She can't go outside without me. She's, uh, trained only for me. You might lose her."

Raven's eyebrows bobbed as if she'd never considered the idea that the hawk couldn't go where it pleased. She nudged Nyx onto his shoulder. "She's beautiful. You've taken great care of her. I've never seen a domesticated hawk before."

He nodded at her, relieved to feel the familiar weight of the bird again. "Who else is here?" he asked, nodding toward the door. "You said there were others."

"Rowan, her mate, Nick, and Tobias," Raven answered lightly.

"Rowan is mated?"

Raven gave him a soft smile. "So is Tobias but his wife is not able to travel like the rest of us."

Pain radiated from the center of Alexander's chest, and he doubled over in his chair, his breath coming faster. "*Everyone* is mated?"

Gabriel grumbled, "Raven..."

She glanced in his direction and spread her hands. "I'm sorry, Alexander. I wasn't thinking. I shouldn't have unloaded that on you all at once."

Sweat broke out on his forehead, and he swallowed hard. "Please leave."

Raven backed away, and he heard the door open and close.

"She was just answering your question. She didn't realize—"

"I know." Alexander closed his eyes against the wrenching pain. "How far along is she?"

"About four and a half months."

"Congratulations. I didn't know dragons could impregnate humans." He shook his head. "Is she human? Her scent is unfamiliar. I can't put my finger on it."

Gabriel's expression closed off like Alexander had sprung a trap, and he found himself no longer staring into the face of his brother but a deadly dragon warrior. *Whoa!* That was a face he'd never wished to see again.

"I'm not here to talk about my wife."

Made uncomfortable by the intensity of his older brother's stare, Alexander shifted in his chair. "Why *are* you here, Gabriel? Really?" He'd had just about enough of this crazy visit. Enough of being tied to a freaking chair. And enough of feeling helpless. He lowered his voice. "You know as well as I do that I'm not strong enough to take you, but I am crazy enough to shift and wreck what few possessions I have here if you don't get to the point and untie me now." He leveled a deadly serious stare on his brother. "You may be stronger, but I've got a helluva lot less to lose."

"I'm here to tell you we were wrong," Gabriel said in a voice so low and gritty it reminded Alexander of asphalt. "About everything. Paragon. Mother. Brynhoff."

"I heard you the first time you said it, but I don't understand. How could this be true?"

"Eleanor didn't send us to this realm to save us. She sent us here to get us out of the way."

Alexander stilled, waiting for the punch line or at least an explanation. He hadn't heard the name Eleanor in over three hundred years, not since he was a prince of Paragon and palace guests would address his mother as Queen Eleanor. It was disconcerting to hear it fall from his brother's lips.

And he'd mentioned Brynhoff, the king and also his uncle, their kingdom having been ruled by brother and sister for millennia. Brynhoff had murdered Alexander's eldest brother, Marius, at what was supposed to be Marius's coronation. The bloody coup had been the last time he'd seen his parents or his uncle and had changed everything for him as well as his seven remaining siblings.

"What the hell are you talking about? Mother saved us. She used her magic to send us here. It would have drained her. It cost her life as well as Father's." Alexander's last memory of Paragon was of his father, Killian, defending their mother from Brynhoff as her ring glowed and her magic plowed into him.

"It was all a lie." A muscle in Gabriel's jaw twitched.

"And you know this how?" He'd seen the coup with his own eyes, experienced the shock and terror of being cast between dimensions.

"I returned to Paragon."

It was a good thing he was sitting down, because Alexander could've been knocked over with one of Nyx's feathers at the confession. He planted his feet and scooted the chair back from the table, placing space between himself and his brother. "Why the fuck would you do that?"

There was a long pause while his older brother seemed to choose his words carefully. "I was dying. I thought magic from Mother's spell book might cure me." His eyes snapped to Alexander's. "She was there, Alexander, on the throne, next to Brynhoff. She was ruling by his side. They call her empress now."

A pounding pain started in Alexander's temple. This couldn't be real. If it was, they'd separated for no reason. Everything that had happened with Maiara was meaningless. He couldn't accept that. There was too much guilt wrapped up in that package for him to bear.

"Why are you here? What do I care what's happening in Paragon?" he said.

Gabriel's mouth twisted. "She sent Scoria to kill us—me, my wife, and Tobias too."

"Scoria was here?"

"Was. He's dead now."

*"By the Mountain,"* he swore. Scoria had been a fierce warrior, devoted to his mother. To Paragon. If he'd truly been in this realm and been defeated, then Gabriel spoke the truth.

"But Eleanor and Brynhoff will send others. Far from keeping us safe, separating us was meant to keep us weak and vulnerable. When we killed Scoria, we became a threat to Mother's seat of power. You know what will happen next. Eleanor will try to pick us off, one by one. Our only hope is to unite and prepare an offensive so we're ready for an attack."

Alexander scoffed. "Won't our collective magic make us easier to find?"

Gabriel shook his head. "What I'm about to tell you may be hard for you to accept, but you must."

Blinking slowly, Alexander couldn't help but laugh. "I threw myself off the side of a cliff this morning." He watched his brother recoil. "What exactly do you think you're going to tell me that I won't be able to accept? I'm no one to judge."

Gabriel nodded in understanding. "My wife, Raven, is a very powerful witch. She can use her abilities to hide us from Eleanor."

Of all the things Alexander thought his brother might say, he was not expecting this. It explained why he'd clammed up earlier when Alexander had asked about Raven's humanity though. Dragons were expressly forbidden from mating with witches. It was said that the offspring of such a union would be a monster capable of leveling Paragon and everyone in it. Dragon-witch pairings had been outlawed in Paragon since the early fourth century when the Witch Queen of Darnuith had attempted to overthrow the kingdom of Paragon.

He laughed. "A... a witch? You've gone and married an actual spell-casting witch?" He locked eyes with his brother. When Gabriel didn't deny it, Alexander laughed, his eyebrows reaching for the ceiling. "And she's pregnant! No wonder Paragon wants you dead. The favorite of the kingdom has shattered the crown's most sacred edict."

"I wouldn't call it the most sacred," Gabriel murmured.

Alexander grew serious. "I'm in no place to tell you what to do, Gabriel. If you came for my blessing, you have it. As for the other part, the part about Mother coming to kill me, let her come. She'd be doing me a favor." He leaned back against the chair and closed his eyes. "Now untie me."

"You really want to die?" The disapproval in Gabriel's voice raked Alexander's skin.

"It's more complicated than a yes or no answer." Alexander opened his eyes to find Gabriel untying his wrists. He tugged them free and rubbed the circulation back into his limbs.

"Can I ask you one thing?" His brother frowned at him from above.

"Why not?" In for a penny, in for a pound, right? The sooner he answered Gabriel's questions, the sooner he'd get back to his solitude.

"How did you find a hawk that looks exactly like Maiara's?"

Alexander glanced at Nyx and then back at his brother. "I didn't. This is the same hawk."

# CHAPTER THREE

*December 1699*
*Port of Philadelphia*

T he Owl's Roost Public House was a seedy establishment, even by human standards, and Alexander had learned more than he wanted to know about human standards. He'd spent the past year traveling up the coast of Europe from a place called Crete, to the port of Genoa, to Barcelona, Marseille, London, sometimes by sea on vessels whose accommodations were suitable only for the rats who inhabited them, and sometimes by land, riding on beasts of burden and bedding down anywhere they could find.

They'd wound up in a place called the Isle of Wight, where a man named William Penn convinced Gabriel to board a merchant vessel for the New World. After seeing port after vermin-infested port in the area they called Europe, all of them had longed for a new world, and so they'd boarded a ship called the *Canterbury* weeks ago and ended up here.

"I don't think Penn was a reputable source." Alexander scowled. "This New World is even filthier and wilder than the old one." He took pencil to paper and continued his sketch of the place. At the front of the Owl's Roost was a bar that housed kegs of beer and whiskey shipped in from Europe, manned by a gray-haired chap with a tangled beard who also served as the innkeeper. The light in the place was courtesy of candles. Their table was circular with a half dozen simple wood chairs around it.

"Don't tell me you miss the palace." Rowan smoothed the heavy wool of her dress. He wondered how she could stand the fashion here for females. The sheer weight and cumbersome nature of what she wore would have driven him mad. He sketched her straight back and mischievous grin, taking great care to capture the impish sparkle in her eyes.

"Don't you? Maybe not the palace, per se, but the conveniences. I haven't been able to paint in months, and my skin is itching to shift." He'd purchased paper and charcoal pencils in Italy, and in his sketchbook, kept a record of the people and places they'd seen, but it wasn't the same as paint and canvas, two things that didn't lend to constant travel.

There was a pause in conversation as a barmaid with a head of red curls and a bulbous nose arrived, slinging pewter mugs of dark ale to each of them. Alexander gulped a healthy dose of the brew. It was no Tribiscal wine, but its charm was undeniable. Gabriel ordered a course of venison stew from the woman.

After the barmaid had waddled back toward the bar, Rowan answered him. "No, I don't miss it at all. Yes, these humans are strange and sometimes violent. We must be careful where and when we shift as not to attract undue attention from them or from Brynhoff if he's tracing our magic as Mother warned. But at least we are free to do as we wish. The palace was a prison." She shuddered.

For Rowan, Alexander realized, their ancestral home had indeed been a prison, maybe more so than for the rest of them. As the one and only princess of Paragon, their parents had kept her safe inside a gilded cage, only let out to fan her feathers for the social elite. Could he blame her for enjoying her newfound freedom?

Gabriel's mug landed with a thud on the roughhewn table, which rocked on its uneven legs. "This new world will make things easier. Penn told of vast land, miles upon miles of wild forest, fresh water, and unpopulated territory. There will be plenty of room for us to establish our own kingdoms, fill our treasure rooms, and avoid humans so we can shift at will."

Alexander was looking forward to settling anywhere. All this travel had left him feeling unmoored and slightly discombobulated. He longed for structure and normalcy again, and although he didn't miss the palace in many regards, he did miss the routine of palace life. He sampled the ale again and daydreamed of his own palace and his own kingdom.

"I *borrowed* this from the captain of our vessel," Tobias interjected, removing a roll of parchment from inside his coat and unrolling it on the table. Invisibility had served them well here, where humans were unaware of their nature as dragons and feared anything that could not be seen. They'd found it relatively easy to avoid detection when it suited them. What Tobias called *borrowing* was more likely slipping into the captain's chambers and removing the item from his desk.

Alexander leaned over the table to get a better look. A

map. Tobias was always the practical one. He wouldn't entrust their fate into the care of outsiders. With this, they would know where they wanted to go and what to ask for.

"These"—Tobias pointed to a series of odd-shaped blocks of land along the eastern coast—"are what they call the colonies. The humans have only recently settled there in any number, are predominantly agrarian and have little available cash. I am told most barter for goods. Our pounds sterling will go far here, but the jewels may be useless if we can find no one to buy them."

Gabriel pressed his lips together and grunted his agreement.

Tobias pointed to a mass of land to the west with few markings. "This is New France. I am told the colonies are few and far between. Wild, unsettled land just waiting to be claimed by our magic. All we need is someone who has been to this area, who can tell us where there is game to eat and materials for a proper domain."

A laugh came from behind them, and the barmaid slid bowls of stew onto the table. "That ain't nothing but soldiers and fur trappers," she said, nodding at the place Tobias's finger pressed into the section of the map. "Everything else is filled with savages. No place for civilized folk."

"Savages?"

She wiped her hands on her smock in an act of exasperation. "The filthy Indians! They'll scalp you as soon as look at you. Skin your hide if you step where you don't belong." She pointed at the expanse to the west. "You go there, you better arm yourself. It's no place for a lady if you don't mind me saying so, especially not now with the cold and the snow coming." She looked pointedly at Rowan.

"Where is a good place for a lady?" Rowan asked quickly.

"Aye, if it were me, I'd go to New York. I've heard things are nice there. Plenty of meat and ale. Young strapping lads with good solid homes who would be interested in a wee thing like you. If I were younger, that be where I'd go."

Rowan leaned back and crossed her arms over her chest. "That's where I want to go, the place with the food and warm strapping lads." She waggled her eyebrows.

"Rowan!" Gabriel boomed.

Alexander flared his eyes at his sister, who laughed and drank her ale around a smirk.

"She's a feisty one, she is." The woman nodded and retreated toward the kitchen.

"You can't control me here, Gabriel," Rowan said, suddenly earnest. "I'll go on my own if I have to. I have no desire to wade through forests and valleys of unsettled territory."

This unleashed a painfully intense lecture from Gabriel about the need to stay together despite their plan to settle apart. As their oldest living sibling, Gabriel had named himself their leader and took pleasure in bossing them around. King Gabriel of the nonexistent dragon land of exiled Paragonians.

Alexander rolled his eyes and sketched his brother standing on his chair, dressed in a robe and powdered wig and banging his fist upon his opposite palm. He bent the page so Gabriel would not see and chuckled as he added a bit of sprayed spit to his drawing. By the Mountain, his brother could be an overbearing cockalorum.

"If it's so great, go on your own, Gabriel! I'll be in New York," Rowan said, her unyielding stare matching their older brother's.

Alexander smiled at his sister's pluck. In Paragon, Rowan had been silenced by the expectations of the crown.

She'd suffered her entire life, bearing the burden of other people's wants and needs, especially their mother's. Only through art had Alex succeeded in bringing his sister out of her shell, coaxing her personality forth in the form of oils on canvas.

But the next hour, she'd be at some royal function once again performing her duties like a trained dog, all the fire drained from her spirit. He saw that fire now. It had awakened more every day they were away from Paragon, and he, for one, was happy to see it.

Gabriel, however, seemed much less enthused about the change in their sister. "Living among the humans is risky. They will expect you to conform to their ways."

"I'll get by," she replied, chin raised. "Anyway, I think we should all split the remainder of the jewels and choose one of these colonies to settle down in. They cover a considerable area, plenty far apart. If each of us chooses a different one, Brynhoff will never find us."

Gabriel's response was undermined when the front door opened and an icy wind blew through the establishment, ruffling Alexander's hair. He looked up to find a slight, hooded figure had stepped inside, layered in furs and skins with a bow and quiver slung over one shoulder and tall moccasins fitted below the knee with strips of leather.

The person—he could not tell if they were male or female—reminded him of the elves of the kingdom of Rogos in his home world, built small with long, lean limbs. But the most unusual part of the stranger's ensemble was a red-tailed hawk perched on the thick animal hide covering the person's shoulders. The bird of prey had eyes of amber, an impressive wingspan, and talons that Alexander thought the man or woman must still be able to feel through the pelt.

The background din in the public house suddenly quieted, and all the patrons turned to face the door.

"Filthy savage," a man muttered.

Alexander shot the man a nasty glare and gripped his ale tighter. The stranger wasn't filthy or savage. In fact, he found the visitor rather enticing and mysterious. A strong urge to sketch the newcomer overcame him, and he flipped his paper over to start a new drawing. He wished he could see the stranger's face. Would they have the pointed ears of an elf as well as the stature?

Two hands emerged from the fur cape and brushed back the hood, and Alexander's pencil stopped.

The stranger was a woman with long, dark hair that fell glossy and sleek to her shoulders and beyond, disappearing inside her cape. High cheekbones marked a face notable for its strong, proud edges, with luminescent amber skin that seemed to radiate sunlight.

Her eyes were deepest ebony and shaped more like the elves of his world than the humans they'd met in Europe, although her ears were not elvish. Her hollowed cheeks suggested she was hungry and had been for some time.

Instantly, deep within his torso, Alexander's dragon stirred, creating a visceral tug in her direction. He sniffed the air to appease its curiosity. That was strange. Since they'd arrived here, his inner dragon hadn't taken an interest in the human population. This one, though, was different.

His nostrils flared. Fallen leaves, oak bark, pine, and fresh crisp air. She smelled of freedom and the wild. He blinked slowly, taking it in.

She strode toward an empty table, the hawk shifting with her movement, followed by the judgmental gazes of the other patrons. Alexander didn't understand. How could they all not be as taken with her beauty as he was? Why did their mouths twist in distaste? She was a breath of fresh air in the otherwise stale room.

The barmaid who'd served them rushed forward and blocked the empty table with her body. "That one's reserved." She stood with an irritable expression, arms spread wide.

The stranger turned and headed for another table, this one both empty and in a shadowy corner of the hall. Alexander scowled. She was giving in, trying to place herself out of sight to avoid the obvious scorn of the other patrons. But she had no reason to hide. It was these people who should be hiding.

"That one's reserved as well," the barmaid said without a hint of a smile. No sugar to ease her poisonous words.

The barkeep piped up. "We don't serve your kind here." As if to pound in his point, he retrieved a musket from behind the bar and dropped it on the counter.

The woman and her hawk pivoted to face the gray-haired man and considered him, her gaze as cold and hard as ice. Alexander thought the man might turn to stone under the power of that gaze. This woman might have been small in stature, but she was strong of will. He immediately respected that.

The barkeep raised his chin defiantly and placed his hand on his weapon.

Hot ire flushed Alexander's skin. He thrust to his feet, his chair scraping the floor as his knees drove it back from the table. Every eye in the room turned on him. He didn't shy away from the stares but stood straighter, using his above-average size to maximum advantage. "This woman is with me," he stated decisively.

"Alexander, what are you doing?" Tobias said under his breath.

Gabriel hissed a note of warning.

Ignoring his brothers, Alexander extended his hand toward the stranger. "Please."

# CHAPTER FOUR

Despite the pained expressions of his family and the hateful outrage of the patrons in the Owl's Roost, Alexander gestured for the native woman to join him.

"Are you listening? She ain't allowed in here!" the barkeep bellowed.

He turned the heat of his stare on the plump, bearded man. "Are you suggesting that my brothers and I must find another establishment to spend our coin?"

They'd rented all the rooms in the small inn and, Alexander suspected, had paid for them overmuch. Considering his and his brothers' size relative to that of the human population, Alexander was counting on the barkeep's reluctance to start trouble. He was relieved when the portly man moved the musket under the counter.

"Fine. But the bird waits outside," the barkeep insisted, pointing his thumb toward the door.

Alexander focused on the Indian woman, his fingers still extended toward her beseechingly. For a moment she seemed frozen, her gaze tracing the line from the tips of his fingers to his face before locking onto his eyes. The hall became so quiet Alexander could hear the ragged inhale of his own breath. Did she understand English? Did she understand he was inviting her to dine with them?

Finally, as if she'd made a momentous decision, her shoulders drooped and she marched to the front door. With more force than necessary, she threw it open, allowing in a gust of cold that drew hateful snipes from the other patrons. The hawk flew off toward the darkening sky with a shrill cry that pierced the late afternoon chill. The native woman released the door, cutting off the rush of cold, and returned to his table.

Dragons had a way with languages. Their magic allowed them to understand and be understood with little effort. Not knowing what language she spoke though, he gestured for her to join them and shoved Tobias out of the chair beside him. Due to his inherent good nature, his brother chuckled and switched to one of the open chairs at their table. Gabriel wasn't as accommodating. He glowered at Alexander in warning.

The woman took a deep breath before sitting. Alexander waited as she removed her bow and quiver, a leather satchel, and her outer fur cloak. She piled them beside her chair. Underneath it all, she wore deerskin breeches and a belted tunic. By this world's standards, her manner of dress might be uncivilized compared to the dress Rowan wore, but she was as pleasant to his eye as any woman he'd ever seen here. He cared nothing for this world's traditions anyway.

"I need food and drink," she said in perfect English. Her chin was high, but he did not miss the way her jaw clenched under her hollow cheeks. She was proud, this lone woman. For her, it wouldn't be easy to ask for help. "I have come a long way, and I am afraid they will not serve me."

Her voice wavered marginally on the last words. Without a doubt she'd felt the edge of hunger.

He intended to see her belly full before the end of this night. Without a word, Alexander slid his own bowl of venison stew in front of her. Gabriel, after a flash of momentary surprise, raised his hand to get the barmaid's attention and ordered more stew and another round of ale.

"You speak English," Alexander said.

"Yes. Very well. My father was a fur trapper."

"My name is Alexander," he said, extending his hand toward her. She eyed it skeptically.

"I am Maiara." She did not shake his hand but began eating the stew before her.

"The people here, why do they call you savage when you speak their language and your father is English?" Alexander pushed aside politeness to ask. His curiosity drove him to find out more about this mysterious woman. Her nearness exaggerated the pull he'd felt toward her earlier, and he flattened his hand on the table to keep from touching her.

She looked at him from beneath her lashes and smiled without showing any teeth. "My mother's people are not well understood by white men. I look like my mother."

Rowan nudged him, widened her eyes, and tapped her fingers against her cheek. This was an aspect of this world Alexander was still trying to understand. People here divided themselves by the color of their skin. He found the tradition odd, inconvenient, and unjust.

Dragons had the ability to transform themselves into any color they desired, but their natural complexion varied widely in hue. Their magic had chosen their current pale appearance; magic designed to help them blend in to their new surroundings.

"It is wrong for them to treat you as they have," he said.

Maiara took another bite of stew. The barmaid returned with another dish and a pint, dropping them in front of Alexander from enough of a height that the spoon rattled against the bowl and a bit of the ale splattered over the edge. He wiped up the mess before pushing the extra pint toward her.

"You are welcome among us, Maiara." Alexander said her name with reverence. Their eyes locked again, and he had to swallow down the rising rush of intrigued dragon.

Always focused on practicalities, Tobias cleared his throat and smoothed his pale blond hair. "Maiara, my brother meant only to help you, but I wonder if I may ask you a favor. You said your father was a trapper. Do you know the wilds of New France?"

She swallowed what was in her mouth. It was impossible to miss how hungrily she devoured the stew. He hadn't touched his bowl in case she desired a second helping.

"Where do you wish to go?" Her grip trembled around the handle of the spoon, and he wondered how long it had been since she'd last eaten.

Tobias pointed to the blank space where the map blended into uncharted territory.

"I know the ways, but that place is not for you. Very few of your kind have the ability to survive there. The tribes will not be welcoming to outsiders."

"These people are not our kind." Alexander interrupted with a broad gesture toward the other patrons.

Tobias elbowed him hard in the side. It was forbidden to tell humans what they were. It was too dangerous to share their secret. "What my brother means is that we are interested in establishing our own land and way of living. We want to go somewhere there are no other people."

Her brows furrowed over a frown. "How will you survive? Even if you waited until spring, you are too few to work the land."

"We cannot wait until spring," Gabriel said. "We must go soon."

A sound like a muffled laugh came from Maiara, and Alexander watched her hide her amusement by taking a long drink of her ale. "No guide will take you there now. Winter approaches and the path you must take is rough and narrow. If you don't freeze to death, you will likely starve to death. If you stray from the path, either the French or one of the Iroquois tribes will kill you."

"Iroquois?"

"There are many native tribes that count themselves as Iroquois. Here, we are surrounded by Mohawk trading routes, and they will not tolerate ignorance of their boundaries."

"Are you Iroquois?"

She shook her head. "I am Potawatomi. We are Algonquian. These are the names the white men call us. In my language we are *Anishinabe.*"

Alexander leaned in, fascinated by Maiara's story. Question after question formed in his mind, and he was about to inquire about her people, when Rowan blurted, "Can you take me to New York?"

That inspired a frustrated groan from Gabriel, who brought his mug down on the table with unnecessary force. "Ignore my sister." Gabriel pinned Rowan to her seat with a warning stare. "She is confused and ignorant of our goals."

Distaste twisted deep in Alexander's chest, and he opened his mouth to defend his sister. They were no longer in Paragon. Rowan should be able to do as she wished. And who had named Gabriel as their leader in this new land anyway? In the end, the conditioning of his childhood won out. As to why exactly, he wasn't sure. He was afraid to examine the coil of emotion that kept him silent. But he didn't like it. He didn't like any of it.

Which made it all the more impactful when Maiara, a stranger in every sense of the word, spoke for him. "Your sister is wise. New York is the more sensible trip."

Gabriel smoothed his hand over the map. "You only say that because you think we are not suited to the hardships you've pointed out. What if I were to tell you the cold is not an issue for us, nor is hunger?"

Maiara tilted her head as her eyes traveled from sibling to sibling. Her sharp gaze missed nothing. "I don't understand."

"My siblings and I are abnormally resilient to the cold and are excellent, experienced hunters. It is part of the reason we desire land of our own. We are also trained warriors and do not fear these Mohawks you speak of."

Becoming very still, Maiara dropped her spoon into her empty bowl and seemed to consider his words. When her eyes fell on Alexander, her gaze felt hot where it moved over him and made his dragon coil and stretch inside him. He rubbed his torso to settle the beast. *Down, boy.*

"I do not have the provisions to make this journey. I cannot guide you," she stated simply. There was a hint of steel in her words, and Alexander was left to wonder why she was determined they not go into the wilds of New France.

"We would pay you handsomely," Gabriel said. "One hundred pounds."

"One hundred—" She narrowed her eyes. "Pounds sterling are limited in the colonies. If you have this amount, you should invest it here. Your return will be greater. I'm sorry to have wasted your time. Thank you for the food." She moved as if to stand.

Alarm rang through Alexander. If Maiara left now, he might never see her again. He placed his hand atop hers on the table. Instantly a spark like internal lightning flowed up his arm and sent his dragon roiling. He had to breathe deeply to keep his beast contained. Peculiarly, Maiara was not unaffected. She blinked at him like she was seeing him for the first time.

"You are not from here," she murmured.

"No, we are not," he agreed. "We need space and privacy."

"Where you wish to go, many places are occupied by peoples who have survived in these lands for generations. Some are friendly. Some are not. There are places where the people will tolerate you if you live harmoniously with them and the land. Other places are guarded by evil ones who will kill you before they speak to you." She paused to sum them all up. "If what you say is true, and you have money for provisions, can survive the cold, and can keep yourselves fed, I can guide you safely to these lands."

"After you take me to New York," Rowan said.

Gabriel and Rowan exchanged glances. As always, Tobias was the voice of reason. "As you can see, we have much to discuss among ourselves, but we would like your help settling here, a different place for each of us, far apart and far from the general populace. Can you help us?"

Maiara remained silent for a moment, so long that Alexander feared they'd insulted her in some unknown way. He was relieved when she swallowed and looked him squarely in the eye.

"I will guide you."

CHAPTER FIVE

*2018*
*Sedona, Arizona*

R owan cradled Alexander's face between her hands, trying to ignore the angry squawking of his pet hawk on his shoulder. His gaze never met hers. He stared, unseeing, across the filthy apartment as if his body was there but his mind had checked out. His skin felt clammy and his pupils were dilated.

Throat thick with emotion, her mind raced. For years she'd suspected Alexander was in a dark place. As the owner of Zelda's Folly, a New York gallery that frequently bought his artwork, she'd watched his paintings grow darker in both color and content. The letters she'd sent him went unanswered. It was one thing to presume her brother was depressed, quite another to see this. It was like he was trapped inside his own head.

Sensing her increasing despair, Rowan's mate, Nick, rubbed her back in a show of support. "Stay strong. We knew it wasn't going to be easy."

"Yeah. I just didn't expect him to be catatonic." She focused the full weight of her attention on Gabriel. "How long's he been like this?"

"Since right after I told him about Mother and Paragon." Gabriel crossed his arms over his chest and leaned against the kitchen counter. "Wait, no, that's not exactly true. He wigged out after he explained to me that this is Maiara's hawk." He pointed at the bird.

Rowan flinched back slightly and frowned when it was clear Gabriel was serious. "Obviously he meant a descendant of Maiara's hawk. Her actual hawk must have died centuries ago."

Gabriel shrugged. "Unfortunately, I do not believe our brother has a strong grasp on reality at the moment."

She sighed heavily. How often did he have these spells? And how exactly was she supposed to tear down the invisible walls he'd built around himself? Her stomach hurt. Alexander deserved better than this, and she, as the one who'd always been closest to him both in Paragon and this world, should have seen it coming. Any sister worth her salt would have thrown caution to the wind months ago and checked on him. She'd been an idiot.

"I don't know what to do," she confessed. Gabriel looked as helpless as she felt.

"Tobias took Raven into town with him to find a pharmacy that will fill a prescription for him. He thinks he can help Alexander snap out of it if he can get his hands on some human medications."

Her brother Tobias was a talented human doctor and an exceptional healer, but that didn't mean he could deal with dragon-size depression. "Since when do human medications work on dragons?"

"Tobias doesn't think it will work on Alexander the way

it would work on a human. On the contrary, he believes the drug will simply disrupt whatever thought pattern is stuck on repeat inside his head. With our metabolism, it will be out of his system in a matter of minutes, but the hope is that it will reboot his wiring."

Rowan placed a tender kiss on Alexander's forehead. "I'm here, little brother. You're going to be okay." Alexander did not respond.

An ache began in her chest. She'd always been closest to Alexander, ever since the day she'd been beaten raw by their mother for refusing to perform her duties as a princess, a responsibility that had included entertaining a much older dragon who couldn't keep his hands to himself.

Her punishment had been solitary confinement, a forced adoption of the ruse that she could not participate in the social function due to illness. She would have gone insane alone in that room day and night if not for Alexander. Her dear brother had snuck in with canvas and oils and taught her to paint. Those sessions had been her lifeline, her sanity. He'd cared for her then at great personal risk. Now she would care for him.

Her head felt hot, and she whirled on Gabriel, crossing her arms to avoid striking out. "This is your fault."

"How so?" Gabriel spread his hands as if the idea perplexed him.

"You pushed him too hard. You always push too hard. Not everyone is a hardened soldier like you. Alexander has always been sensitive. You know that." She pointed a finger at Gabriel's face. "You should have been more careful with him."

Jaw tightening, Gabriel slapped her finger away from his nose. "At least I did *something*. You've known he was mentally disturbed for years and have done nothing but buy the evidence of it and sell it to the highest bidder."

Rowan inhaled sharply as the barb hit too close to home. Yes, she'd purchased his paintings and sold them in her gallery in New York, but that was because she wanted to make sure he was taken care of financially. A niggling of guilt wormed its way inside her. Was her brother right? Had she purposely chosen to ignore the signs?

"Hey! Don't touch my girl like that." Nick's New York accent grew stronger with his anger. "Rowan thought she couldn't be in the same room with Alexander without risking your uncle killing them both. Give her a fucking break already."

"Your *girl* needs to keep her finger out of my face," Gabriel snapped. "She also needs to remember that Alexander's so-called sensitivity is debatable. He trained with the rest of us, and I've personally seen his dragon eat a man's head like it was a cheese puff."

"Those were extreme circumstances," Rowan protested.

"He ate someone's head?" Nick's eyebrows shot up, and he studied Alexander like he'd been given a new window into his character.

"It was a long time ago," Rowan said. "And the head in question belonged to an evil bastard who had it coming." A scuff on the back of his jacket caught her eye, and she ran her hand along his shoulders. Her fingers caught in a tear in the leather, freeing a lodged pebble. She grimaced as it bounced off the chair and onto the floor. "It looks like he was in an accident."

Nick frowned. "What kind of accident would be responsible for these lines on his wrists?" Rowan saw the detective in her mate rising to the surface. He examined Alexander's arms as if he were at a crime scene.

"Those are marks from the rope I used to tie him up," Gabriel admitted.

"What?" Rowan's voice came out high and sharp. "Why did you tie him up?"

"I needed something to hold him to the chair while he was unconscious." Shame rippled through her older brother's expression but disappeared in an instant. Just like Gabriel to dismiss his part in this. He hadn't expressed near enough regret for what he'd done. Her older brother could be a stinking brute on the best of days.

"Are you telling me that you first knocked him out and then bound him to a chair? What the hell is wrong with you?" She punched Gabriel in the bicep and was rewarded with a small sense of satisfaction when he grunted in pain.

"Oww! His fuckin' bird bit me!" Nick pulled his hand away from Alexander, blood bubbling on his knuckle. The hawk flapped her wings and repositioned herself on Alexander's shoulders.

"There's something odd about that bird," Gabriel said.

"Ya think? Who keeps a hawk as a pet?" Rowan led Nick to the kitchen sink and ran his finger under cold water, then grabbed a take-out napkin from a pile on the counter and pressed it to the bite.

Gabriel planted his hands on his hips and cocked his head slightly as he squinted at the hawk. His nostrils flared. "Do me a favor and smell her."

Rowan nudged Nick. "Would you mind waiting outside for a minute? I can't smell anything over your scent."

"Sure." He placed a light kiss on her lips before he slipped from the apartment.

She drifted toward her little brother, keeping a wary eye on Nyx, who watched her with blazing amber eyes surrounded by smooth russet feathers. Rowan focused on the bird and inhaled deeply through her nose. Her inner dragon sorted the scent.

There was the tang she associated with a natural predator. Nyx smelled like any bird of prey, like she was supposed to smell. She was about to tell Gabriel as much when a secondary metallic odor hit her palate. An aftertaste. Underneath the layers of wild fowl was an unmistakable scent of magic. She inhaled deeper.

"It just hit you, didn't it?" Gabriel said.

"She smells like Maiara's magic."

"Exactly."

"The question is why?" Exhaustion overcame her, and Rowan rubbed her eyes. Their early-morning flight to Sedona had been overly long and subject to delays, and she desperately needed a cup of coffee. Although Gabriel had procured rooms for them at this retreat compound, she hadn't had a chance to rest and hadn't eaten anything either. No matter, she hardly felt hungry. Her younger brother's withdrawn state had chased away her appetite. The unease left behind created an uncomfortable sensation low in her belly.

"We never fully understood Maiara's abilities. We were new to this world. We didn't know it was unusual for a human to practice magic back then. If she was a witch like Raven, perhaps this bird was her familiar. She might have used her magic to make it immortal."

Rowan reached for the bird but withdrew her hand just as quick when it snapped at her fingers. "Immortal and crabby." She backed off and crossed her arms, tucking her fingers out of view of Nyx.

A knock came on the door, and Gabriel opened it for Tobias, Raven, and Nick, who entered, arms full of groceries.

"What's all this?" Gabriel said. "I thought you were going to the pharmacy?"

Tobias flashed a dazzling white smile. "Food, drinks, cleaning supplies. Once we wake him up, we're going to need to get him to eat something. I've never seen a more emaciated dragon."

Rowan dropped her shoulders and rolled her head to stretch her neck in an effort to relieve some of her stored-up tension. A small sense of relief filled her. Tobias would know how to snap Alexander from his unresponsive state. He seemed to have a solid game plan.

"And if we don't clean in here soon, I'm going to be sick. It smells like something died, and the baby makes me hyper-sensitive." Raven dug into one of the bags and withdrew a bottle of disinfectant.

"Where is Willow?" Gabriel asked, seemingly irritated by the idea of his wife cleaning. Willow, Rowan remembered, was Alexander's oread, one of the nymphs they'd met when they'd come to this world. Oreads and dragons had a symbiotic relationship; the nymphs fed off dragon energy, and in return they served them in a domestic capacity. Rowan had left her oread behind in New York to maintain her residence there. She had no idea what had happened to Alexander's.

Raven shrugged. "Gabriel, it's not going to hurt the baby if I wipe a counter."

Gabriel started to object, but Nick interrupted him. "No, ahh, I got it." He plucked the spray bottle from between Raven's hands. "I need something to do to stay busy or I'll get my fingers bit off sticking them where they don't belong." He gave the hawk a sideways glance. "You, take a load off."

Rowan gave him a quick peck on his cheek. Despite the

trials of his past, he maintained a generous spirit. It was one of the many reasons she loved him.

"Here goes nothing," Tobias said. He injected a clear liquid into Alexander's arm. Her brother's eyelids fluttered, but he didn't respond to Tobias's prodding.

Rowan knelt in front of her younger brother and gazed up into his still face. "Why isn't he snapping out of it?"

"Give it a chance," Tobias said.

Alexander groaned.

"Oh, thank the Mountain," Rowan said under her breath.

As if on instinct, Alexander turned his head to check that Nyx was on his shoulder. He rubbed his palms along his thighs. When he spoke, his voice was low and threatening. "All of you, get the hell out of my house."

Rowan spread her arms and forced a light note into her voice. "Is that any way to greet your favorite sister?"

His face softened and he rose to embrace her in a quick hug that included three firm thumps at the center of her back. "Okay. Now, get the hell out."

It was such an Alexander response, she snorted. "I'm not going anywhere. We need to talk. Did you know I'm mated?" When he hung his head like he was exhausted, she went on. "Come on, Alex. Talk to me. Please."

His eyes narrowed as if he were deliberating between flashing her the middle finger or tolerating her for a few minutes more. After a long pause, he raised his chin and said, "Fine. Just you." He glanced at Gabriel. "Everyone else, out!"

Rowan leveled a stare on Gabriel and he relented. He and the others left without another word.

Alexander rubbed his wrists. "He can be such an asshole."

"Undisputed," she said. "Now it's just you and me. Tell me where you went just now. You scared the hell out of me."

He nuzzled the bird on his shoulder and stroked her feathers. "I was thinking about Maiara."

"What about Maiara?"

"There's something I never told you about the night we met her."

# CHAPTER SIX

*1699*
*Port of Philadelphia*

No respectable excuse existed for Alexander to follow Maiara from the Owl's Roost, but he could not resist. He told himself he was concerned for her well-being, but there was nothing incapable about her. On the contrary, she exuded strength and understood this world better than he did. But night had fallen while they discussed their plans, and he felt strange allowing her to go into the freezing darkness on her own.

Whatever had caused this deep need to protect her was unreasonable and uninvited. But it was also undeniable. All he wanted to know was that she was safe and sound and had found a decent place to spend the night.

After how they'd treated her at the public house, he was afraid all the inns would be similarly resistant to her occupying their rooms. And if that were the case, he planned to offer her a room even if he had to sneak her inside.

His concern for her increased exponentially when she

exited the boundaries of the town and walked into the forest by the light of the moon, which tonight was round and full in the star-filled sky. He cloaked himself in invisibility and followed at a distance, careful so she wouldn't hear his footsteps.

Raising her arm, she released a long, low whistle. A few moments later, he heard a rustle of feathers and her red-tailed hawk swept in, landing on her offered perch, and chattered at her.

"Shh, shh, Nikan. I am sorry it took so long, but I brought you something." She fed the bird a strip of meat she must have squirreled away from the stew she'd eaten. The bird gulped it down. "It's not much. I hope you were able to hunt while you waited for me."

The hawk swallowed and chattered once again.

"No. There will be no bed for us tonight. This place is inhospitable to our kind." Nikan squawked and flapped on her arm.

Alexander didn't like the sound of that. Did she plan to sleep outside? That wouldn't do at all.

"Yes, I do think he was the one I dreamed about," she said to the bird, and his skin tingled. Was she talking about him? "His energy is... unusual." The bird cooed in response. "I'm not sure what it means, but Mother wanted me to meet him. I am certain. Besides, we need the coin for winter."

Deep among the trees, she stopped before a large twisting oak. "Here we are."

He froze when she began to undress. What was she doing? It was far too cold for this. She removed her pack and weapons, then each layer of her clothing quickly, folding the pelts and skins carefully beside the base of the tree.

Her silky skin gleamed in the moonlight, the mounds of her breasts, tips lusciously peaked, visible between the shadows of the trees. She turned and the light caught the spread of her shoulders, lean but muscled like a dragon's, and the taper of her back down to a slim waist. The tops of her buttocks, smooth and round, were visible before the rest of her disappeared into shadow. He watched her shiver against the chill night air.

He swallowed hard, his mouth suddenly dry. He should look away. What sorry excuse for a dragon watched an unsuspecting woman undress? No matter how much he chastised himself, he could not do it. Everything about the woman intrigued him. It took all his effort not to rush forward and wrap his wings around her to protect her from the chilly December wind.

Battling his dragon against this inappropriate temptation, Alexander planted his feet, dug his nails into the palms of his hands, and concentrated on staying exactly where he was. If he couldn't force himself to look away, the least he could do was not interfere. Maiara rested both her bare hands against the bark of the oak and suddenly and abruptly disappeared. He blinked and blinked again. Had he consumed too much ale? One moment she was there beside the tree, the next she was gone. Completely gone. He stumbled forward, dropping his invisibility and rushing toward the tree.

Right, then left, he searched the woods for her. Her scent lingered in the air. He tried to follow it but only ended up back at the tree. He ran his hand along the fur cape she'd folded at the base, her deerskin clothing beneath it. She'd definitely been there. How far could she travel naked as she was?

Perfectly still, he held his breath and listened. A rabbit scratched its ear a few yards away, and a bird ruffled its feathers directly above him. He looked up. The red-tailed hawk was in the branches of the oak, staring down at him with intense, knowing eyes that had no business being in the head of a bird.

"Where is she?" he whispered.

The hawk blinked twice, flapped its wings, and jumped to a higher branch, turning its back to him. No help there. He stared at the gnarled bark of the ancient tree, and a chill that had nothing to do with the cold traveled through him. No wonder they called this the New World. This was a strange land indeed.

Feeling uneasy, he backed away and hurried to return to the Owl's Roost. He pondered telling Gabriel what he'd seen but was relieved to find all his siblings had abandoned the main hall for their rooms upstairs. That gave him an excuse to wait and consider his options. For reasons he didn't quite understand, he wanted to keep her secret, perhaps confront her about the tree and her nakedness. He wanted to know more, to know everything about her.

What sort of magic had led to her disappearance? Could she make herself invisible? Dissolve into the moonlight? Did all the Indians in this new world have these abilities? The white men had called them savages. Was the term born of fear because they'd witnessed such phenomenal magic?

When he entered his room, he found his oread, Willow, preparing his bedchamber. The creature's skin shone like polished pearl in the flickering light of the candelabra, and Alexander wondered again at this strange world and its creatures. But his sense of wonder soon gave way to concern. Often the nymph carried his gossamer wings high, raised above his shoulders, but tonight they drooped from his back as if boneless and soaked through.

"Willow, am I mistaken, or do I sense a melancholic air in your disposition?"

The nymph's voice came soft and melodic as he turned from the shelf he was dusting. "The long journey at sea has drained my reserves, my dragon. Our kind require the grounding energy of the mountain or the lush green life force of trees. Even the cool luxury of fresh water can sometimes invigorate our magic. Salt water, though, is toxic to nymphs, and we were a long time at sea before coming here. I will recover in time, with rest."

Alexander changed into his bedclothes, handing his linen shirt and breeches to the oread as he undressed. "When we arrived in Crete and your kind came down the mountain to greet us, I was under the impression that you fed off our energy and this partnership was advantageous to you."

The nymph's eyes grew unnaturally large. "Oh, we do! Your energy has sustained me, sir, and it is my privilege to be in your employ. You've freed me from the prison of my mountain. But we need more to thrive. We need more to feel alive."

As Alexander washed up using the basin Willow had filled, he thought he understood more than he'd expected to. Losing their home in Paragon had been hard enough, but constantly moving over the past year had left him with a perpetual ache behind his breastbone. He was unmoored, rootless, and what comfort he drew from the family he still had would soon be torn apart as they again found permanent homes separated from each other. They'd survive, but could any of them thrive again?

He climbed into bed and reached for his sketchbook. Willow had kindly placed it on his nightstand. Lifting his charcoal pencil, he began furiously drawing Maiara, the slope of her shoulder, her back, her glorious bottom. He placed her near the tree, in profile, her hands resting against the bark. It was a vivid likeness, and he caressed the long sleek darkness of her hair that cascaded down the center of her back. Staring at the drawing in the candlelight, an idea flickered to life in his head. "Willow?"

"Sir?"

"Are there others like you in this land? Ones who... have a relationship with the trees?"

The oread thought for a moment. "Oreads are mountain nymphs, and my family is from Crete, where you found us. I've no idea what magical creatures populate this land although I would suspect dryads, er, tree nymphs and water sprites given the topography. I will say this, these humans you live among have a horrible habit of refusing to see the magic in their own world. I believe it would be stranger to think we are the only enchanted beings here than to assume we are not."

"Hmm." He continued to work on his sketch. "How do you tell in this realm who is human and who is not? How would you know another nymph if you met them? I mean, if they were disguised as a human?"

Willow paused. "I don't understand your question, sir. Nymphs are just like you and me. If you suspect a creature isn't human, why wouldn't you simply ask?"

Alexander rubbed his face. He didn't think it was normal behavior to go around asking strangers if they were nymphs. Willow came from a place with few humans. Magical creatures were more of the norm for him. "Never mind. It was just a thought."

Willow's slender fingers pressed into his chin. "If there were nymphs in this area, I doubt you'd meet them now."

"No? Why not?"

"The weather here grows cold. Once the trees sleep for the winter and the waters freeze, the nymphs associated with those natural sources of magic would either sleep until spring inside their element or be stuck in their human form until the thaw. If the legends we were told as children are true, it's a vulnerable time for their kind. I doubt very much they'd be mingling with strangers now."

As Willow finished cleaning Alexander's clothes and packing them away before extinguishing the candles, all Alexander could think about was the look of desperation he'd seen on Maiara's face when she'd first entered the Owl's Roost. Whatever she was, she needed help, and he wanted desperately to be the one to give it to her.

# CHAPTER SEVEN

2018
*New Orleans*

I f you wanted something done right, you had to do it
yourself. Aborella's patience had long ago run thin with
every subordinate she'd sent to capture the treasure of
Paragon. Now the job was proving far more frustrating than
she'd foreseen.

She'd been posing as a human named Charlotte and
compelling Raven's father, David, since June. It should have
been a simple job, but he'd yet to succeed in luring the
witch and Gabriel to his side. The man was useless. He
seemed to have no power over his children whatsoever.

Power was something Aborella had plenty of. In
Paragon, she was considered the most powerful fairy to have
ever existed, a seer and sorceress to the crown. Sorceress
was a necessary descriptor. She was not a witch. Unlike
witches whose magic came from the natural elements,
Aborella's power originated in life itself. Plants and herbs
were the tools of her trade, but her sorcery was not limited

to potions and poisons. On the contrary, by draining the life force from growing things, she could gain enough power to perform the most complex spells, along with those inherent to her fairy composition.

Born and raised in the fae kingdom of Everfield, she'd excelled at magic from a very young age. But despite her extraordinary talents, no one there had wanted to be associated with her. The ancient runes she tattooed into her skin to enhance her power scared them, and she cared little for shallow social interactions. What need did she have for performing the dance of the five kingdoms when she could reduce a tree to dust with the touch of her finger? Which was why Eleanor was so important to her. The empress and Aborella understood each other, and their friendship had changed their world.

Consequently, she'd agreed to come here. Eleanor wanted her children, and Aborella planned to deliver.

Illusion had always come naturally to Aborella, and tonight was no exception. She watched herself in the full-length mirror— her naturally purple skin, her filmy, gossamer wings. The webbing was the same color silver as her irises and the platinum cascade of her hair. She thought herself quite beautiful, but unfortunately this appearance would not get her what she wanted.

Rolling her neck, she sent a cascade of creamy white skin to cover her true complexion, red hair in place of the white. She folded her wings away and stretched her body to look like the models in the magazines. She constructed a face with a series of angular and delicate bones and colored her eyes a deep shade of emerald.

When she was done, she donned a filmy white tunic and wide-legged flowing pants with a pair of strappy sandals. The doorbell rang. Time to shine.

David had promised her tonight was the night Raven and her sister Avery would finally come to dinner. All she had to do was get Raven to drink the elixir she'd made, and the witch would be her puppet. After that, finding the treasure of Paragon—the eight sibling heirs to the throne who'd been exiled here centuries ago—would be easy.

The elixir was important. Raven had the power to absorb magic. At their first meeting in Paragon, she'd drained Aborella into unconsciousness. It had taken her days to recover. That would never happen again. Now that she knew how the witch's magic worked, she'd keep herself beyond the woman's reach until Raven was under her control.

The doorbell rang, and she heard that lout, David, lumber from the living room. Aborella practiced Charlotte's smile in the mirror and then strode toward the foyer to meet him.

"Avery, come in, honey. Where's Raven?" she heard David say.

Aborella's blood began to boil. Had the witch dodged her trap again?

"Dad, I told you earlier, she messaged me yesterday. They've extended their honeymoon. Gabriel surprised her with yet another excursion." Avery Tanglewood looked so much like her sister that at first Aborella thought the witch was standing before her. But Avery's cheeks held a fullness Raven's did not, and of course, Raven by now would look very pregnant, unlike this woman whose trim waist made her curvy figure seem exaggerated.

David's eyes rolled back and his face turned red. His voice shook as he said, "I told you Raven had to come. You weren't supposed to come without her."

Clearly offended, Avery backed toward the door. "Fine. I'll go."

"Please, excuse your father," Aborella called as she turned the corner into the foyer. "He's only asking for my sake. I'm afraid he's a bit overzealous about finally introducing me to your sister."

"Hello, Charlotte. Nice to see you again." Avery held out her hand politely, and Aborella gave it a practiced pump.

"Won't you join us in the dining room? We were about to open a bottle of prosecco. Would you care for a glass?"

Avery pushed her dark hair off her shoulder, her skin still dewy from the New Orleans humidity, and glanced at her father. "Prosecco, huh? I didn't know my father drank anything but beer."

David blinked, waiting for Aborella to answer for him. She'd have to cut back on the compulsion. The man appeared half-baked.

"Oh, I think you'll find I've expanded David's horizons more than you'd think." Aborella reached the dining room and popped the cork on the bubbly wine, pouring it into the glasses she'd readied. The elixir of Paragonian milkwood she'd dribbled into the bottom fizzed as the bubbly liquor mixed with it.

"Honestly, you're so sophisticated, Charlotte. Sometimes I wonder how you two ended up together." Avery glanced between her and David.

Aborella handed her one of the tainted glasses. "I think you underestimate your father. His mind is more pliable than you give him credit for." She raised her own glass and took a deep drink. Avery brought the glass to her nose but lowered it without taking a sip.

"I'm just happy he has someone. It's great that you two

found each other." She set the glass down and Aborella silently cursed.

"So, where *is* that sister of yours, Avery? It's been weeks since the wedding, and I haven't seen her since." Aborella gave her an exaggerated pout.

"You know honeymooners." Avery shrugged.

Aborella gestured toward one of the dining room chairs, the place already set with a dressed salad tainted with elixir. "Please, sit. You must be starving."

As expected, David sat like a well-trained dog, eliciting a frown from Avery. "Wow, you've got him... trained," Avery said in a tone that was meant to sound light and playful but which reeked of concern for her father.

"Where did Raven and Gabriel go again?" Aborella asked. "Your father has been vague on the details."

"That's because there were no details. Gabriel planned it all, a surprise honeymoon. Even Raven didn't know for sure where they were going. Knowing Gabriel, though, they are probably traveling across Europe or cruising the Virgin Islands. He's not one to spare any expense when it comes to Raven."

Aborella frowned. "Surely she left you some way to contact her. Everyone nowadays stays in constant contact. She must have a cell phone. Can't one of you... communicate with her somehow and find out where she is?" Despite her best efforts, Aborella's voice had become shrill.

Avery wrinkled her nose. "Raven takes her privacy seriously. If she hasn't shared her number with you or my father, I am not the right person to ask for it." She turned to her father. "Dad, are you sure you don't want me to go? It seems like the person you really want here is Raven."

"Of course we want you to stay." He shook his head groggily like he was just waking up.

Aborella forced her shoulders to relax and composed her face again into a jovial expression. "Avery, you'll have to excuse me. I didn't mean to push, and your father and I are so happy to have you here. We simply have some news we wanted to share with the two of you, and we are frustrated we've had to wait this long to do it."

"What's the big news?"

Aborella tucked in her chin and looked at David through her lashes. "Should we tell her? It seems if we wait for Raven, we will be old and gray before the news gets out." She chuckled lightly at the thought. She would never be old and gray. The thought was ridiculous.

David did his duty like a good little compelled human. He lifted his chin and said, "Charlotte and I are getting married."

"Oh! Um... congratulations," Avery forced out. Aborella saw the concern gather in the corners of her cobalt eyes. "But isn't this awfully rushed? You've only known each other a few weeks."

"Your father and I were destined, my darling. You simply can't stop what's meant to be." Aborella gave her a cool smile.

"Dad? How did you ask her?" Avery narrowed her eyes as if she still couldn't believe the news.

Trouble. Aborella had not preprogrammed David to answer that question. She watched his mouth work and a tiny bit of saliva pool in the corner of his lips. Time to think fast.

"I asked him. I've always thought if you wanted something you should work for it, even *take* it if you have to. Right, David?"

He fluttered his lashes and nodded. "Yes. Yes, I think you're right."

Aborella raised her glass. "To David and our future happiness." She held the glass aloft until both David and Avery joined her, then took a long sip. As expected, Avery did the same. Finally.

And spit the liquid back into her glass. "I'm sorry. This tastes off to me."

Aborella frowned. She should not have been able to taste the milkwood. That was odd. Her fist balled under the table. Of course. She'd underestimated the witch. Clearly Raven had placed a spell of protection on her sister. Well, Aborella had more than one trick up her sleeve.

"Oh? I hadn't noticed." She put her glass aside. "Anyway, now that you know our little secret, we have a gift for you."

Under the table, Aborella passed one hand over the other and a jewelry box appeared in her palm, expertly wrapped with an elegant bow. She handed it to Avery across the table.

"Oh, what's this for?" Avery took it, her brows lifting.

"Just a little something I picked up. It reminded me of the color of your eyes. Consider it a thank-you for welcoming me to the family."

Placing the box on the table in front of her, Avery pulled the ribbon and removed the top. Inside, a polished orb glowed blue against the cotton. Old magic, an ordinary crystal enchanted to serve her needs. This amulet acted as both eyes and ears, allowing her to track the activities and whereabouts of its wearer. She would know where Avery was at all times.

Best of all, with extended wear, the crystal would corrupt any protective spell Raven had placed on Avery, making her susceptible to compulsion once more. Under Aborella's influence, Avery would become her tool.

The orb could also be used to find concentrations of magic, although that function had proved unreliable over the years. She'd used a dozen of these polished crystals in the early days without success to try to track the dragon heirs, her latest host being Scoria, the captain of the Obsidian Guard. Scoria had come as close to finding the heirs as anyone she'd ever sent to do so. He'd ended up dead, but at least he'd succeeded in tracing the dragons and Raven here.

"It's beautiful," Avery said.

"Here, let me put it on you." Aborella stood and looped the necklace around Avery's neck, adjusting the chain until it was precisely the right length. "As I thought, it brings out your eyes. Don't you think so, David?"

"Oh... oh yes, it does look beautiful."

"Thank you, Charlotte."

She waved a hand dismissively. "It's nothing. Now, you won't need this because I used the wine in the salad dressing." She swept the plate and her glass from the table. "I'll get the main course."

Aborella grinned as she passed into the kitchen. This would be too easy. The next time Avery contacted her sister, Aborella would be a fly on the wall, or around her neck as the case may be. And this time she wouldn't let her or the treasure of Paragon slip through her fingers.

# CHAPTER EIGHT

*2018*
*Sedona, Arizona*

Rowan's shoulders tensed the moment Alexander stopped talking. She worried the only thing keeping him from a slow retreat into a purgatory of his own making was telling Maiara's story, and his sudden silence unsettled her. As the director of Sunrise House community center, Rowan dealt with children suffering in all sorts of ways: some from the death of a loved one, some from abandonment, some from the loss of a home or stability. The experts talked about stages of grief, but no Kübler-Ross-type model existed for dragons.

Any hope Rowan might have of coaxing Alexander to a place of stability, of coping with Maiara's loss even if he could never recover from it, lay in her ability to keep him talking.

"At this point, did you believe Maiara wasn't human?" Rowan asked. Part of her wondered at his ability to keep this secret. Back then he'd never kept anything from her.

"Why didn't you tell anyone? And what was she? Some sort of dryad?"

He snorted. "I never said she wasn't human. All I said was that I saw her do something magical. She was an indigenous person, and I was still learning about this place the Europeans called the New World. I didn't know what I saw that night."

"Oh." Rowan swelled with hope at his engagement in the conversation. This was good. Getting Alexander to tell her about Maiara was a breakthrough. She was sure of it to the marrow of her bones. His grief was a festering sore, and there was only one way to heal it. "Tell me more. I wasn't with you after New York. I don't know the entire story."

He rose and sauntered to the couch, digging a bottle of tequila from between the cushions. Holding it up to the light, he shook it. Empty. "Fuck, I'm so tired, Rowan." His voice cracked. "I'm tired of this feeling like I'm constantly being torn apart and put back together." Silence imposed on them again.

"I know it hurts, but..." Rowan shifted from foot to foot. She should have known better than to think this would be easy. He was closing off again. The only way this was going to work was if Alexander was an active participant in his own recovery. A person couldn't be tricked into miring through the pain. "You've never properly grieved Maiara's death."

Alexander's eyebrows became two dark slashes in a face much too hollow to be healthy. "What are you talking about? That's ridiculous. It's been hundreds of years."

"No. It's not ridiculous. Yes, it's been hundreds of years. You've suffered, so much, all alone. You are the only one who knows her true story. None of us understood her like you did, Alexander. And because we thought we had to be apart, you had no one to share those memories or your feelings with after she died.

"I bet you've never told anyone the story of how you loved her or how she died. Did you have a memorial for her? You've bottled everything up and let it ferment, and that grief has turned into something bitter and toxic. The only way to make it better is to pop the top and pour it all out. You need to tell me everything. Tell me the rest of the story of how you fell in love with Maiara."

Every part of him tensed, and he gripped the sides of his hair as if his head ached. "No," he said firmly. "That's not going to happen." He reached inside a lampshade and snared a fifth of whiskey. Also empty. He swore again.

The bird on Alexander's shoulder shifted restlessly, staring at Rowan with an unnerving ferocity as if it shared his agitation over the empty bottle. Surely he hadn't trained the poor thing to drink. Maybe the hawk was as strung out as her brother.

No way was she giving up on him. She knew she was right. Pointing a finger at his face, she popped out one hip and unleashed her inner New Yorker. Forget the concerned professional persona. Now she was only his sister and she was about to give him the kick in the dragon ass he needed. "You're a stubborn son of a bitch. I get that. Remembering is painful. I get that too. But this has gone on long enough. Look at yourself. Look at this place! It smells like the floor of a distillery in here, and this abused stray animal thing you've got going on is not a good look on you. You need help, and I'm giving it to you. This is not an offer. I'm telling you how it's going to be."

A low growl percolated up from somewhere deep inside Alexander, and he loomed over her in an unspoken threat. "Get. Out. Leave me alone!"

"No. I'm not going anywhere," Rowan barked. She couldn't leave. If she did, he'd revert to the troubled wraith he'd been before she'd arrived. Her heart couldn't handle that. She needed him to be whole again, this brother who had been her rock in Paragon. "You once taught me to express my emotions using paint and canvas. You saved me. Back then, I would have either gone crazy or offed myself if it weren't for you. All these years I've supported you from afar because I thought that was all I could do.

"Now I know I can do better. It's time for me to return the favor. I'm going to save you the way you saved me. And I'm going to start by cleaning this fucking apartment while you tell me what happened next with Maiara. Because my fucking stars, I have never seen so many empties littering a place in my life."

She strode to the kitchen and dug out a garbage bag from under the sink. At least he had that. She returned and threw the empty tequila and whiskey bottles into the bag. "Start talking."

There was a long pause while Alexander's face alternated between teeth-clenching tension and misty-eyed resolve. Rowan played it cool, acted like she had all the time in the world even though inside she wondered what she would do if he refused to tell her more. She had no plan B.

"Do you remember how we changed Gabriel's mind about New York?" Alexander asked.

"It's been centuries. Remind me."

# CHAPTER NINE

*1699*
*Port of Philadelphia*

When Alexander woke in the Owl's Roost to watery light streaming through his window, his mind was already preoccupied with Maiara. Where was she? What had happened to her the night before? He dressed in the breeches, shirt, vest, and overcoat Willow offered, all designed with hidden panels to accommodate his wings, and thanked the Mountain for the oread's magic and allegiance. While Alexander slept, Willow had cleaned, mended, and reinforced the clothing for the day's journey.

"Shall I carry your bags down for you?" Willow asked. There wasn't much to carry. To this point, they'd traveled constantly, amassing only the necessities.

"No, I'll take them. Last night, Gabriel said he'd procure mounts for the journey. I'm sure he'll be loading a packhorse."

"Very well."

Alexander spread his arms and the oread embraced

him. Energy flowed into the creature. Once Willow had his fill, the pearlescent skin of the nymph flushed with vitality. The oread offered his thanks, then blinked out of sight. He was still there, Alexander knew, and would follow him wherever he traveled. How oread magic worked was a mystery to him, but he was regularly thankful he'd found the creature.

Shouldering his bags, he exited the room and descended the stairs, avoiding the main hall. Slipping out the back entrance, he strode toward the stables, frost crunching under his boots. Once he'd finished what was bound to be an uncomfortable moment with his brother, as all moments with Gabriel tended to be, he was looking forward to a hot breakfast and perhaps a moment to sketch the woman who had occupied his dreams.

At the entrance to the stables, however, he narrowly avoided colliding with Rowan, whose strange appearance made him recoil and look at her more closely.

"By the Mountain, sister, why are you dressed like a man?" he asked, his gaze drifting over the boots, breeches, vest, and coat Rowan wore. With her hair braided beneath a man's hat, she could very well pass as a young male in the right circumstances.

Rowan shot a furtive glance over her shoulder. "Where's Gabriel?"

"I thought he'd be readying the horses in the stable, but considering you've come from that direction, I assume not."

"No, thank the Mountain. This will be easier if I avoid him."

"What will be easier?"

"I'm going to New York."

"I thought Gabriel denied you that request last night."

She pursed her lips and toyed with the end of her braid. "I'm going alone."

Alexander winced. "You can't be serious. You've seen the way these humans treat women."

With a huff, she waved a hand in the air. "I can handle the humans. It's fighting with Gabriel that scares me. He acts like we're still in Paragon and he's next in line for the throne. Defy him and it's off with our heads. No, brother, I'm done allowing him to treat me like his subject."

"You know he'd never hurt you."

Her dark eyes flicked toward the frosty earth. "Do me the courtesy of an hour's head start before you tell him."

"Rowan, please. We must separate if we are ever to have a real life again, but surely you want to say goodbye. You can't leave things like this between you. This could be forever. You both deserve better."

She frowned. Gabriel's insistence on leading the group as if they were a battalion of soldiers was wearing on them both, but Alexander couldn't let her give up on their family. Forced physical separation was one thing, but they all needed each other emotionally even if their contact remained sporadic and from a distance.

"Mark my words, I won't go west. I don't want to isolate myself from the humans. I want to live among them. I want friends. Real friends. The kind I was never allowed to have in Paragon. I want community."

"Give Gabriel another chance. I swear to you, I will help you convince Gabriel to go to New York if you promise to stay with us until we get there. With me." And he would. He'd find a way to give her what she needed. But the thought of her leaving and traveling this new world alone made his chest ache.

She folded her arms. "You are not playing fair, Alexander. I've never been able to deny you a single thing."

"I never promised to be fair." He winked.

"Fine, but know this, if Gabriel refuses me again, I will go, and you must take this as my goodbye because there shan't be another." She turned on her heel and headed toward the main entrance of the Owl's Roost.

Alexander entered the stables and found Gabriel's pack leaning against one of the stalls. He flopped his bags down beside them, then froze as an electric tingle made the skin along his back hot and tight. He whirled to find Maiara standing behind him, holding the reins to a pony laden with supplies. Her hawk steadied itself on her shoulder.

"Your sister should go where she wants." She narrowed her eyes. "New York is safer. It would be safer for all of you."

He released a deep breath. "You heard that? I promise it's not up to me, but I do expect to speak to Gabriel about it."

"Speak to me about what?" Gabriel marched into the stables, a lumpy flour sack tossed across one shoulder that Alexander assumed contained food for their journey. He offered Maiara a hasty good morning.

Alexander shifted, uncomfortable now that the confrontation was nigh. Saying he'd speak to their older brother was remarkably different than actually doing it. Gabriel was an intimidating force of nature. He braced himself against the stomach-churning nerves that always accompanied a desire to challenge his brother, and with a fortifying breath said, "I think we should take Rowan to New York."

Gabriel rested the bag next to their other things before

meeting Alexander's gaze with total confidence. "No." He pivoted and entered the stall, cooing to the stallion inside.

Tempted to let the conversation die there, he sighed, but the nod of support Maiara gave him encouraged him to try again. Wiping his sweaty palms on his jacket, he moved inside the stall door and continued. "She's going to go whether you like it or not. She's an adult, Gabriel. She can make her own choices. Would you like her to do so behind your back or with your blessing?"

A grunt came from Gabriel, who did not turn from the horse he was saddling. "She will do as I tell her to do. Rowan has always been headstrong. She'll fall into line once we are on the road."

The way his brother said it—as if it was a foregone conclusion—made Alexander want to bang his head against the stall door. Honestly, caving in his own head would be easier than getting through Gabriel's thick skull with any idea that wasn't self-serving to the dragon. He should have let Rowan ride off with a hug and his well wishes.

Only Maiara's unflappable voice stopped him from retreating. "I will not guide you if you force her to go with you."

That caused Gabriel to stop what he was doing and advance toward her. "Pardon? Are you addressing me?"

"There is no honor in slavery."

"My sister is not a slave," he boomed. The force of his anger nearly rattled the rafters.

"Then she can go where she pleases. New York." Maiara raised her chin.

Rushing forward, Gabriel moved in a flash, his presence meant to intimidate. Alexander stepped between them. Not that he expected his brother would harm her, but he didn't dare take that chance. "You heard her. She will not guide us if you do not allow Rowan her freedom."

"You are unfamiliar with the dangers of this land," Maiara added. "You will not get far on your own."

Few stood their ground against Gabriel, but despite her diminutive stature, she faced his brother with the unflinching and cool stance of a warrior. Tension thrummed in the air between them. She'd thrown down an ultimatum. Alexander was stupefied when Gabriel seemed to consider it. He bowed his head and paced the length of the stall, twice.

When he looked at them again, he seemed to have come to a decision, one that didn't feel comfortable in his skin if the dark flush on his cheeks was anything to go by. "We go to New York. Then we go west."

Maiara tipped her head. "As you wish."

Stepping around her, Gabriel strode toward the exit and the Owl's Roost.

Once his brother was well out of earshot, Alexander huffed out a breath, amazed by her courage. "That was incredible."

"Why do you allow him to treat you that way?" she asked, her gaze finding his. Her words held no judgment, only curiosity, but they cut him to the quick.

"I don't—" His ears grew hot. He didn't need to explain himself to her. Through a clenched jaw, he said, "If you'll excuse me." He bowed at the waist in lieu of goodbye and followed his brother's footsteps back to the inn.

CHAPTER TEN

Traveling from the Port of Philadelphia to the colony of New York on horseback was expected to take four days and required a ferry to cross the Delaware River. However, Maiara assured them that the King's Highway and Post Road they would follow would be well appointed with inns along the way. She anticipated no hardship finding places at regular intervals to rest their horses, replenish their supplies, or spend the night.

Alexander hoped these inns would be more receptive to their native guide than the Owl's Roost, although he seriously doubted it. He suspected Maiara faced prejudices everywhere she went. He'd save her from the ignorant fools if he could.

"I like this Maiara." Rowan adjusted herself in the saddle. She'd been beaming from the moment Gabriel had announced he would take her to New York. She rode beside Alexander on a mild-mannered Appaloosa while Gabriel and Tobias rode ahead, the packhorse between them. Gabriel followed directly behind Maiara, his clenched jaw indicating his displeasure to not be in the lead.

"Me too."

Rowan sent him a crooked smile. He recognized the mischievous twinkle in her eye immediately and braced himself for trouble. "You fancy her."

He scoffed.

"You do! She makes your dragon shiver, doesn't she? Tell the truth, brother."

"Hold your tongue."

"Are you afraid? There are no rules against it here. No royal decrees against princes and commoners to abide under. We are free to choose. And it's not like she's a witch or something. The law says nothing about humans."

He licked his lips. Was she human? He wasn't entirely sure. "It's folly. Soon we will all go our separate ways. What type of dragon would I be to pursue her when I have no intention of revealing our secret? How can there exist a relationship between two beings when one can never know who the other really is?"

Rowan frowned. "I suppose you speak the truth, although I find it quite sad to think the lot of us are doomed to a long and lonely life on this infernal planet." When Alexander didn't respond, she nudged her horse into a jog and engaged Tobias in some unheard conversation.

They'd made good use of the short daylight hours, stopping only for necessary breaks and to partake in the cheese, dried fruit, and bread they'd packed from the Owl's Roost. Twilight descended upon the road and in a blink gave way to the dark of night. Weighed down by the cold, they were all relieved to come upon a small inn called the Green Gate.

Each of them made haste to dismount and lead their horses to the stables, anxious to take part in the warmth of the hearth and a fair meal. But before Alexander could follow his siblings inside, Maiara tugged his arm.

"I am sorry, Alexander, if I offended you with my words about your brother."

He frowned. "I am not offended. You simply do not understand the ways of my family."

Her face fell. "This is your way?"

Was it? Alexander didn't know. It certainly was the Paragonian way for the eldest living heir of Paragon to rule the kingdom. But in the New World there were no such rules. The truth was he had been afraid to face his brother, and her question about why he tolerated Gabriel's authoritarian manner was warranted. It simply wasn't something he was ready to bring into the light of day. He wasn't sure he could explain the comfort in letting Gabriel lead. A very small part of him wondered who exactly he would become now that he was no longer a prince of Paragon. Gabriel's presence, however overbearing, gave him the luxury of not having to think about it... yet.

Which reminded him, he'd never asked her about that night he'd seen her vanish. He turned the tables and answered her question with his own. "What is your way, Maiara? I saw you that first night at the Owl's Roost. I followed you into the forest and saw you... near a tree." He looked behind him and lowered his voice. "You disappeared."

"It is rude to follow someone."

"Yes. I am sorry about that. But I need to know... I think we could come to understand each other if we were honest—"

"I am Maiara, half Potawatomi from my mother and half English from my father. I was a healer for my people once, and now I am your hired guide. Nothing more." Her jaw was tight as she spoke.

"You were a healer? I thought you said you were a trapper." He was growing frustrated trying to figure out the enigmatic woman.

"My mother was a healer, my father was a trapper. I have been both."

"Where is your family now?"

"Dead." Her teeth clenched and she looked away from him.

A weight settled over Alexander's heart, and he felt like a brute interrogating her as he was. He lowered his voice. "I... lost my parents as well, and my eldest brother. They were murdered for political reasons. That is why we left our homeland and came here."

That seemed to surprise her, and she returned her gaze to his face. "I am sorry."

They stood with each other as grief snaked around them. He inched toward her and placed a comforting hand on her elbow. "I should join the others. Will you dine with us?"

"I may not be welcome here." She frowned.

"You are welcome. I just welcomed you. And if anyone takes issue with that, they shall take it up with me." He lowered himself to her height. "Please."

"Yes. I will eat with you." She whispered to her hawk, and the bird flew into the rafters of the stable.

He took a step in the direction of the inn but stopped short when he realized she'd never actually answered his question. "Maiara, that night in the woods..."

"Yes?"

"I saw you... vanish."

She shook her head. "People don't vanish."

"But I did see you in the woods."

Her face became an impassive mask. No secrets would

be forthcoming. "My people sleep in the trees." She pointed up.

"In the trees. You mean in the branches. You were in the branches?"

She answered only with a soft smile before leading the way inside.

Maiara's reception was no better at the Green Gate than at the Owl's Roost. She was met with murmurs of "savage" and worse. And although they served her the same supper as the rest of them, she was not allowed any ale.

"We abide by the law here," the barmaid said. "No Africans or Indians may be served ale or whiskey, and don't even try takin' her upstairs."

Alexander promptly ordered two pints and gave her one as soon as he was served. Although Maiara seemed to appreciate his generosity and ate and drank her fill, Alexander felt tension in the silent way she held her space. It was as if she wasn't there at all. And although he tried to engage her in conversation, her curt responses kept their exchanges short.

Tobias entertained them with the story of how they'd survived an attack by a band of pirates on their way to the New World, and Gabriel followed it up with his own tale of winning at dice in the south of France. Neither triggered a smile from her, although the patrons within earshot were overtaken with boisterous laughter. It saddened Alexander that she showed so little joy, and he wondered if it was their surroundings or something else that bothered her.

Whatever it was, when each of them made to retire for the night, she headed for the door.

"Where are you going?" He followed her to where the shadows gathered far from the hearth and the flickering candles.

"To make camp." Her chin was high, and nothing about her expression suggested she was fearful or disappointed to be heading into the cold night.

Alexander wouldn't have it. "It's too cold to sleep in tree branches. I can get you a room."

"It's not allowed."

He reached for her, his hand landing gently against her cheek where the tips of his fingers brushed the sleek edge of her silky hair. Their eyes locked, and the same electric charge built between them as the first time he'd seen her.

It was like being underwater, pushed toward her by an opposing current that promised their eventual collision. It left him semibreathless and sure that at some point, the force would topple them over a waterfall or draw them into a whirlpool. After all, his head was already spinning.

"You could stay with me," he said softly, then clarified, "I have a suite."

Her ebony eyes warmed, and she gave him a hint of a smile. For a split second he was sure she'd say yes, that the feeling was mutual and as undeniable as a force of nature. Yet she peeled his hand from her cheek and said, "Rest well, Alexander. We have a long journey ahead."

She bowed her head slightly and slipped out the door into the night. After a moment's hesitation, he tried to follow her, but she was already gone, another shadow in the inky darkness. Even her hawk had disappeared from its roost in the stables.

This pattern repeated itself the next two nights. Once,

he found her things beside a tree, although he never found her in that tree's branches. The next night, he found nothing at all, not a single footstep to mark where she'd gone. Until the third night a vicious storm moved in. The temperature dropped and the wind roared as if winter was a scorned goddess who wanted her revenge.

That was the night of the attack.

They'd finished supper at an inn called the Lion's Head. Alexander and Maiara were alone at a table near the hearth, Gabriel, Tobias, and Rowan having already retired to their rooms, when a man's guttural scream cut through the building's warm interior. Alexander, along with several other patrons, rushed outside to find a British soldier staggering toward them. From the back of his red coat, an arrow protruded, not deep by the looks of it but having the effect of straining the man's breathing. He collapsed face-first in the snow. Above them, Maiara's hawk screeched and circled, the ominous sound sending a foreboding shudder down his spine.

"Help me remove it." Maiara knelt at the soldier's side and pressed her fingers along his back, feeling the bones.

"It is between his ribs. We must pull it out." She gripped the arrow with both hands but recoiled when her gaze fell on the fletching. To Alexander, the arrow seemed ordinary enough, except that bloody fingerprints stained the white feathers. Decorated for death.

"What's wrong?"

"Help me."

He winced, knowing the barb would tear the man's flesh, but squatted beside her and wrapped his hands around hers. "One, two, three." Together, they yanked the arrow from the stranger's back. Blood gurgled from the wound.

Maiara dug under her cloak and brought forth an otter skin pouch. After untying it, she removed an amulet—a white shell of a type Alexander had never seen. Its lustrous exterior reflected the silvery moonlight with colors that seemed to dance across its surface. She rolled the soldier over, opened the collar of his shirt, and placed the shell in the hollow of his throat.

"What is that?" Alexander asked.

"To heal him," Maiara said.

Before Alexander could question the effectiveness of Maiara's amulet, the mouth of a musket appeared before him, pointed at Maiara. "What you doing there, injin?" The ruddy-faced owner of the Lion's Head scowled behind the gun's barrel. The hostility twisting his features made it easy to read his thoughts. The arrow was from a native weapon. He believed she was responsible for the attack.

Enraged on her behalf, Alexander shoved the barrel of the musket aside. "Sir, lower your weapon. She's providing assistance to this man."

The soldier began to cough, sucking in deep lungfuls of air. Maiara removed the shell from his chest and returned it to her bag. Alexander raised an eyebrow as the man's breathing evened out and his pale features pinked to the picture of health. Awestruck, he helped the soldier into a seated position but was appalled when instead of offering his appreciation for Maiara's efforts, the man turned accusatory eyes on her.

"You," he said through his teeth. "She's a savage, I tell you!" He glanced around the circle of onlookers and pointed at her. "I watched a man of her kind strip the flesh from my horse with his bare hands!"

Horrified gasps greeted his words.

Alexander protested to the contrary and stated Maiara

had, in fact, saved his ungrateful life. The crowd barked their skepticism; they hadn't seen what he had. The argument heated to the point of his distraction, and Alexander didn't notice Maiara slip away. But once the skirmish broke and the soldier sauntered inside, he looked for her in the crowd. She was gone.

Blending into the night, he made himself invisible and took a deep breath. He could smell her on the wind. The snow fell thick and heavy, increasing until he struggled to see an arm's length ahead. If he weren't a dragon, he would have lost her in the storm. But her scent was unmistakable to him now. Plus his speed and agility far outpaced the mortal's. In minutes, he'd closed the distance between them.

Into the thick of trees he followed her, deep into the woods until she found another tree like the one in Philadelphia but with a narrower trunk. He watched in abject horror as she began to remove her clothing.

Dragons could feel the cold, but it wasn't dangerous to them. They were born of flame, and fire blazed within them. Humans did feel it, he knew, and he'd seen the way the tavern workers had huddled against this storm as if their exposed skin ached from the stinging air.

The discomfort he felt on her behalf warred with the desire to watch her again as she lowered her deerskin tunic from her shoulders. Her hair flowed like spilled ink down her back where a shiver traveled the length of the silky skin over her spine. She planted her hands on the tree, but this time nothing happened. She removed her hands and then tried again. Nothing. She began to slap the bark frantically, the hawk in the branches above her shrieking into the wind.

In the distance, a roar cut through the storm and turned her head. Alexander had never heard such a sound, not in

Paragon or in this world, and it made the hair on his neck stand on end.

"No. No." Maiara's words cut through the howling wind. Frantic, she searched the trees. What was she hoping to find?

Alexander didn't know what to do as she trembled visibly, the snow gathering in her lashes and hair. That was until her sobs reached him. She bent down and tried to dress, but her fingers were stiff and she fumbled with the skins and pelts. The roar came again, closer. The sight of her tears solidifying on her cheeks drove him into action.

A protective nature was a dragon's prerogative. To be blessed with strength, speed, flight, and immortality came with a certain responsibility, the same that made him stand up that first night in the Owl's Roost. He could choose. He could rise above this world and its cruel expectations, and he could help her. He would help her.

He dropped his invisibility and stepped forward, the snow bombarding his cheeks, his dark hair, his breeches and waistcoat. Her head turned and she panicked when she saw him, her eyes becoming wide, dark pools as her numb fingers worked hopelessly to gather her skins against her naked breast. The roar came again, closer still, and she shook violently at the sound.

Alexander's wings punched from his coat, and in one mighty thrust, he closed the space between them. Her eyes met his and she collapsed. He caught her in his arms, his wings wrapping around her to protect her from the storm.

The weight of a stare raised his head. There was a man, an Indian, standing in the woods in the distance. Even with his dragon sight, he could hardly see him. The snow was too thick. But a strange blue light glowed from the indigenous man's neck. The Indian raised his bow and notched an arrow.

Alexander blinked out of sight, cloaking Maiara in his invisibility and moving her behind the protection of the tree. Gathering her things, he carried her back to the Lion's Head, swearing to protect her to the snow, the moon, and the hawk that followed him home.

# CHAPTER ELEVEN

*2018*
*Sedona, Arizona*

"I'd forgotten that Maiara was the reason Gabriel let me go to New York." Rowan drummed her fingers on the table. "What was she doing naked next to the tree again? The explanation of her sleeping in the branches makes no sense. She'd freeze to death. And what did she say after you revealed yourself to her? When you showed her your wings, you basically pulled the dragon out of the bag. What happened to swearing to keep our secret?" She returned to cleaning as she spoke, scrubbing the counter while waiting for Alexander to answer.

When the silence drew her attention back to him, he ran his hands through his wild mess of dark hair and said, "I love you, my sister."

He looked positively wrecked. She'd been so wrapped up in the story she'd almost forgotten why it was important that he tell it. "I love you too."

"I need a break." He frowned. "And a shower."

"And a square meal," she added, heartbroken to see him like this.

He nodded. "I'm tired. I can't do this anymore."

She tossed the rag she was using into the sink and approached him, pulling him into a hug, which he thankfully returned. "You did so well today. That's enough for now. Go take a shower. I'll finish picking up around here and maybe scrounge us up some lunch."

Alexander walked toward the window, opened it, and let Nyx take flight.

"I'm relieved you don't shower with her." Rowan gave a low laugh.

Alexander raised his eyebrows. "She's all I have—the only thing left of Maiara—and I've had her for a very, very long time."

"Right." She watched him lumber toward the bedroom, his shoulders hunched. Time had not been kind to her brother. "I do want to hear the rest," she called after him. "I would be honored if you kept the memory of Maiara alive by continuing to share with me, once you've had time to rest."

He gave her a placating wave.

No sooner had he closed the door behind him than she texted Nick and was soon joined by him, Raven, Gabriel, and Tobias inside the small apartment. Raven got to work cooking lunch while Rowan relayed what she'd learned from Alexander to the group.

Perhaps it was because of Nick's turbulent past that her mate tended to take the supernatural in stride; his childhood reality of being abused was far scarier than learning there were dragons, witches, and vampires living among humans. But while his exterior seemed calm, she knew he was analyzing everything she'd told him with a detective's mind.

"So, we have a three-hundred-year-old bird who used to belong to an indigenous guide who may or may not have blended into living trees, had survived in the wilderness alone for some time, and feared other Indians who had presumably butchered her people. I'm going out on a limb and saying she wasn't human." Nick rocked back on his heels and surveyed the rest of them as if they had the key to solving this mystery.

Rowan tied off one full garbage bag and grabbed another. "I met her. She seemed human to me, but she had magic, that's for sure."

"We knew she had magic. I used her healing amulet this year to cure one of my patients." Tobias rubbed the back of his neck.

"You have it? I thought it was burned with her." Rowan frowned. She was almost certain Alexander knew nothing of the kept amulet, and she could feel her hackles rise at the thought of what finding out about its existence would do to his already fragile state.

Gabriel confirmed her worst fears. "Yes... He doesn't know."

"You fucking bastard. How could you keep this from him?" Rowan gave Gabriel a withering stare.

"I'm sure that's going to go over well when it comes out," Nick murmured. Rowan widened her eyes at him in agreement.

"Do you have it with you?" Rowan asked Tobias.

Gabriel growled. "No. We agreed he'd keep it locked away. It's too powerful to risk it falling into the wrong hands."

"Actually..."

"Tobias?" Gabriel hissed. "Don't tell me you did something stupid."

"I wasn't sure what we'd be dealing with here with Alexander." He shrugged. "I'm a human doctor. It seemed prudent to have it in case we needed it."

Gabriel opened his mouth to tear into him, but Raven held up her hand.

"No, I'm glad he did," Raven said from the kitchen where she was wrapping what looked like enchiladas and tucking them into two large lasagna pans. "I'd like to analyze her magic. See if I can understand it better. The hawk shouldn't have survived this long after her death."

Rowan glanced toward the bedroom door, all her protective instincts waking up. "I don't care what you do with it. Just keep it to yourself until we get him in a better place."

RAVEN UNDERSTOOD WHERE ROWAN WAS COMING from. Until recently, Gabriel hadn't known where Alexander was and couldn't have returned the amulet even if he'd wanted to. But now that they were here, it seemed both wrong to keep it from him and terribly cruel to give it back. Alexander was clearly in a fragile state of mind. Learning what Gabriel had done and seeing the amulet might do more damage than good.

She slid the two pans of enchiladas she'd made into the oven and rubbed her growling belly. Baby was hungry again, and he liked things spicy. She'd learned it was common in dragon pregnancies, the hotter the better. She opened the cupboard next to the fridge. With any luck, Alexander kept some hot sauce on hand.

Her phone vibrated on the counter. She frowned at the screen. Avery again.

"Who keeps texting you?" Gabriel asked from where he was helping his siblings clean. "I swear that's the hundredth time today."

"Avery." Raven sighed. "She thinks we're still on Maui, celebrating our honeymoon. I haven't told her about Sedona. Too hard to explain why we're here."

"What does she want?"

"Remember how my father brought that woman to our wedding?" Raven asked. Everyone nodded, even Nick who had met her entire family that day. The red-headed woman stood out in a crowd. "Her name is Charlotte. Apparently their relationship is serious and Dad desperately wants me to meet her. Avery keeps putting them off, but she's running out of excuses. She's wondering when we'll be home so she can get the two of them off her back."

"Maybe we *should* go back," Tobias said. "You are over four months pregnant, and frankly, things seem further along than they should be at this point." He looked worriedly at her ever-growing abdomen. "I'd like to get you under an ultrasound and see what's happening."

"Uh, I think you should know I've been this large for a while. You simply didn't see it because I used a cloaking spell to conceal it until the wedding. It's just exhausting using that much magic anymore." She spread her hands and shrugged. "This is me in all my glory."

Tobias's eyes widened. "You should have said something. This is a high-risk pregnancy. You have a dragon egg growing inside your human uterus, Raven. This is nothing to mess around with."

Raven sighed. "We have time, right?"

Tobias's expression turned clinical, the doctor in him

coming to the surface. "If you were a dragon, I'd say you had two more months, but there's no record of a dragon being born to a human. With this pregnancy, I think we have to expect the unexpected. Sabrina has a fully equipped medical ward lined up for us in Chicago, but it won't do us any good if we're still here when you go into labor."

Predictably, Gabriel's protective mating instinct kicked in at Tobias's words, and he placed a hand on her shoulder. "Tell Avery she'll just need to deal with your father. We should go to Chicago and stay with Tobias and Sabrina until the baby comes."

"What about Alexander?"

"Alexander has Rowan."

"I feel like we made progress today," Rowan said. "It might be better if I have him all to myself for a while anyway. He seems to get overwhelmed easily."

Gabriel placed a kiss on Raven's temple. "You have to think of your health and that of the baby first."

"You're right. We should look into flights," Raven said, more to appease her mate than because she thought there was any rush. "Will the end of the week be soon enough?" That would give her time to analyze Maiara's amulet. Maiara's abilities were unique. The idea that she could keep the hawk alive beyond her death was remarkable, and Raven longed to better understand her magic. If she couldn't use this understanding to help Alexander, perhaps she could use the knowledge to help someone else.

"As long as you're not having any symptoms, I think that will be just fine," Tobias said. Gabriel smiled at Tobias as if he considered her agreement a victory. He pulled out his phone and started checking flights.

Everyone quieted as Alexander emerged from his bedroom, dressed in a fresh pair of jeans and a black T-shirt.

Hair still wet from the shower, it dripped onto his shoulders in two dark patches. After an impromptu staring match, Alexander spoke first. "I thought you said something about lunch?"

Raven peeked inside the oven to confirm the shredded cheese had been reduced to melty goodness, thinking she could eat at least half of it. She was relieved both pans were ready to go and pulled them from the oven. "Come and get it."

She dished out a generous helping and held out the plate to him. "Alexander, can you help me understand something?"

Slowly he took the plate and gave her a tentative nod. Behind him, Rowan shot her a warning glance, but she ignored it. If Alexander would tell her this one thing, it would save her so much time. "Did Maiara identify as a witch like me?"

He stared at the enchilada on his plate like he was trying to decide whether to ditch it and run for the hills or answer her question.

Rowan spoke up. "Alexander, you don't have to—"

"No. I'll answer her," he said, finally meeting Raven's eyes again. "The answer is no, but she did practice magic and it was a type I'd never encountered before."

# CHAPTER TWELVE

*1699*
*Colony of New Jersey*

Alexander hurried back to the Lion's Head Inn with Maiara in his arms. Her body was limp and cold despite wrapping her in her clothing as best he could. Using his invisibility, he snuck past the innkeeper and hastened to the room he'd let.

"Willow, stoke the fire. She's chilled through," he ordered. His oread hurried to the fireplace and tended the logs. Alexander stretched Maiara out on the bed and tucked her beneath the blankets.

He'd hastily collected her clothing from beside the tree, and now that she was covered, he discreetly withdrew them from under the linens. He cringed when he noticed a star-shaped scar below the collarbone of her right shoulder. What past hardships had this brave woman encountered?

"Shot by an arrow," Willow said from the place where he squatted beside the now blazing fire.

"You know this mark?" Alexander folded her things and

set them on the chair beside the window before layering another blanket over her. He hated the dusky color of her lips.

Willow approached the bed, perusing Maiara with a tip of his head. "I've never been shot myself, you understand, but I have seen it. A knife would create a slice." He made a sawing motion across his arm. "An arrow makes a star."

Alexander's eyes narrowed. "Do you know what's wrong with her?"

Willow turned surprised eyes on him. "I have no idea. If she was simply human, I might suggest she was suffering from exposure but—"

"What makes you think she isn't human?"

"Oh, she's human, but she has employed strong magic. Can't you smell it?" The oread beckoned him closer.

Alexander leaned over her until his nose was temptingly close to her ear and drew in her scent. She smelled sweet as spring grass with a hint of wildflowers. Previously, he'd also smelled the deerskin she wore along with the faint residue of horsehair. Not any longer. Now that she slept naked beneath the blankets, he sorted her scent from the others in the room. Her skin carried the freshness of new green life. The first night he'd met her, she'd smelled of pine, bark, and fresh air. This scent was different. This scent held the crisp tang of magic.

"What is she?" he asked. "A witch?"

Willow rubbed his marble-smooth chin. "No, I don't think so. Perhaps she is like me, a nymph, but not of the mountain—of the forest. A dryad. Although..."

"What is it, Willow? Please tell me."

"As I mentioned to you before, if she were a full dryad, she should be hibernating right now. It's winter and her kind is normally associated with deciduous trees. Once the leaves fall, their spirit goes home and sleeps until spring. Besides, her flesh is undeniably human. That much I know."

Alexander watched her chest rise and fall, wishing she'd open her eyes. The room had warmed to sweat-inducing temperature, but her hands remained cold and her lips still held that unsettling dusky tint. "Do you think a warm bath would help?" he asked Willow.

The oread was distracted from answering when a slap at the window turned his head. A dark shadow beat against the warped glass. Alexander turned the pewter lock and eased the casement open on its hinge. Maiara's hawk flew inside, landing on the bed beside Maiara.

"Oh dear," Willow said. "Poor thing must have been attracted by the light. Would you like me to help you chase it out?"

"No." Alexander closed the window and locked it. "The bird is her pet. Perhaps its nearness will benefit her recovery."

After a moment by her side, the hawk fluttered to the pile of her things on the chair and burrowed into them. A moment later she emerged with the otter skin pouch in her beak.

"You brilliant, brilliant bird," Alexander said. Of course, he'd watched Maiara heal the soldier with her shell. With any luck, he could use the same magic to heal her now. He untied the bag and removed the amulet, again admiring the multicolored sheen that reminded him of the surface of a clear spring pool in the morning sunlight.

He positioned it in the hollow of her throat, the same place he'd observed her place it on the soldier. The hawk bobbed its head as if she approved. At once, Maiara's lips pinked, and then the tone of her skin corrected to its usual sunny radiance. Inhaling deeply, he slipped his hand inside hers, now warm and pliant. "Maiara?"

"She wakes," Willow said, blinking out of sight.

Her lashes fluttered against her cheeks and then flew open. Air flowed into her lungs. Maiara jackknifed into a sitting position, clutching the blankets to her chest.

"Where are we?" Her eyes widened, and she surveyed the room with barely contained panic.

"In my room at the Lion's Head."

"I am not supposed to be here." She started to climb from the bed, but his hand landed gently on her shoulder.

"No one saw. I—" How much did she remember about seeing him with his wings extended? "I used discretion."

She nodded her understanding. The shell had flown from her neck when she'd sat up, and now she swept it from the quilt and into her palm.

"Your bird reminded me about the amulet. It healed you," Alexander said, glancing at the hawk who now perched on the headboard.

Maiara stared at him as if she were reading his soul, her expression taking on a faraway quality. "Please?" She pointed at the otter skin pouch.

"Of course." Alexander handed it to her, and she returned the amulet to it, tying the strings tightly before looping them around her wrist. When her gaze met his again, the intensity made Alexander flinch.

"You had wings."

He swore under his breath. Gabriel would be livid if he shared his secret, as would the others. Then again, they'd shared their true identity with the oreads. If Maiara had magic, perhaps telling her the truth wouldn't be his worst mistake. Who was he kidding? Gabriel would be furious.

"You were disoriented. Naked in a storm. There was a beast roaring in the distance and a native man."

"You saw an Indian man? A Mohawk warrior?" She hugged the blankets tighter to her chest.

"I don't know what tribe he was from, but he wore his hair roached and had a stone around his neck that glowed blue in the moonlight. I saw him from a great distance." Alexander hated the flash of terror she saw in Maiara's eyes. "He aimed an arrow in our direction, and that is when I took you and brought you here before he could do any harm. Is he the one who shot the soldier?"

She lowered her chin. "Yes. That man is very dangerous. I never thought he would follow me here among the *cmokmanuk.*" Before his magic could translate the word, she did it for him. "White men. I thought he would avoid the white men."

"What were you doing naked in a snow storm, banging your fists against a tree?"

She raised her dark brows, and the corner of her mouth lifted slightly. "I told you my people slept in the trees."

He gave her a frustrated look. "What does that mean?"

"Tell me why you have wings?"

He stared at the fire. "It seems we both have secrets." When he turned back to her, he searched her face. Their gazes met and held. The same arresting force from the first time he'd seen her came again, like standing at the bottom of a cliff and feeling the wind shear off the side, thrusting him forward, driving him toward her.

She must have felt it too, because her lips parted and her expression held the same wonder he thought his must. Did she want to know him as he wished to know her?

"Tell me what you are, Maiara," he asked softly. "And I will do you the same courtesy."

Licking her lips, she considered his offer. "It is hard to describe in your language, but I will try. I am a *Midew*... a medicine woman. Among my people, certain women and men gifted with mystic abilities by the *kshe'mnIto*... the Great Spirit, join a society called the Midewiwin among whom we study healing and other *mide*."

"Mide?"

"Mmm... Magic."

"What does that have to do with the tree?"

"*Kshe'mnIto* has blessed me with great magic. Magic that allows me to hide inside the trees."

"Inside the trees. Are you a nymph? A dryad?"

She shook her head. "I don't know these words. I am *Potawatomi* and I am *Midew*. My magic comes from *kshe'mnIto*."

"The one you call the Great Spirit."

She nodded.

"Why is that man after you... the Mohawk man?"

She shook her head. "Tell me about your wings."

"Dragon," he said softly.

"Dra...gon," she repeated slowly. "I do not know this word."

Approaching the bed, he sat beside her, his stomach flipping at the thought of what he was about to do. He took a fortifying breath. A dragon's wings were intimate, private. It was, he supposed, like any body part that was normally kept hidden away. Showing his wings was akin to removing his clothing in some ways. And maybe he owed her this given that he had watched her undress beside the tree like the letch that he was.

He allowed his wings to unfurl and extend, slowly at first and then with a snap that gave them a much-needed stretch. Big mistake. Nikan started from the headboard, flapping wildly and circling the room to the sound of Maiara's ineffective attempts to calm her until finally Alexander opened the window and let her out. When he turned back, Maiara's ebony gaze was a palpable thing.

Almost palpable. Without any sudden moves, he returned to her side and lowered himself to sit beside her. She didn't scream or run. That was a good sign. Her trembling fingers lifted toward the bony edge of his left wing. He stilled, another part of his anatomy twitching with anticipation. It had been a long time since anyone had touched his wings.

Swallowing hard, he closed his eyes as her fingertips connected with the sensitive flesh and caressed along its length. He stifled a moan. And then the touch turned firm. He opened his eyes when she tugged firmly on the talon at the joint and winced when she went about unfolding its natural bend. "Maiara..." She poked the webbing with her fingers as if she were testing its elasticity. He cleared his throat and jerked the wing from her grip. "Maiara... please, that's quite uncomfortable."

Her eyebrows rose as if this surprised her. She nodded her head. "Dragon," she mumbled under her breath.

He nodded. "I can change." He tapped his chest and then reached for his sketchbook and flipped to a page where he'd drawn a fully shifted dragon. It wasn't him, exactly, more of a combination of dragons he'd known, straight from his imagination. He showed it to her. "I can change into this."

To demonstrate, he held up his hand, curled his fingers, and allowed his talons to sprout from his first knuckle. She inhaled sharply. He folded both his talons and his wings away. "I'm sorry. I didn't mean to scare you."

She shook her head. "I am not afraid. You are... We have

a different word for it. *Piasa.* Only, I did not know you could look like a man." She stared at him for some time, and he wondered what she would tell her people about him when she returned home.

"So, why was the Mohawk warrior following you, and why were you hiding in the tree?"

She looked down at her fingers tangled atop the blanket between them. "My people, the Potawatomi, are part of a larger group white men call the Algonquians. It is from these clans that the *Midewiwin* society"—she tapped her chest—"was formed. The Algonquians are at war with the Iroquois, a confederacy that include the Mohawk."

"War? Why?"

"Our territory is home to many animals prized for their furs. The French pay and they are good to trade. The Iroquois want our land and the wealth it will bring them. Already they have forced my people south from where my ancestors once lived."

"And this warrior is hunting you because you are Algonquian?"

She shook her head and tears spilled from her eyes. "He is hunting me because I am the last of my kind. The last *Midew.*"

Alexander's chest contracted at the sob in her voice. He desperately longed to comfort her, but she spoke on. "This warrior traded his soul to an evil spirit for the power to slay my kind. He is a monster, a *wendigo*, with an insatiable appetite for blood. Very fast and very hard to kill."

"A *wendigo*?" Alexander wasn't familiar with the word or the creature.

"The *Midewiwin* protected my people with their magic. Now they are dead. He murdered all but me."

Alexander raised a hand toward her scar. "Is that how you got this?"

"Yes."

He thought about the morning she'd stood up to Gabriel for Rowan. More than bravery was at work that day. "You said you didn't believe he'd come near the white men. That's why you believed we'd be safer in New York. But you didn't anticipate that the weather would make it impossible for you to use the trees to hide."

"You are large men. White men. Until the soldier, I thought we were safe." Her lids drooped from exhaustion.

"You're tired. You should rest," he said.

She attempted to rise. "Of course. It is too cold for the trees, but I will try to find a place."

He shook his head and nudged her shoulder toward the mattress. "No. You will sleep here tonight with me," he said. "From now on, you will have my protection."

She relaxed into the mattress, her dark hair spilling over the side of the pillow. "Why are you helping me?"

"I am a dragon. I protect what is mine," he said, and indeed, his inner dragon stirred and chuffed, eyeing Maiara as if she were a valuable jewel.

Far from comforting her, Maiara's eyes narrowed and she shook her head. "Yours?"

Alexander chided himself. The fear he saw in Maiara's expression was the kind he'd seen in Rowan's time and time again at the palace in Paragon. Any kindness or love Rowan received from their parents had been transactional, and it had made her weary of the cost of any sliver of happiness. Did Maiara fear that Alexander would expect something in return for his protection? Her body or her magic? The thought turned his stomach.

"I mean only that you are my guide, Maiara, and, I

think, my friend. I will protect you as long as we are together. That is all."

He sensed by the jut of her chin that she didn't fully believe him but was too exhausted to fight. Her shoulders relaxed and she sank deeper into the mattress.

"Sleep, Maiara. I will keep watch over you," he said. It was enough. She slipped into oblivion, and he kept his promise.

# CHAPTER THIRTEEN

2018
*Sedona, Arizona*

"I think we made huge strides with Alexander today." Raven lay next to Gabriel in the queen-size bed in the apartment they rented at New Horizons, a copy of *Kill the Queen* propped up on her massive stomach, possibly the only convenience afforded her by her pregnancy. She'd chosen the book precisely for the title, which made her smile every time she read it. There was nothing Raven would rather do than kill Gabriel's wicked mother, former queen of Paragon, now evil empress. "Sharing what he did about Maiara couldn't have been easy. The fact that he did it anyway means we're gaining his trust."

"I certainly hope so. Rowan seems to think sharing is good for him."

"Do you think you can convince him to return to New Orleans with us?"

"At this point, I'm happy he's eating." Gabriel threaded his fingers behind his head and stared at the ceiling.

She tapped her thumb against the page of her book. "Tomorrow I want to spend some time experimenting with Maiara's amulet and maybe do some research on the *Midewiwin* society of the Algonquians."

Gabriel groaned. "Raven, don't get too deeply involved. Remember that you promised to return to Chicago with Tobias and me on Friday. I have purchased our tickets. Rowan will handle things here with Alexander."

"Don't you want to know the source of Maiara's magic and how her power remains in the amulet and her hawk? It's an incredible accomplishment to create a spell that outlasts your death."

He turned on his side and propped his head up on his hand. "Honestly, no."

She did a double take. "No? What if there's something there we can harness to help Alexander or your family in the future? This is unique magic, Gabriel. It's not something you run into every day."

He blinked slowly. "For once, Raven, can't you just worry about you?"

She waved a hand dismissively. "I promise you, I'll be on that Friday flight and everything will be fine. But until then, I'm going to figure out this Maiara thing. I think Alexander will really appreciate it."

He rolled onto his back, mumbling something about her being as stubborn as a mountain horse. "Birds of a feather," she mumbled back at him.

Her phone rang and she swept it off her nightstand. "That's weird. It's a voice call from Avery."

"How is that weird? She's been texting you nonstop all day."

"Exactly. Texting. If she's voice calling, it must be serious." Raven's mind flashed to her mother, and she tapped the screen, instantly worried something was wrong.

"When are you coming home?" Avery asked before she could even greet her.

"Hello to you too." She glanced at Gabriel and mouthed, *She seems upset.* He rose from the bed and headed for the kitchen, closing the door behind him.

"I'm sorry to be so abrupt, but I really need you." Avery's voice quaked over the line, and Raven closed her book and sat up straighter.

"What's going on?"

"It's Dad and Charlotte."

"Yes, I know, you've been texting me about them all day."

"There's more, something I was going to wait to tell you because they asked me not to spoil the surprise, but I can't wait anymore. It's just so... unexpected."

"Why? What's going on?"

"He says he's going to marry her. And it's weird, Rave, but I swear she's got some kind of hold on him. I mean, Dad? Married again? It makes no sense. And he follows her around like a puppy!"

While Avery spoke, Raven flashed back to meeting Charlotte on her wedding day. The moment she'd shaken the woman's hand, a shock ran up her arm, one she usually associated with magic. She didn't think Charlotte was dangerous. At the time, she'd talked to Gabriel about it, and he suspected she was a natural witch. But if she was a natural witch, her subconscious magic might be influencing her father. She didn't like it, especially with Avery close enough to get pulled into it.

"Stay away from her," Raven said, interrupting Avery's story about her dinner with the two of them.

"Huh?"

"Stay away from her. I don't trust her. I'll help you when I get home. I leave Sedona Friday. Oh wait." She cursed and slapped her forehead. She had to go to Chicago so Tobias could monitor the growth of the baby. She didn't know when she'd be back in New Orleans. "I'm sorry, Avery. I forgot Gabriel and I have another stop to make on our trip."

"Sedona? You're in Sedona? I thought you were honeymooning in Hawaii?"

"Only for a day or two. Gabriel's honeymoon plans are taking us all over the place." She forced a laugh.

"So what am I supposed to do about Charlotte? I can't exactly avoid her. She comes into the Three Sisters with Dad on a regular basis."

"I don't know. Just play it cool. Hang out with Mom. Lord knows Dad won't stay around long if Mom is there."

"All great ideas. But seriously, Raven, when do you think you'll be back?"

She thought about that. "I'm not sure, but I'll let you know as soon as I do."

Avery sighed heavily. "All right. I hope you are having fun at least. Get it in now before the baby comes. Who knows when you'll have time after that?"

"Right." Raven laughed. "And, Avery, I'm sorry I'm not there to help you with Dad."

"I forgive you. I suppose you get a pass considering it's your honeymoon and everything."

"I love you."

"I love you too."

She hung up the phone but couldn't get Avery off her mind. She put her book aside and called for Gabriel. He returned and slid back into bed beside her.

"Everything okay?" he asked.

"Avery says my father is engaged to that woman, the one we thought might be a witch."

"Hmm. Good for him."

"Avery seemed really upset about it."

He kissed her on the forehead. "Do you want me to ask Richard to stop in at the Three Sisters and check on her?"

She curled into his side. "No. I think it's just a shock to both of us. It's so soon after the divorce."

"From what you've told me. He's always been... flighty."

"True," she said, resting her head on his chest. "I'm sure it's nothing to worry about." She closed her eyes, and the sound of his purr ushered her to sleep.

# CHAPTER FOURTEEN

The next morning, Rowan accepted an extra-large cappuccino from Nick and kissed him with more force than absolutely necessary. "Have I told you how much I love you today?"

"Just today?" He winked at her.

"Always. Thank you for this. I couldn't sleep last night. I am so worried about Alexander."

"How come? I think it's going well. He ate with us. Showered the stink off. We cleaned up his place." Nick shrugged. "Frankly, I was surprised how much he shared. When we left him, he seemed okay."

"I know it appears that way, but I know Alexander." She toyed with a curl of her hair. "At least I used to know him. We spent a lot of time together as children, and even though I haven't seen him in centuries, we've communicated through his art and by letter. I think he's sharing to placate us. He's in a dark place."

Nick sipped his coffee. "How did you two reconnect? I mean, after you separated back then, what year was it?"

"It was 1699. I was the first one to leave our party. The others were with her into 1700."

"So how did you find him again?"

"The gallery. His art. He painted under a variety of identities. His work gained popularity in New York in the early 1900s. By 1920, everyone was talking about him. He's changed his name since then, but his work has always found a market, and because I owned a gallery, it was inevitable it would find its way to me." She laughed. "All his paintings were pure Alexander. I knew his work right away, the shifting patterns in the texture, the short, abrupt strokes, the color spectrum—he paints with colors that are common on Paragon. I knew it was him. So I wrote to him, and then I bought his paintings, and I kept buying them even when his depression robbed him of the ability to manage his own business. There was a stretch where I was the only one buying his work. I kept him afloat."

"And now you think his sharing is just a way to put you off the scent that he's basically suicidal."

She nodded. "That's what I'm afraid of."

A knock came on their apartment door. Rowan opened it to find Tobias waiting on the other side. "We have a problem." Rowan followed her brother to Alexander's apartment next door. "He wasn't answering, so Raven used her magic to pop the lock and get inside."

Rowan found Gabriel cursing in the door to the bedroom. Past the simple bed, the window was open. Both Alexander and Nyx were gone.

"He knew if he went out the front door one of us would hear him," Rowan said. "We were stupid not to watch him more closely. Fuck!" She could kick herself.

"What could we have done, Rowan? Watch him while he slept?" Tobias said. "He's a grown dragon."

"Are you kidding me? He told us he was exhausted, and we pushed him to tell us more. Now he's gone. With how much hurt we dredged up yesterday, I wouldn't be surprised if we never see him again," Rowan said.

Gabriel asked Raven, "Can you do a locator spell? If we can find him, we can capture him. He won't get away next time."

"We're not trying to capture him, Gabriel! He's our brother, not the enemy. We're trying to help him." Rowan's voice rose with her anger. "And honestly, all of you coming at him at once is the last thing he needs."

"You know him best, Rowan. Where do you think he'd go?" Tobias asked.

She shrugged. She was wondering the same thing herself. Closing her eyes, she tried to think if he'd ever mentioned anything in his letters about a favorite hangout or bar. All she could think of were the funny stories he had written to her about living here and all the new age trends that had come and gone. Her mental light bulb clicked on, and she grabbed Nick's hand.

"Where are you going?" Gabriel asked as she headed for the door.

She turned to them and cleared her throat. "I have an idea where he might be, but I think Nick and I should go alone." The warmth of Nick's body beside her bolstered her resolve. For as much experience as she had facing off against Gabriel, she never enjoyed it.

Thankfully, Tobias backed her up. "Makes sense. You can do this. You were always his favorite. If anyone can convince him to come back, it's you."

"Of course she should go." Raven turned toward Tobias. "And we should examine the amulet and start researching Maiara's magic."

And just like that, Gabriel's full attention was on Raven again, grilling her and Tobias on exactly where they planned to go and what they planned to do and if it was safe for Raven. Nick opened the door for Rowan, and they slipped into the Arizona heat.

"Where do you think he went?" Nick asked.

Rowan jogged down the stairs and walked through the parking lot toward the meditation center. "In all the time I've been buying Alexander's paintings, the subject of most of his work has revolved around a handful of things: Maiara, Nyx, the Sedona landscape, but a few decades ago he painted something else, something that stood out to me—a mysterious cave. I have always wondered about that cave. It seemed like the perfect place for a dragon to hide and recharge."

"You think it's his treasure room?" Nick raised an eyebrow.

"Exactly."

"So why are we heading toward New Horizon's meditation center?"

"To see the man who runs this place, Mr. Gu. Alexander has rented this apartment for a decade. He's a hermit, but he talked a lot about Mr. Gu in his letters. Alex often said that Gu noticed things other people didn't. I have a hunch he'll have an idea where Alexander goes when he's not here."

Rowan entered through double glass doors into a vast air-conditioned space filled with light and polished white furniture. A glass room at the center was filled with people sitting cross-legged on red silk pillows, eyes closed, thumb and forefingers touching in the sacred om mudra. She scanned the rows of heads but didn't see the man she was looking for.

"Can I help you?" Mr. Gu emerged from one of the offices that lined the south wall. "I hope you are enjoying your stay with us. This meditation has already begun, but there will be another beginning in an hour."

"Actually, we're here about my brother Alexander," Rowan said. "He's missing."

Mr. Gu smiled. "I never knew he had a sister, but then Alexander is a man of few words."

Rowan extended her hand. "I'm Rowan and this is Nick." Mr. Gu shook her hand with a firm, confident grip.

"It's a pleasure."

"Thank you. But please, do you have any idea where my brother might have gone?"

Mr. Gu frowned. "Your brother has been in need of healing for as long as I have known him. I've tried to help, but his soul is damaged in ways only he can fix."

Rowan nodded. "I know. We're trying to help him."

"There are places in Sedona called vortexes, swirling, concentrated energy that calls to those like Alexander who desperately need its healing power. I have noticed when your brother's aura has become exceptionally dark, he has, in the past, mentioned visiting a local place called Shaman's Cave."

Hope bloomed in Rowan's chest, and she squeezed Nick's hand excitedly. "How do we get there?"

"I have a map. Take water. It's a two-hour hike from the parking area at Coconino National Forest. Be aware that the trail is unmarked in places and can be hard to follow." Mr. Gu handed them a trifold guide. "May peace find you."

"Oh, thank you. I appreciate this so much." Tugging Nick's hand, Rowan turned to leave.

"Yours is nice."

"Huh?"

"Your aura. The two of you have the same hue. A beautiful rose color. Nick's is darker than yours, but they go together perfectly."

Rowan grinned. "Thank you. That's very sweet." She followed Nick out the door.

"Good to know our auras are a matched set," Nick said lightly. "I'd hate to have to color mine to match. Even when the results are good, the upkeep is a nightmare!" He gave her an exaggerated scoff.

Rowan giggled. "Was there ever any doubt?" She held up the map, her expression growing serious. "Let's pray this is the place."

A DRAGON'S ABILITY TO HIDE ITS TREASURE WAS unparalleled. Rowan expected Alexander's cave to be unreachable by humans and magically warded against supernatural beings. If they had any hope of finding Alexander, Rowan and Nick would have to work together.

As a supernatural, Rowan could find the cave but not enter it without Alexander's permission. Nick could enter it, but Alexander would have chosen a location inaccessible to humans. If Alexander had cloaked the entrance in invisibility, neither of them would be able to see it. Luckily for Rowan, she had the best of both worlds and knew her brother better than anyone.

After making the hike to Shaman's Cave, Rowan sensed they were close. The metallic tang of magic hung in the air. She smiled. If it had been her, she would have chosen this area as well. "Are you game for a ride?" she asked Nick. "I need your help."

He clucked his tongue. "Always, baby."

Sweeping Nick into her arms, she unfurled her wings and cruised around the red crags, searching for Alexander's hiding place.

"But if it's invisible," Nick asked, "what are we looking for?"

"Tell me if you see any irregularities in the stone. It's here. I can smell my brother's magic; I just can't pinpoint it."

"There!" Nick pointed to a place where the reddish hues were broken and incongruent as if someone had folded the rock in half. She flew toward the side of the mountain and broke through Alexander's invisibility charm. Landing on a projection of stone, she could feel the buzz of his protective ward coming from the dark opening of a cave, but she couldn't see inside.

"It's homey," Nick said.

"You can see in?" she asked.

He nodded.

"Do you see Alexander?"

"No."

"I can't go any farther. His cave is warded," she said to Nick. "If I call to him, he might run from me."

"You want me to find him and try to convince him to talk to you?"

She grinned and spread her hands. "He's a softy for humans."

"I'll take care of it." Nick kissed her on the mouth and moved past the magical barrier, disappearing into the darkness.

Alexander's voice boomed a moment later. "Come in, Rowan. By the Mountain, you're a pain in the ass."

She tentatively stepped forward and felt the protective ward bend around her, then give way. Alexander strode from a side room that, from what she could see through the door, appeared to contain a notable amount of treasure along with more traditional bedroom furniture. He wrapped a silky black robe tighter around himself and tied the belt.

Nick flashed her a self-satisfied grin.

"I was in my dragon form, Rowan. For Mountain's sake, you're lucky I didn't burn him to a crisp or worse, eat him alive," Alexander said.

"Give me a little credit," Nick said. "It's not like you're the first dragon I've met. You're not even the scariest."

"How did you find me?"

"Master Gu. Plus that is your motorcycle in the Coconino parking lot."

He looked up at the ceiling. "Gu. That guy has an uncanny ability to annoy the hell out of me, even from afar."

"Hmm. He had only nice things to say about you." Rowan rested her hands on her hips and looked around. The cave had been seriously enhanced to the point of being far nicer than his apartment. Extra was the word that came to mind. There was a full living room, complete with a fireplace that housed a crackling fire. To the right and behind the sofa grouping was a nicely appointed kitchen. Rowan could see more rooms down a hall behind the kitchen. And, of course, the treasure room to the left. "Nice place you got here."

"It's been a labor of love."

"I thought you were practically destitute! You told me your paintings weren't selling. And given the state of your apartment, I thought you'd completely stopped taking care of yourself." She pointed her thumb over her shoulder in the general direction of New Horizons. "All this time, you've had this?"

"To be honest, I'm not very good with money. But the proceeds of all those paintings you bought had to go somewhere. Plus you collect things over the years." He glanced at his treasure room.

She nodded slowly, then stared at him for a long breath. None of this was what she'd expected. This cave was well cared for, and far from being distraught, Alexander looked better than yesterday. "So... why did you take off like that?"

He scrubbed his fingers through his hair. "I'm sick of Gabriel's bullshit. I'm not going to New Orleans. I'm not going anywhere."

"I love you, Alexander, but you're being a pill. Why not come back with us? You need help. You're obviously hurting. It's not like it will be forever. Gabriel will figure this thing out with Mom, and you'll be back here in no time."

"I'm not going."

"You can bring the bird." Rowan wasn't sure how Nyx would do with Raven's cat, but she was sure Gabriel wouldn't bitch about her offer if it was what pushed Alexander to come with them.

He looked at the hawk and scoffed. "If you can figure out a way for me to leave her behind, let me know. Even if I tried, she'd catch up with me."

For a minute she stared at her brother, wondering what to do next. Eventually she simply walked to the sofa and sat down, propping her feet up on the coffee table. Nick fell in next to her.

"Don't you have somewhere to be?" Alexander said with a note of annoyance in his voice.

"Nope." She tipped her head back to look at him. "I was

wondering what you did about the monster you said was following Maiara?"

"The *wendigo*..." He took a seat in the chair beside the fireplace. "It's not an easy story to tell."

"I've got time."

# CHAPTER FIFTEEN

*1699*
*Colony of New Jersey*

He woke beside her, the sunlight coming through the slats in the window. Alexander hadn't intended on sleeping with Maiara, only to watch over her, but he'd rested his head in the wee hours of the morning and drifted under.

Anyway, the bed was large and he was an honorable dragon. He'd remained fully dressed and didn't cross the centerline of the bed. Still, in her sleep, she'd sought him out, moving to him and curling into his side. In his slumber, he must have embraced her because when he woke, she was wrapped in his arms, her head on his heart and the scent of spring in his nose.

"I'm sorry," he murmured into her hair when he felt her wake. He never saw her eyes open, just sensed a change in her breathing. "I should have asked permission to sleep beside you."

She lifted her torso until she hovered over him, her hair

cascading from one shoulder like a sheet of dark silk. One of her hands came to rest on his chest. "This is your room."

Looking into her eyes, his jaw tightened. "Last evening, I did my best to make it clear to you my invitation did not come with additional expectations. There are no requirements of you, Maiara. I simply wanted you out of the cold."

With a deliberate grace, she folded her hands on his sternum and lowered her chin to his chest. "Do you find my nearness unpleasant?"

"No."

"Does it bother you that I touch you?"

"No."

"Good. I like to be near you. You are warm like sunlight on my skin." Her full lips smiled softly.

Alexander's dragon rolled under his skin, excited by the idea that Maiara longed for his nearness. His heart pounded and his mouth turned dry as a stone. Was it possible that by some miracle Maiara felt the same inexplicable attraction to him as he felt to her?

Languorously he trailed his fingers along the bones of her spine. Their eyes locked and held. She did not move away. She floated above him like a dark angel from some otherworld, and he basked in her breath-of-life beauty.

"Alexander." His name sounded strange on her lips, broken in odd syllables.

"What is it?"

"As I told you last night, the monster who killed my people is here. If you hadn't come for me, I—"

"I won't let the *wendigo* hurt you."

She nodded. "I thought I'd outrun it. I thought it would never come this close to the land of white men. I was wrong. It's here, and it is tracking me. And now the trees are dead for the winter and I can no longer use them to hide."

"You have my protection now," he said. "Last night, I used my invisibility to bring you here. I can do it again. I will keep you safe."

She blinked slowly and made a sound low in her throat. "You can become invisible?"

Demonstrating, he blinked out of sight and she scrambled back, taking the blanket with her. He appeared again, reaching out to her. "I didn't mean to startle you."

Her face turned serious, and she ran her fingers over his sketch of the dragon on the nightstand. Dragons had a heart of stone, one that glowed from behind the scales of its chest. It had been difficult to capture this glow, using only charcoal pencil. If he'd had paint and canvas, he could better do it justice. But her focus landed on the pale shading he'd depicted, and he could tell she understood. "You have fire in your heart."

"Yes, more or less. All dragons can breathe fire. It's part of what we are."

"The *wendigo* won't stop with me. It won't stop until every Algonquian is dead."

He studied her face. She was on the edge of something, an idea, and the fortitude he saw in her eyes made his heart swell with respect. To have a woman like her... Deep inside, his dragon twisted again.

Her fingers toyed with the corner of the blanket wrapped around her, reminding him she was naked beneath it. Desire took root and branched through him. He tried to tamp it down, to rein in his inner dragon. He failed. Every inch of his skin came alive at the thought of tasting her, being inside her, marking her as his own. A fierce, overwhelming need burned within him, hot enough to raise the temperature in the room.

The moment she felt it, her gaze locked with his. But

she did not address the heat. Instead, she broached something else entirely. "What remains of my people live west of here. They call themselves the keepers of the fire. With your help, your fire, we could defend them against the *wendigo* and the rest of the Iroquois."

He understood now what she was trying to ask him. Now that she knew what he was, she wanted his protection, not only for herself but also for her people. His answer came immediately. "Then we go there."

She blinked at him in surprise. "It will not be easy. It is a long distance, straight through the territory of my enemy. The way will be dangerous, and there will be more snow."

He cupped her face. "We will go to these keepers of the fire. I will take you there. We will leave today."

"What about your sister?"

"We can't be more than a day's ride from New York."

"A day's ride. Yes."

"Rowan will go alone. She is dragon as well and stronger than she looks. You will draw her a map, and she will make her own way."

"I cannot repay you for this," she said, her voice cracking.

He sat up, bringing his face close to hers and spread his wings behind him. "You won't have to."

By the time they'd dressed and descended for breakfast, Gabriel and the others were already seated. Alexander joined his siblings at a long wooden table in the Lion's Head Inn where they were partaking of a breakfast of sausages and porridge. While he'd hoped not to call attention to the fact Maiara had spent the night in his bed, however innocently, Gabriel noticed her position by his side immediately, put down his fork, and raised an eyebrow in his direction.

"We need to talk." Alexander forced back the familiar anxiety that came from facing his brother. Maiara was counting on him. He decided the best course of action was to share the least amount of information. Knowing Gabriel, the dragon would abandon Maiara if he thought she endangered their passage in any way. That was an unacceptable scenario.

Tobias and Rowan stopped eating and looked up.

"About what?" Gabriel eyed Alexander as if he didn't like where this was going.

"The storm last night was just the beginning. More snow will come. We must move west now or stay in New York for the winter. If we wait or go farther north, Maiara says the way may be impossible to traverse."

A barmaid with an overlong jaw and buckteeth brought Alexander tea but conspicuously ignored Maiara. Alexander handed his mug to their guide, then made a show of the fact he'd not been served. The horse-faced woman reluctantly brought another.

Gabriel grunted. "We've agreed to take Rowan to New York. Besides, you know as well as I do that we can handle any weather this land delivers to us."

"We can. Maiara can't." Alexander's dragon rose to the surface, this time out of anger. He wouldn't allow Gabriel to plow over him this time. Maiara and her people were too important. And although the promise he'd made to her was not something he was ready to share, he refused to back down. "Rowan can advance to New York on her own. We must start west today."

Rowan and Tobias froze as if he'd just revealed he'd

grown a third arm overnight. He'd never spoken to Gabriel in that tone before. Outwardly, he steeled his spine. Inwardly, Alexander prepared himself for the inevitable backlash that came at anyone who threatened Gabriel's role as leader.

Gabriel's hands fisted on the table, but the pounding never came. He simply frowned and perused Maiara like she were a rare specimen of plant or animal he'd not encountered before.

"Agreed," he said. "The weather here is unpredictable, and these people are fragile. If Maiara wishes to go now, we go now."

Rowan squealed.

"So happy to continue on your own, sister?" Gabriel shot Rowan a disapproving glare.

Immune to his judgment, she smiled wickedly and stood from the table. She was wearing breeches again and a man's shirt, although the delicate bones of her rouged cheeks could not be mistaken for a man's. She swept her long black hair off her shoulder before answering. "Oh yes, brother. Being on my own is something I've waited for a long, long time. Give me my cut, and I'll be on my way."

Gabriel sneered, reached inside his satchel, and produced a small purse. But when she attempted to take it, he clutched her fingers in his own. "Despite your haste to leave us"—his face grew serious—"you will be missed. Brutally, desperately missed. I love you dearly."

They stared at each other for a moment, hand in hand, and Alexander was sure he saw tears brim in both sets of eyes. And then she embraced him. Tobias was next to take her in his arms. At last Alexander had his chance to say goodbye, holding his dear sister and friend longer than the rest.

"Once you are settled, send word. Find me when it's safe," she whispered in his ear.

He nodded. They had to stay apart. They did not have to forget each other. "I will. I promise." She took one last look at all of them and then rushed from the Lion's Head before the tears Alexander saw welling could spill over the dam of her lower lids.

The table grew quiet, the group reeling from the loss of yet another of their kin. This was why they were here, but it was harder than any of them expected. Beneath the table, he felt Maiara's hand come to rest on his own, and the touch of her comforting fingers traveled straight to his soul.

CHAPTER SIXTEEN

An hour later, Alexander found himself on his horse again with the dull morning light at his back. Although the snow had melted, a thick, cold fog had settled among the trees, concealing patches of ice that occasionally caused the horses to trip along the slick trail.

He couldn't help but think the fog was a good metaphor for where he was at the moment. For the first time in his life, he was staring at a blank page without the benefit of imagining what the future might bring when he brought pencil to paper.

Everything was new. New world. New, intense feelings for a woman whose possible indifference could not be overestimated. New relationship with his brothers. No longer was he forced to act the younger brother, the follower, the quiet obedient one. He could be anything. He could be himself, whoever that was.

Today he was a dragon on high alert for a *wendigo*. Had it waited outside the tavern last night? Was it following them? The forest was alive with birds and tiny animals that skittered beneath the thick white cloud that clung to everything. He feared the *wendigo* would be upon them before anyone noticed its presence. Considering he hadn't told his brothers about the creature, it was possible, even if they did notice, they wouldn't register the danger immediately.

Telling them, however, wasn't an option. If they discovered she was a Midew and that a supernatural monster wanted her dead, they might choose to abandon her. Gabriel had made a point of avoiding human drama and violence. It was too tempting to reveal what they were under such circumstances.

Maiara led the way beyond the last tavern onto narrow trails that weaved between the trees. Now it made sense why everything they'd brought with them had to fit on horseback—in the saddlebags, the large bedroll on the back of the saddle, or the packhorse. There was no room for a cart on these narrow trails. There was barely room for the broad shoulders of his brothers.

Fog or not, he couldn't miss the trembling of Maiara's fingers. He rode close to her, Gabriel and Tobias falling to the rear. Even though she was covered in fur, he longed to pull her into his arms and protect her from both the cold and the monster that hunted her.

At first Maiara stopped to break every few hours until it was clear Alexander and his siblings did not share the fragile compositions of human travelers. After that, she picked up the pace, her hawk following in the sky above them, and rode into the mist until it turned into a cold rain and soaked them through. She only stopped when the horses needed water.

The trail ran along the side of a mountain, the rain gathering in a waterfall that pooled at the base. The horses dipped their heads and drank greedily, but Maiara seemed distracted by something in the woods. Alexander noticed the hawk circling silently above the same spot that drew her attention.

In one fluid motion, she drew her bow from her back and nocked an arrow. Was the *wendigo* here? Alexander readied himself for the worst. His wings punched from his back and talons extended from his knuckles.

But when her arrow flew, it did not target the *wendigo*. Instead, a few yards into the woods, it protruded from the body of a hare. Her marksmanship awed Alexander, who noticed she'd pierced the creature through the eye, killing it instantly. She lifted it from the shaggy underbrush and held it proudly above her head.

"*Wiyas*," she said. "To eat." She motioned toward the sticks and branches that riddled the ground. "We will make fire."

"Alexander," Gabriel growled.

His desire to protect Maiara had superseded any ruse of keeping what he was a secret from her. There, in full daylight, he stood before Maiara and his brothers, wings stretched and talons out. Gabriel's expression was nothing short of livid. Tobias's jaw dropped, his eyes narrowing as if he couldn't quite believe Alexander's stupidity.

"She knows," Alexander admitted, squeezing his eyes shut for a long blink.

"You told her?" Tobias's accusing stare might as well have branded him a traitor.

Maiara drew her knife and gutted the rabbit in the practiced way of an accomplished hunter. She grunted at Gabriel and gestured at him with the bloody blade. "Humans do not begin journeys at the mouth of winter. Humans do not say they cannot freeze to death or starve to death. You are dra-gon." She skinned her kill. "I have eyes and ears. Do not blame Alexander."

Alexander swelled with affection for her. It was true he'd broken his promise to his brother and told her what he was, but he did not regret it. They needed her and she needed them. If he had any influence at all, this was how it would be.

"We won't hurt you," Tobias said.

Maiara's dark brows crowded together on her forehead, and she started to laugh. "I am not afraid of you, dra-gon." She raised the bloody knife between them once more. "But I think the time for hiding is done."

She pointed to an opening in the side of the mountain. "We camp here. Others use this place. One of you must check that it is empty and for dry wood inside for cooking. We need fire."

Alexander retracted his wings and claws. "We have fire."

Tobias glanced between Alexander and Gabriel. "One of us will need to hunt. We are going to need more than one rabbit."

Alexander removed his coat. "I will hunt. You start the fire."

"And I will check the cave," Gabriel said. Something about the way he said it made Alexander believe he'd be quite happy to find a bear to wrestle within its depths. He was still furious with him.

"A nice young stag sounds delicious," Tobias called to him before following Gabriel.

"You'll get what you get," Alexander muttered toward their backs. His gaze fell on Maiara. "I have to... change... to hunt."

She paused what she was doing long enough to shrug.

Moving for the cover of an outcropping of stone away from the horses so as not to spook them, Alexander undressed, doubled over, and dug his claws into the ground. He allowed the transformation to take hold, his forearms shingling with turquoise-blue scales, his spine stretching into a tail. When it was done, he moved out from the shelter and, as silently as possible, slipped toward the woods.

Maiara's head snapped up and her mouth gaped. The skinned rabbit dropped from her hand.

As he'd feared. A sketch of a dragon on a page was nothing compared to seeing one in person. This could change everything.

Gently, as gently as he could in this form, he lowered his head and nudged her shoulder with his nose, the shoulder where he knew the *wendigo*'s scar marred her flesh under her tunic. A reminder, he hoped, that they were different but the same. Both creatures of magic.

Each heartbeat seemed to echo in the quiet of her perusal. He held absolutely still. Could she accept what he was, or was seeing his dragon in the flesh too much for her human mind to handle? But her hand rose and stroked his cheek. Secure in that reassuring touch, he backed away, spread his wings, and started to hunt.

Later when his kill—he had found a young stag after all —was roasting over the fire, Maiara chose to sit beside him near its warmth. At first she stared at the fire in silence. Who needed to speak when Tobias and Gabriel chatted on about the differences between a Paragonian forest and those of this realm? Besides, Alexander had never been the chatty sort, preferring to express himself with his art rather than his words. He picked up his sketchbook and started drawing Maiara while he waited to eat.

"You are beautiful as a drag-on," she said softly.

He paused his pencil. The light of the fire cast shadows along her face and neck. How he'd love to trace that long, smooth trail from her ear to her shoulder with his fingers, feel the hollow of her throat, the soft curves that no doubt led to her navel. The fire had raised the temperature in the cave, and her skin glistened in a way he knew he'd never fully capture in his sketches.

"You weren't afraid?" he asked.

"At first." She looked down at the cave floor. "Then I saw you inside." She pointed to her eyes. "It is still you, through the eyes."

He nodded. That was one way to think of it.

"Your brother started this fire with his breath," she said, her brow crinkling as if the memory disturbed her.

"That explains the smell." There was a moment's hesitation before she laughed.

"You have fire inside. You truly cannot burn." The playful curiosity on her face was irresistible. He reached down and removed his boot and sock and rolled up his pant leg. While she watched in obvious horror, he extended his bare foot until it rested on the burning logs. Beside him, she inhaled sharply. After several breaths, she began to squirm until she had to cover her eyes. Eventually her hand shot out and landed on his forearm.

"It doesn't hurt me," he reassured her.

She tightened her grip and laughed nervously. "It hurts me."

He pulled his foot out of the fire. To his disappointment, her fingers trailed from his arm.

"You are a good shot with that bow." He rolled down his pants and reached for his sock.

"I learned to hunt as a child."

"Is that common among your people?" In Paragon, only elves hunted with bows and arrows. And while they did learn as children, the weapon was used for self-defense rather than hunting in most cases. Only a select few of their kind actually hunted for meat.

"In many tribes, women do not do the hunting. It is left to the men. The women take care of the home. But my father insisted that I learn."

Interesting. Every time he thought he understood humans, he turned out to be wrong. "You said your father was an English trapper. Did your people accept that he wanted you to be different?"

She sighed. "I was always different. My father loved my mother, but he did not live with us. Their spirits were not joined." She held two fingers together. "Not... married."

"Is that difficult for a child in your culture?"

"It was allowed because my mother was a *Midew*. Otherwise she would have been pressured to marry and raise me with a warrior of our tribe."

"All the women who are not healers must marry?"

"It is considered rude for a woman to turn away too many warriors. It is not a law, only an expectation."

"Where I come from, there are fewer women of our species than men. It is unheard of for women not to marry, usually at a young age. I understand what you mean about societal expectations."

The fire danced in her dark eyes. "My father came to our village several times every year and would stay with us, and then when I was old enough, before I'd become a woman, he started taking me with him on his expeditions. He taught me to hunt, to trap, and to speak English."

Alexander stared into the fire. "It sounds like he loved you very much."

"He did. And I loved him. He believed in my magic even though he had different gods."

Alexander thought he would have liked Maiara's father.

"I do not have so many memories of my father, and few of them are pleasant."

She frowned. "What was it like when you were a child?"

He leaned back on his elbows, wondering if he could distract her by putting his foot back in the fire. But in the end, he answered her with a story that summed up his childhood.

"From the time we can walk, dragon boys are taken to fighting rings called pits. Because my mother was the queen of our kingdom, I went to a special pit where I trained with my brothers only."

She placed a hand on his arm as if she wasn't sure she'd understood him correctly. "Your mother was queen? You are prince?"

"Yes, but not anymore. We were exiled during a coup that overthrew our kingdom."

"I am sorry."

He couldn't interpret the tightness that gathered at the corners of her eyes and mouth, but he continued.

"Girls don't train in the pits, but nearly all of them learn to fight on their own. Parents recognize that they, of any of us, need to know how to defend themselves, but the training is all done in private and no parent would ever admit it."

"It is secret?"

"Secret."

"But not for the boys."

"No. For the boys it is very public. And for boys of noble birth, it is nothing short of torture." Alexander looked across the fire to where his brothers were still laughing, telling stories, and paying him and Maiara no attention. He leaned his head closer to hers. "The eldest brothers receive all the training, but the younger of us are made to fight. So being the third in line for the throne, and a boy with a soul for art rather than war, I spent a lot of time on my back in the dirt or on a training mat. And it was all publicized. My failure was used to make Gabriel and my brother Marius look stronger to our people." He frowned at the humiliating memory.

"Is this why you fear Gabriel?"

He did a double take. "Why do you think I fear Gabriel?"

Her eyes flicked across the fire. "You hesitate to speak to him. You often follow behind. Even now, you lower your voice as if you fear displeasing him."

An undesirable truth. He hated that she was right. He kept his eyes trained on the fire, the weight of her stare heavy on his cheek.

She nudged his elbow. "No pit here. No reason to be afraid." When he looked at her, her brows lifted and he returned her smile.

"Right. You're right about that." The smile faded from his mouth as a thought crossed his mind. "Maiara, do you have a mate among your people?" He held his fingers together as she had when describing her parents.

Her eyes narrowed as if she was struggling with a word.

"A husband? A lover? Someone who is courting you?" he clarified.

She shook her head. "No. Among my people, I spent much time developing my skills as a *Midew* like my mother. I had no time for... marriage games."

Marriage games. He'd cared little for those in Paragon as well.

"Do you have a... mate where you are from?" she asked.

"No," he scoffed. "In Paragon, my family did not play...

marriage games often. And when we did, it was for political reasons."

Her dark brows became two slashes over her obsidian eyes. "Paragon is the name of your land."

He stared into the fire, an old sadness bleeding into his disposition. "It's not my land. Not anymore."

This she seemed to understand to the depths of her soul. Staring straight into the fire, she slid her hand down his arm and threaded her fingers into his. No further words were spoken. None were needed.

# CHAPTER SEVENTEEN

*2018*
*Sedona, Arizona*

Rowan stood and stretched, cracking her neck. The emotional toll of Alexander's storytelling was bleeding over onto her. She remembered the pits and what it had been like to reveal her true form to Nick for the first time. While she knew this was helping Alexander, she needed a break and was pleased that he'd paused where he did.

"Can I interest either of you in a drink?" Alexander asked.

"Yes," Rowan said quickly.

Alexander moved into the kitchen. "I have some tequila and mix. How does a margarita on the rocks sound? I don't have a blender out here."

"Heavenly." Rowan looked at Nick. "Honey?"

"Beer?" Nick asked.

Alexander hooked a Dos Equis from the fridge and slid it across the counter to him.

The sun was setting outside the cave, and the view of Sedona with its bluebell-colored sky and rusty red terrain was postcard perfect. Rowan wished she could fully enjoy it, but she was distracted by the way Nick studied Alexander as if his detective background was kicking into gear again. She nudged him and raised an eyebrow.

"Uh, the way you ended that story, it almost sounded like Maiara didn't have a home, but weren't you headed to be with and defend her people?" he asked.

Rowan rubbed her temples. Guess they weren't taking a break after all.

Alexander stared out the mouth of the cave at the setting sun as he squeezed a lime into Rowan's drink. "Both her parents had been killed by the *wendigo* as well as the rest of her *Midewiwin* society. I learned later that her extended family unit had been killed as well, some of them in the war with the Iroquois, others trying to defend the *Midewiwin* society during the attack. She was taking me to her people, her tribe, but they were not her close family. And her arrival there was not exactly welcomed with open arms."

"Are you saying her people didn't want you there once you arrived?" Rowan couldn't believe it.

Nick interrupted. "Where was the bird during all this?" He gestured toward Nyx. "That thing you said about it coming to your window when Maiara was half-frozen, that ain't normal."

"Nick..."

"I'm just sayin' people don't usually talk to their hawks like that. Or *have* hawks as pets for that matter."

Alexander turned from them to stare at the hawk and then handed the margarita to Rowan. He poured himself one, stronger than Rowan's. He never answered Nick.

Rowan noticed. "Alexander, do you keep anything to eat out here? We haven't eaten since breakfast."

Blinking rapidly, Alexander snapped out of whatever revolving thoughts had sent him staring into his drink and looked at Nick. "Yes, I do, and she's right, you need to eat and drink something. I can hear your stomach growling."

Rowan noticed for the first time that night Nick looked truly exhausted. She'd been so caught up in Alexander's story she hadn't properly cared for her mate. Thankfully, a few moments later, a pot that smelled like chili and some crusty bread appeared on the kitchen counter.

"Whoa!" Nick said. His eyes blinked rapidly.

"Willow?" Rowan asked.

"Yes."

"After the state of your apartment, I thought you'd sent him away."

Alexander shrugged. "I did. I sent him here to the mountain where he feels at home. He's an oread, Rowan. A mountain nymph. He belongs here, not picking up after a ghost of a man in a filthy one-bedroom apartment over a smarmy spiritual retreat."

Her heart warmed. Perhaps she had been wrong about his suicidal tendencies this entire time. "You did it out of compassion for him, not because you wanted to turn him loose before you died."

He whirled on her then, his dark hair wild around the sharp bones of his face. A dark cloud moved in behind his eyes. Rowan had never seen a person burned at the stake. She'd heard about it over the course of her long life but had never seen it. The way Alexander looked at her then, she would've sworn he was burning alive. The darkness in that look made her take a step back and hold her breath.

"No one wants to die, Rowan," he said, his voice lined with grit. "They want the pain to stop."

She didn't know what to say. She held his gaze, wondering how to help him.

It was Nick who spoke up. "Pain is nothing to be afraid of." There was no pity in the look he gave Alexander. "Pain is a reminder you can feel. Fear the day you no longer feel anything. Numb is the worst. Numb is empty."

"Nick...," Rowan said.

"No. This guy needs to hear this." He pointed a finger at Alexander's chest. "The reason you feel pain is because you had love once and you lost it. That's horrible. It's a horrible thing that happened to you. But you had love, all right. You have happy memories. That's why you feel the pain. That's something to hold on to."

The two men stared at each other, each one shifting as if they might either hug or let fists fly. Rowan prepared herself to break it up if she had to, but there was something good happening here. Her brother's shoulders drooped in surrender, and he started ladling some chili into a bowl.

"Where the fuck did you find this guy?" Alexander asked Rowan.

"Manhattan." Rowan accepted a steaming bowl and returned to the couch in front of the fire. Nick did the same.

Alexander returned to his chair and started eating. "I can't tell you more tonight."

"It's okay. You don't have to," she said.

"Don't go back to the apartment. Gabriel will give you shit if you go back, and you'll end up cracking and telling him where I am. Just... I need some time."

Rowan threaded her fingers into Nick's. "We'll stay and won't tell Gabriel a thing."

"Perfect."

"Anyway, you can tell us more of the story tomorrow morning." Rowan stared at him over her margarita, the way she used to when they were kids and she was trying to get him to do something for her.

Alexander rolled his eyes. "I promise you, I'll try."

## CHAPTER EIGHTEEN

The next morning, Rowan woke beside Nick as the sunrise cut through the cave opening and showered the sofa bed they slept in with golden rays that made the azure sky and red mountains in the distance seem to glow. The sight was bright and glorious, and Rowan could tell Nick was fascinated. The ward protecting the cave also acted as a window, keeping the inside warm and free from bugs or critters. It made for cozy sleeping and a perfect view.

In the next room, the light glinted off the pile of treasure that Alexander slept beneath. A shower of coins and jewels clattered to the stone floor. Rowan watched a turquoise-scaled paw retract into the dark recesses of the pile.

"I don't think she's dead," Nick mumbled, his eyes never leaving the mountains.

"Huh?" Rowan snuggled in close to him under the faux fur blanket. In the morning light, she traced the scar that cut through his lip and trailed her nail over the stubble of his chin.

"I don't think Maiara is actually dead."

Rowan's hand pressed flat to his chest. "Shhh. Don't say that so loud." She glanced back toward the next room where she hoped Alexander was still asleep under his pile of treasure. She lowered her voice to a whisper. "Gabriel, Tobias, and Alexander saw her body burn. She's definitely dead."

"It's incredible to me that I am the newest addition to this family but the only one who seems to appreciate this thing you all call magic." He scrubbed his hand through his whiskey-colored hair.

"What are you talking about?"

"Do dragons commonly have relationships with their pets like Alexander has with his bird? Or is this as crazy as it seems?" Nick gestured in the direction of Alexander's room where Nyx was asleep on a perch beside the pile of treasure.

"It's crazy for sure, although if what Gabriel and Alexander said is true, it makes sense. If Nyx is truly the bird that once was his mate's familiar, then she is the last piece of his relationship that remains."

"Uh, yeah, explain to me how a hawk can live to be over three hundred years old again?" Nick turned on his side and reached around her to run the tips of his fingers down the length of her spine. If he kept doing that, she wasn't sure she could explain anything. Her mind would go completely blank.

"Obviously magic was involved in making her immortal. Maiara must have enchanted the hawk before she died."

Nick's eyes narrowed contemplatively. "And why would she do such a thing? What was Maiara's motivation for making her hawk immortal?"

Rowan opened her mouth to answer, but the truth was she had no idea. It was highly unusual.

"After you fed me your tooth and we were bonded, you

explained to me that if you ever died, I would die too. My immortality is tied to your magic."

"That's right."

"So if Maiara used her magic to make her familiar immortal and Maiara is dead, shouldn't the bird be dead too?"

"Maybe. That's how dragon magic works, but we never really understood Maiara's magic."

"Because she was human but had some really insane *Midew* powers given to her by the Great Spirit, right?"

"Right."

"Even Alexander doesn't seem to understand her magic."

"He said she melded into the trees. Maybe she had some type of nymph blood we never knew about."

"And if nymphs make something immortal and they die, the magic remains?"

Rowan sighed. "The magic dies too. Actually, I don't think nymphs have the type of magic to make something immortal anyway, now that you mention it."

The corner of Nick's mouth twitched. "Do you see what's bothering me? I'm new to this magic and immortality thing, but I haven't heard you talk about even one creature whose magic outlives them."

"I don't know of any. But what other explanation could there be?"

The question hung in the sliver of space between them, the whisper landing heavy on Rowan's heart. She should have thought of those questions, but she'd been too focused on reconnecting with Alexander and saving him from drowning in despair. She'd never assumed the hawk in his painting was the same hawk that was Maiara's. This was new information. But Nick was right. It was more than a little strange. No wonder Raven had been so intent on studying it.

"You know how you locked Verinetti inside his animal form?"

How could she forget? A former boyfriend and shifter, Michael Verinetti had betrayed Rowan to the New Amsterdam vampires. She'd retaliated by having a witch make an enchanted cuff that she'd had her friend seal around Michael's leg when he was in the form of an owl. The magic stopped him from shifting back into his human form. Verinetti would remain an owl for as long as he lived. "Of course I do."

"Well? Maybe something like that happened to Maiara."

Rowan tucked her chin in to get a better look at Nick's face. "You think Maiara was actually a shifter and she's somehow stuck in her bird form and that's why the bird has lived so long?"

Nick shrugged. "Tell me why I'm wrong."

"For one, I personally saw the hawk and Maiara together at the same time back in 1699. Maiara definitely did not shift into the hawk."

"Okay."

"Second, shifters can't meld into trees. That's a nymph thing. And nymphs can't shift."

"Hmm. And nymphs can't do magic, but Alexander says she was a healer and she enchanted the bird."

Rowan frowned. "Maybe she was a natural witch."

"Can a witch's spell outlive them?"

"No. I don't think so. Not something like immortality."

Nick sighed. "It doesn't take an NYPD detective to figure there's something worth investigating here. I, for one, would like to know exactly how Maiara died and the events leading up to those circumstances." In his excitement, Nick had raised his voice, and Rowan cringed at the sound of the pile of treasure shifting behind her.

Metal clinked against metal. She rolled over in time to see her brother emerge from his pile of treasure in his human form and draw his shiny black robe around his naked body.

"I promised you the rest of the story, Nick," Alexander growled. "And I won't go back on my word. I just hope you'll allow me a cup of coffee first."

The coffee machine started to run, and the scent of oread filled Rowan's nose. "Would you and your guests care for breakfast this morning?" Willow's voice whispered from somewhere near the kitchen.

Alexander's gaze darted between Rowan and Nick. "Why the hell not? The human would like to hear the rest of the story, and he might as well do it with a full belly."

# CHAPTER NINETEEN

*1700*
*New France*

D ays and then weeks melted away in the rhythm of travel. As Maiara had predicted, the snow moved in and the days grew short. Between Gabriel, Tobias, and Alexander, they ate well of hunted game and always had a bit of meat left over for the trail. Along with the dried grain, fruit, and nuts they'd brought and rationed and the wild onions and acorns Maiara found and prepared for them, no one went hungry.

But as the temperature dropped, water became harder to come by. The trails, carved by migrating people and animals, bordered streams and waterfalls, but that afternoon everything was frozen.

The snow had started again, white flakes the size of dandelion blooms that floated down and coated them and their horses. Everything white. Everything frozen except for Alexander and his brothers, who were noticeably steaming.

Maiara dropped from her pony beside a river coated in

a thick layer of ice. She picked up a stone and struck the surface, but she could not break through to the liquid below. "We need water for the horses."

"Stand back. I'll melt it," Alexander offered.

Gabriel scoffed. "No need, brother." He slid off his horse and shuffled a few yards out onto the ice. Extending the talons of his right hand, he lowered himself to one knee and punched into the frozen surface. A spider's web of cracks extended from his fist. Jaw clenched in determination, he leaped into the air and punched again, this time plunging through with a splash. Maiara gasped, undoubtedly fearing for his safety.

Alexander shook his head and laughed. "Show-off."

Gabriel's head broke the surface in a steamy rush, his beard dripping. His eyes glowed red from his inner dragon rising to the surface, and steam rose from the water as he warmed the space around him. Wading to shore, he extended his wings and shook like a wolf shaking off rain.

An icy drop hit Maiara's cheek, and she grunted before leading the horses to the water. "It grows dark. We must make camp here."

Alexander frowned at the way she shivered. Even under every fur she owned, she couldn't keep warm. There was no cave or shelter along this part of the trail, and the winter storm had grown until he could barely see her through the falling snow. He would start a fire, but keeping it burning through the night would require constant tending. Nodding his reassurance to her, he started gathering wood in the clearing next to the stream.

"This isn't good," Tobias whispered to him. "She's already shivering, and keeping a fire going in this weather is going to be nearly impossible."

He didn't say a word but piled the wood high. Nearby,

Maiara removed the simple tent she'd acquired in Philadelphia from the packhorse and began to pitch it in the mounting wind. She had used the tent many times during their travels but never in cold such as this. The canvas bent and bowed in the storm. He finished with the wood and helped her stake it down. Together, they reinforced the supports with ropes tied to nearby trees.

It was completely inadequate for the weather.

While Gabriel and Tobias started the fire, he followed her inside the tent, where she'd spread a pelt over the icy ground. "You're shivering," he said.

"I need the fire." Her teeth clacked together. His dragon twisted in discomfort, and he could stand no more.

"Let me help you." He spread his arms and his wings, as much as the small space would allow, and she did not hesitate to enter them. His eyelids sank as her fresh, green scent filled his nose and the softness of her hair brushed his cheek. Enfolding her in his wings, he lowered both of them to the floor of the tent, using his arms to pull her fur cloak tighter around her. After only a few seconds, her shivering quieted and she leaned her full weight into his chest.

"Do you never grow cold?" she asked.

Alexander thought about the question. "I feel the cold. It's not as if I can't tell ice from fire. I can, and I much prefer the latter. But the cold isn't dangerous to me. It's never made me uncomfortable to the point I couldn't eat or sleep."

"You are always this warm. All of you?" Her gaze darted toward the tent's flap, beyond which the silhouettes of his brothers worked to build a bonfire and prepare stew from their reserves.

"Yes. Sometimes hotter. We were born in the belly of a volcano. We thrive in the heat."

She sagged against him. With the weather coming,

Maiara had ridden hard with few breaks, trying to get them to the Potawatomi village as quickly as possible.

"Are we close?"

She opened her eyes and peeked up at him. "Two days' journey."

"But you're tired."

"Yes. I have never traveled so far so fast."

"Rest now. I will wake you when the food is done."

"I should help cook."

"My brothers will do the cooking tonight."

Tension melted from her body and she sank deeper into his arms. Contentment softened her cheeks, bringing back the radiance he'd seen the first night he'd met her. He tried his best to commit every detail to memory so he could draw her as soon as he could get his hands on his sketchbook.

"Tell me about Paragon."

He adjusted her in his arms while he considered what would make sense to her. "Paragon is a land divided into five kingdoms. In the ruling kingdom, the kingdom of Paragon, it never snows. I grew up in a palace built into the side of a volcano that we call Obsidian Mountain."

"Are there trees there?"

Alexander raised his eyebrows. "Oh yes. Our forests are tropical and our flora and fauna are different from what grows here. In the forests of Rogos, that's the Kingdom of the Elves, it is said every variety of tree grows, one from every realm in the universe. The first time I saw you, I thought you reminded me of an elf, although to be honest, we were never allowed to spend much time in Rogos or with its people."

"Why not?"

"My siblings and I..." Her eyes were closed and he tightened the wrap of his wings around her. "As I mentioned before, we were heirs to the throne, the sons and daughter of the queen."

Her eyelids cracked open. "I remember. My people do not have kings and queens."

"What do you have?"

"There is a leader, white men call him chief, we call him *ogama*. The *ogama* has a wise council, one of whom is the healer or *Midew*. Most of the time, these leaders are men. My mother was a *Midew*, and she taught me the ways at her side. She was once part of my *ogama*'s council. They have passed into the Land of Souls now."

He stroked her hair back from her face, and she closed her eyes again. "I'm sorry."

She swallowed. "She is the reason I survived. She taught me to hide in the trees."

Alexander wondered why her mother hadn't used her power to escape the *wendigo*'s attack, but if she'd been trying to save the other *Midew*, some of whom weren't strong enough to use that type of magic, it was possible she just didn't have the chance. "How does that work?"

She smiled up at him and narrowed her eyes. "It takes years of training. I cannot teach you."

Of course not. He tucked a strand of her hair behind her ear.

"If you were royalty in your land, why did you come here?" she asked.

Alexander pursed his lips. This was not something he liked to think about, and he hadn't shared it with anyone outside his family before. He longed to share it with Maiara though. He wanted to be known by her. He wanted to know her. "My brother Marius, the oldest of our siblings, was meant to take over as king. On his coronation day, our uncle, the current king, murdered him so that he could retain control of the throne."

This time her eyes opened wide and her lips parted. "He would have killed you too?"

"Yes. Our mother, the queen, used her magic to send us here. We assume our uncle killed her and our father as well. That's how it is in Paragon, the oldest brother and sister are king and queen and each take a consort as their mate."

Maiara narrowed her eyes. "This uncle who killed them, he continues to rule your land?"

"Yes."

"You said the queen used her magic. Do you have magic too?"

He held up his right hand and wiggled the finger wearing the large turquoise ring that was the source of his magic in his human form. "Yes. Dragons are magical beings. We are born with the ability to protect what is ours. We can make ourselves invisible, fly, have superior strength and speed, and we can also lay protective wards around an area, keep it hidden from view and inaccessible to anything supernatural. It comes from our origins, our nature to hoard and protect treasure."

"But you said the queen used magic to send you away."

"Yes, but that's different. As magical creatures, we can perform spells. We aren't like witches, mind you. We can't naturally control the elements with our intention. But we can follow a spell, like a recipe, and it will sometimes work because of our magic. Before her death, our mother had amassed a great book of dragon spells. She enchanted our rings before Marius was murdered. We believe she suspected our uncle's treachery and prepared the spell she used to save us in advance."

Maiara sighed and burrowed deeper into the nest of his

jacket. "Thank the Great Spirit you came. I would surely be dead if not for you."

He scoffed. "I don't believe that. The girl who speaks to hawks and hides in trees would have found a way to survive."

"Many of my kind, *Midews*, have animals that help them bridge between this life and the next. Nikan is mine. She came to me when I reached the level in my training where I understood the thin line that separates us from our ancestors. Nikan and I are bound to each other."

Alexander looked up then at the silhouette of the bird on the roof of the tent. He sometimes forgot Nikan was there anymore, but she rarely moved far from Maiara. "Should we invite her inside?"

"No. She is happy where she is. She prefers not to be contained."

"I see."

"You are a good dragon for asking," she said. "And for coming with me to protect my people."

"Maybe. Maybe I have my reasons for being good and they are not so innocent as you might think." Immediately he regretted saying it. Why had he? It was a deep secret he should have kept to himself.

"No? What reason could you have to help someone like me? Other white men call us savages."

He tapped her nose. "The white men who say those things are filthy dolts. The only things savage about you are your intelligence and your beauty." Her ebony eyes locked with his, and the smile faded from his face. "Perhaps my reasons for helping you have more to do with that than pure benevolence."

The way Maiara looked at him then was raw and transparent. In that moment, he wanted her as males of all peoples wanted their females, and she must have seen it in him, because she brought her hand to his face. He made no attempt to hide the hunger in his eyes. The way she tipped her head and parted her lips only encouraged him.

"You are a man of honor," she said. "Being here with you, warmed in your arms, is as natural as breathing. It reminds me of summer."

"I couldn't agree more." He touched his forehead to hers.

"I had a dream. Before I met you." Her voice wavered, and he got the sense she hadn't expected to share this with him. He pulled back so he could see her better.

"What happened in this dream?"

"After my father was murdered by the *wendigo* and I escaped into a tree, I waited two days to come out. I had to make sure the creature was gone. I only emerged when it was clear if I did not I would starve to death. After that, I hunted and existed and survived until I knew the weather would soon be too cold to support this way of life.

"One night, while I slept in my tree, I had a dream. I saw my mother's face, and then a thunderbird picked me up in its talons and dropped me in the land of the white man. There I found a box, and inside was a stone like the one in your ring. I took the stone between my hands, and its magic felt hot.

"It glowed as bright as the sun. I recognized this as a great gift because a cold and dark force had captured my people. I wanted to give the stone to the keepers of the fire to protect them from the evil they were enduring. But when I arrived in their village, the stone cracked like an egg and inside was a bird I'd never seen before. The bird became fire and then dust and then a bird again, and no warrior could best its magic."

"A phoenix?"

"I do not know that word."

He shook his head like the name didn't matter. "What do you think this dream means?"

"I think it means I was meant to meet you, Alexander, and meant to take you back to the Potawatomi. I think the fire is you. You will protect my people against the Iroquois and the *wendigo*."

"Oh." His gaze drifted away from her.

"In my hands," she murmured.

"Pardon?"

"You were meant to go there, in my hands. In my arms. Your heat, in my blood."

His breath caught. She slid her hands around his neck and pulled herself closer to him.

Kissing her was as natural as taking his next breath. He held her loosely, allowing her to come to him on her own terms, at her own speed. When their mouths connected, the crackle of magic coursed through his blood, from his mouth to his chest and then low in his abdomen. He felt himself harden beneath her and wondered if she could tell through the layers she wore.

Oh, how he wanted to be the man of her dream. His inner dragon coiled and stretched inside him, made happy by the feel of her arms. He cradled her head and tickled her upper lip with his beard. The closeness tore down any barriers left between them. He had nothing to compare this to. He'd never felt this way about a female, even in Paragon where his social calendar had allowed for a number of physical relationships. This was different. This was intimacy.

Her lips parted and he tasted her. By the Mountain, this was a fire he had never known before. She returned the taste, licking inside his mouth and adjusting herself in his lap. She paused to shed her outer layer of fur and positioned a knee on either side of his hips. Indeed, the tent had grown hot, even with the snow and wind blowing beyond its walls.

"You taste of smoke, fresh cut wood, and pawpaw fruit," she said.

"What's a pawpaw fruit?"

She didn't answer but kissed him again. Chest pressed to chest, he swallowed her moan and stroked along the place where her braid cascaded down the muscles of her back. He raised his hips, grinding against her. There was no hiding his desire for her now, and she didn't move away. He could only imagine what it would feel like to be inside her. He longed to have nothing between them, to join with her, maybe even bond with her. Yes, his dragon liked that idea.

*Mine.*

She dug her fingers into his hair and kissed him harder, her body rising and falling above him. He cursed the layers of clothing between them.

"Stew is ready," Tobias yelled from the fire.

"Best eat it quickly," Gabriel said. "The fire won't last in this."

By this he meant the blizzard. The snow cascaded in heavy blots beyond the canvas, collecting in a thick shadow around the base of the tent. He would have loved to ignore his brothers and continue kindling the fire he and Maiara had started inside the tent, but she had grown thin, the traveling harder on her than the rest of them. He steadied her, his thumbs braced on the bones of her hips.

"You need to eat," he said. Her stomach growled its agreement.

Reluctantly she pulled away. He reached for her fur and drew it around her shoulders and then spread his wings to free her from his embrace.

"Two more days until we reach your people. I will see you safely into their arms."

She narrowed her eyes and smiled in understanding, their earlier intimacy extending to this moment. This was for the best. Alexander wanted more than a tent in the snow. If he had her, if she gave herself to him, he wanted forever. He wanted a home.

"Two more days," she repeated.

He moved toward the flap. "It's cold. Stay. I will bring you food."

"It is cold. Won't you keep me warm when you return?"

The smile he gave her was laced with wanting. "It would be my honor."

# CHAPTER TWENTY

Two days later, with snow peppering his horse's mane, Alexander followed Maiara through a passageway of tall sandstone ridges toward the Potawatomi village. The Potawatomi lived most of the year in the lake basins on the edge of the Great Plains, but in the winter, Maiara had explained, families journeyed into the hills for protection from the harsh winds. At the same time, they abandoned their dome-shaped wigwams for homes called teepees or *nsoegen* in their language, conical houses covered in hides and sheaves of reeds, abodes better suited for the cold.

It was these homes he noticed first as they approached, followed by the strange and foreign symbols carved and painted in the sides of the stone. The teepees were erected in a circle around a central gathering place, curls of smoke rising from the pointed tops. His heart leaped knowing Maiara was now home. Although he'd kept her warm these past nights sleeping by her side, he'd shared nothing more than a few passionate kisses with her.

He wanted more. His dragon wanted more. The thought of making her his mate caused his blood to throb in his veins. She was wild, bold, and free, braver than most of his kind. He longed to worship her as she deserved to be worshipped.

But he would not take advantage of her need for his warmth or have their first time be in the mud in some tent or cave. He wanted her, but if she accepted him, he wanted their mating to be forever. Which meant that he needed these people to accept her as their own. He needed her to have a home so that she could invite him into it, not choose him out of some feeling of necessity.

His reverie was broken by a rush of native men armed with knives, axes, and spears who surrounded them, yelling in Maiara's native language. While Alexander waited for the magic of his ring to analyze the language and give him a translation, Maiara shouted back at them through the falling snow.

"I am Maiara, healer and last living member *Notawkah's* tribe. My people were slaughtered by the *wendigo*. I ask for the protection of your fire for me and my friends."

Alexander stared down at the angry natives circling them. The men were not lowering their weapons. Instead, three of them broke from the others and grabbed their horses' reins, leading them into the village.

"I'm not comfortable with this," Tobias grumbled. "Didn't that barmaid from the Owl's Roost say these people have ripped white men's hearts out? We should have changed our appearance before coming here."

Alexander growled. "They're protecting their village. Pay them your respect."

"For now," Gabriel said. "Maiara needs shelter. For her sake, let us give these people the benefit of the doubt."

"It's the least we can do," Alexander said, holding Gabriel's gaze.

They were led into the center of the village to the largest teepee, big enough for a group of men to gather inside. The warriors stopped and gestured for them to dismount.

Maiara slid off her horse. "This is a sacred place where their chief rules on important matters with his council. They have invited us inside. Please come in but do not speak."

"Don't speak?" Gabriel scowled and glanced toward Tobias. "I think they would prefer words to what I might do if they don't get those spears out of our faces."

Flashing his crooked half smile, Tobias added, "Are you sure you are even capable of it, Gabriel? You haven't kept your mouth shut in some two hundred years."

Alexander growled under his breath. "Do not ruin this for her."

"You mean for us, don't you, brother?" Gabriel narrowed his eyes.

Ignoring him, Alexander dismounted and stood beside Maiara with his hands folded. Praise the Mountain, his brothers followed suit, although Gabriel's countenance suggested he wasn't happy ceding the floor to anyone, including Maiara.

They entered the teepee together under a flap of animal skin. What animal, Alexander was unsure. He did not recognize the pelt as anything he'd become accustomed to during their travels in Europe. Inside, the round room was dark, warm, and smoky, with a fire crackling at the center of a circle of straight-backed men. *Homey. Not unlike the mountain.*

Among the humans, one man looked of particular

import, adorned in silver rings, beads, and porcupine quills that nearly covered his deerskin leggings and tunic. *This must be the chief.*

The man raised his chin and gestured to the others in the room, murmuring something to Maiara Alexander didn't quite catch. She, however, must have understood what he was asking, because she took a deep breath and stepped toward the fire. Reaching into the folds of her cloak, she removed the otter skin pouch where she kept the white shell she'd used for healing. "I am the last of the *Midewiwin* society."

There was an audible intake of breath as they gazed upon the pouch she held above her head. Their eyes widened as she drew the shell from inside. Whispers twisted between the flames. "The *Midewiwin* society was attacked by the Iroquois at our curing ritual. The Iroquois are angry that the French men trade with us for furs. They are not satisfied with the animals on their own lands. They want the lands of the Anish'ina'beg too. They want all the lands for their own."

A loud murmur rose among the elders, and they nodded as if these facts were well known.

"The *Midewiwin* have protected the Anish'ina'beg since Great Rabbit of the Good Spirit sent Otter to bring us magic. The Iroquois knew they could not defeat us without eliminating the *Midewiwin*. No mortal man could defeat our magic."

An uprising of agreement welled around the fire. "One of their warriors invited a demon into his heart and now walks the earth as a *wendigo*. With this added power, the warrior was able to defeat the magic of the society. I alone survived."

The men cried out at this news and murmurs filled the teepee.

The chief silenced them with one raised hand. "When our *Midew*, Keme, did not return from the ritual, I dreamed he had crossed to the Land of Souls, but if what you say is true, how is it that you survived?" the chief asked. "And why are you coming to us only now? The curing was before the leaf fall."

Alexander watched Maiara's face flush. Whatever she was about to say was a source of shame to her. His heart felt heavy and he almost took a step forward to comfort her, but her eyes found his before he moved and she gave her head one firm shake.

"My father was a white man, a trapper," she said to the men. "He witnessed the *wendigo* set upon my village. He was there with my mother. He begged my mother to flee with him, but she insisted on protecting her tribe. The last thing she told him before the *wendigo* took her life was that I was on my way to the curing on foot as is our custom. My father rode hard to intercept me. He told me what had happened, delaying my arrival at the ritual. We tried to warn the others, but we were too late. The sacred place of the curing was already soaked in blood."

The men roared and beat their chests, tears forming in their eyes. "I did not see Keme, but the *wendigo* left nothing alive in its wake. The creature spotted me, and my father tried to hide me. But it hunted me. After some time, it found us and my father gave his life to save mine. Only by using the great magic was I able to escape and hide among the white men until these three guardians agreed to protect my journey here."

Alexander did not miss the dagger-filled stare Gabriel and Tobias gave him when Maiara gestured toward them.

Gabriel especially looked like he'd eaten something bad. But then this was the first time his brothers were hearing about Maiara's magic and the *wendigo*. He ignored his brothers and turned his attention back on Maiara.

"My village, my family, my tribe, my society, are dead. I ask that you take me in as your own and give refuge to my guardians until the snow melts and the crocus blooms."

The chief stared into the fire, looking particularly perplexed. "The *wendigo* will come for you."

"Yes."

"If you stay, the village will be at risk."

"Yes."

"If the society of *Midewiwin* could not stop the *wendigo*, how will my people? We are few and the winter makes us vulnerable. *Wendigo* hunts day and night and is not susceptible to the cold as we are. If we allow you to stay, the blood of our clan will be on my hands." The chief pointed one gnarled finger at her as he spoke.

There were sounds of agreement from the circle of elders.

Maiara's head sagged on her shoulders, and her eyes glistened with unshed tears. "Please."

"You will stay the night. We will provide you with provisions and fresh horses. Then you must go."

Alexander's blood heated in his veins. This was unacceptable. They must take her in. Maiara didn't just need protection; she needed a home.

"I will protect you from the *wendigo*," Alexander announced in their language. The men quieted. No sound but the crackle of the fire accompanied the stares that burned into him. Every mouth sagged with disapproval.

"Alexander, no," Maiara whispered. But there was also

a look of respect in her eyes. She did not know he could speak her language.

Removing his coat and shoes, Alexander gave Maiara one last reassuring nod and tapped his chest. "I will protect this tribe." Then he stepped into the fire.

The men cried out, rising and turning to each other in confusion as Alexander's clothing caught fire. His breeches blackened, then burned away, as did his shirt. At one point, the flames were so high they swallowed his head. He spread his hands and turned, showing them that although the last wisps of his clothing were consumed, his skin did not burn. Then he spread his wings.

Now the entire council fell into total chaos.

"Alexander!" Gabriel howled. But he ignored his brother's angst.

"I will protect your tribe," he said, louder now, allowing his dragon to infuse his voice with rumbling grit. "Only as long as you allow her to stay." He pointed at Maiara, whose dark eyes had turned into pits of wonder.

The men spoke among themselves for only a moment before the chief said in a trembling voice, "You are welcome here, spirit. A place will be prepared for you. Maiara, I take you as my daughter."

Aware of his nakedness, Alexander stepped out of the fire, picked up his coat and boots, and left the teepee, his skin still steaming.

# CHAPTER TWENTY-ONE

A lexander paced, his dragon ready for a fight. After he'd left the tribal council, he'd dressed and waited near the horses. Within moments, he was shown to a dwelling where he, Gabriel, and Tobias were invited to stay. Maiara was offered a smaller teepee that used to be the tribe's *Midew* Keme's, before he was killed by the *wendigo*. As he understood it, it doubled as a sacred healing room.

At first Gabriel and Tobias remained silent as they unloaded the horses and started a fire, more for light than for any need for heat. But once they were alone, Gabriel could no longer hold his tongue.

"Do you intend to reveal our true identity to every human in this realm?" Gabriel fumed.

"They would have rejected her," Alexander snapped. "I couldn't let that happen. These people are all she has now. Her life is at stake."

"Right. The *wendigo*," Gabriel snapped. A vein in his neck bulged and his hands balled into fists. "When were you going to tell us our guide was a healer with a monster hunting her? Or did you intend we find out when it tried to murder us in our sleep?"

"That didn't happen. We were on horseback. The creature is on foot. We outran it," Alexander mumbled. He actually didn't know for sure how fast the *wendigo* could travel, but it was his best theory.

"No wonder you demanded we change course." Tobias shook his head. "How could you keep this from us?"

"I couldn't risk you turning her away! She needed our protection and we needed her. I was afraid you wouldn't do the right thing."

Gabriel charged at him until his face was less than an inch from his own. It took everything in Alexander not to take a step back. "We didn't have a choice. You didn't give us one."

"Don't tear him apart yet, Gabriel. Not until we get to the bottom of his stupidity." Tobias crossed his arms. "You do realize, you promised to protect this tribe for as long as she lives among them. When do you plan to explain to them that your stay here isn't permanent?"

Alexander stared into the fire and didn't say a word. Oh, he had things to say. But where did he start when it came to his feelings about Maiara?

"By the Mountain." Tobias squinted at him from across the fire. "You do intend to stay. Permanently."

Gabriel harrumphed. "That's ridiculous. He can't stay with these people. He needs his own territory, a place to hoard treasure, a place to fly and hunt without interference from humans." He pointed at Alexander's chest. "Tell Tobias he's mistaken."

Alexander was done taking orders from Gabriel. "What does it matter to you? The two of you can go anywhere you wish. I made the promise, and I plan to deliver on it."

Gabriel made a sound deep in his throat like he couldn't believe what he was hearing. "You would sacrifice your happiness for a human woman?"

With a heavy sigh, Alexander decided to tell his brothers the truth. There was no point in lying now. Not to them and not to himself. "My happiness *is* the human woman."

"In what way?" Tobias asked.

"My dragon wants her."

Gabriel laughed. "You can't mean—"

"I am drawn to her to the depths of my soul and wish to mate with her."

"Are you mad, brother? You are an immortal! She has a human life. If you bond with her, you will be tying yourself to a sinking ship." Gabriel lowered himself onto the layers of fur that would serve as his bed and pulled a piece of jerky from his saddlebag.

"It's not like I chose it consciously." Alexander stared at his brother and tried to explain. "When it happens to you, if it happens to you, it's like the entire universe is converging to bring her to you. She is mine. Mine to protect. Mine to care for. It is like how we feel about treasure when we have it. Even stronger."

Tobias crossed his arms. "That's never going to happen to me."

Alexander shrugged. "Maybe not, but it isn't an unpleasant experience."

"Does Maiara share your feelings?"

"I don't know." He sank to his own bed and pulled off his boots. "But I've decided it doesn't matter. I will stay with her until she either agrees to be mine or sends me away. It is the only thing I want." He finished undressing and tucked himself between the pelts.

"Don't get too comfortable, brother," Gabriel said.

"Why not?"

"You promised to protect the tribe, remember?"

"So?"

"The *wendigo* hunts at night. Do you plan to wait until it claws one of the men or women of this village apart before you do the protecting? Or will you do your duty and patrol the perimeter?"

Fatigue from their long journey came to rest like a sandbag across his shoulders. Gabriel was right. During their journey, he'd protected Maiara by wrapping his body around her as she slept. He could not do such a thing with the entire village. The only way to do his duty was to stay awake and watchful.

He sat up and reached for his boots, then thought better of it. His senses were more alert in his dragon form. He'd shift and watch over the village from above. Rubbing his eyes, he moved for the flap in the teepee.

"Brother," Gabriel said.

"Yes?"

"We'll take shifts. Come back in three hours and wake me. I'll take the second shift. Tobias will take the third."

Tobias raised an eyebrow. "I will?"

"Of course you will," Gabriel said. "Because we're family and because this frozen wasteland will be the last time we're all together for..." He turned his face away, unable or unwilling to finish the sentence.

Alexander had almost forgotten that the longer they stayed together in one place, the greater the risk that Brynhoff would find them. They were taking a big chance staying here, but until spring, there was nowhere else to go. And Gabriel was right. This would be the last they were together for what could be a very long time.

Funny, neither Gabriel nor Tobias looked angry anymore. Only exhausted.

"Thank you, brothers," he said, moved by their understanding.

Tobias shrugged. "It's your heart. I just hope you take care of it."

THE WENDIGO DID NOT SHOW ITSELF THAT NIGHT OR the next in the forests surrounding the village. But Alexander barely had time to reassure Maiara of this. There was little time to discuss much else either. Her teepee was overflowing with patients in need of healing. Many illnesses and injuries had festered in the absence of the tribe's regular healer, Keme.

He told himself her withdrawal from him was a consequence of her compassion. Maiara had simply become distracted with caring for the tribe. But when Tobias demonstrated a special affinity for healing and Maiara invited him to assist her, Alexander burned with jealousy. Somehow his brother intuitively knew which patients would benefit from being packed in ice or from spending time in the sweat lodge. He also understood how to set a bone and learned quickly how to make a paste to heal rashes and abrasions. This freed Maiara to use her healing amulet on the sickest patients, those injured while hunting or suffering from debilitating infections. It left Alexander to pine for her.

Although Alexander would have liked to take Tobias's place to be closer to Maiara, the language of healing made no sense to him. He found it difficult to be around the sick without being drawn into their stories by his creative brain.

Talk to them, sketch them, feed them, those were things he could do, but hurt in order to heal? Tobias was far better at that than he was.

So he and Gabriel were relegated to patrolling and occasionally fetching water or wood for her fire. He would watch her when he could, linger in her teepee after bringing her what she asked for, or brush her hand with his own when she asked for help binding a wound. It never went anywhere, and during mealtimes, she would often sit near the chief and his council.

After weeks of this, he was convinced he'd made a terrible mistake. All this time, her affection for him had been transactional. She'd needed safety. He'd wanted her. But now that she had a home and everything she needed, she had no use for him.

He wouldn't go back on his word to the tribe, but his dream of having her as his mate had grown foggy around the edges.

"Tell her how you feel," Tobias said one night. Alexander hadn't complained, but he supposed his withdrawn and sulky mood told its own story. "You can't go on like this. Tell her. Then you will know for sure."

Resolved to do just that, Alexander made a point of lingering in Maiara's presence the next day.

"Hold this here," she ordered him, pressing his hand to a scrap of cloth covering a nasty gash on an elderly woman's hip. "Pressure." She nodded at him and he complied. The old woman moaned softly. "She fell on the ice. We need to stop the bleeding. This will give me time to heal her from within."

"The cloth is soaking through. What do I do?" Alexander asked.

"Rinse it in the bowl. There." She pointed toward a

silver vessel that looked like it came from a white man's table. Then again, he suspected the scraps of cloth they were using as bandages came from trading with the white man as well.

"Always silver," Tobias said from where he was helping another patient. "It impedes infection."

"Right. Infection...," Alexander mumbled. He understood nothing about healing. Quickly he rinsed the cloth in the bowl and pressed it against the wound. Maiara removed her amulet from one warrior, who was holding his head as if it ached, and placed it around the neck and against the skin of the old woman. Raising her hands, she chanted a healing prayer. The resulting power that coursed through the room raised the hair on Alexander's arms.

"The bleeding slows." Although he'd observed her healing before, it never ceased to amaze him.

She placed her hands on the woman's forehead and spoke soothing words to her.

"Maiara," he whispered. "When you are able, I'd like to speak with you... alone."

Her gaze met his. She checked the woman's wound, then removed the bloody cloth from the woman's healing hip and dropped it back into the silver bowl. With a few words to Tobias, she gestured toward the exit. Alexander rinsed the blood from his hands before following her outside.

"It is time we spoke," she said, her expression serious. "I have never thanked you for your help."

"It's no inconvenience." He glanced back toward the teepee and the woman inside.

"No. I never thanked you for speaking for me and offering your protection to the elders. You are the reason I am welcome here."

He met her gaze and held it. "I wanted you to have a home. You've lost too much." He rocked back on his heels, warring with himself over what to say.

"I have sensed for many days that there is something your spirit wishes to say to my spirit." Her lips pressed into a flat line, into an expression he found impossible to read.

He took a deep breath and let it out slowly. Reaching out, he ran his hand along the sleeve of her deerskin dress. "You're starting to shiver."

"I left my pelt inside."

"Come closer. I will warm you." He extended his wings, and she moved into the harbor of his arms. "Better?"

She tipped her head back to look up at him. "Like the height of summer. Why was it important to you that I have a home? I would have continued to guide you to lands where you could settle if the council refused me."

He swallowed the lump forming in his throat. "You needed a home so that you could be safe and warm and in need of nothing. And once you had all you needed, then you would be free to decide about what you wanted. If you might want one thing more. One... person more."

She drew back to get a better look at him. After a long pause, she said, "You hoped it was the will of the Great Spirit that I would want you?"

He sighed. He did not know this Great Spirit. In Paragon, they worshipped the goddess of the Mountain. But he supposed he understood the sentiment, and he couldn't agree more. Nodding slowly, he placed a hand over his heart.

"I will stay and protect you, no matter your feelings for me. To my dragon, it is done."

"It is done?"

"You are mine."

"Yours?"

He placed his hands on her shoulders and brought his face close to hers. "When dragons mate, they mate for life. I want you as my mate, Maiara."

"Your... mate." Her eyes shifted away.

"Connected... Mated... Married... Joined?" He hooked his fingers together. Not side by side as she'd described marriage once, but intertwined. "Bonded."

"You want to join our spirits?" she clarified, her face remaining impassive.

He nodded. "I... love you, Maiara. And I will stay and protect this village no matter what you decide. But you are *why* I agreed to stay. I needed to tell you that. I needed to ask you to be mine."

She studied him as if she truly saw him, saw his soul. This woman of the trees understood every fiber of his being without sharing a single word. She knew the root of him, and he found himself fantasizing about their nights on their journey here, when she would sleep under his wing and curled into his side.

"You've given me much to pray about," she said, her face serious. "I am glad you shared this with me. What is the polite way for me to respond to your request for this mating?"

He frowned. "If you reject me, you should do nothing. Go on about your life. I will vex you no further."

"And if my answer is yes?"

"Lie with me."

"I have already lain with you," she said seriously.

"As a husband lies with a wife."

Her lips formed into a tiny *O* and her eyebrows knit. "This is your way?"

"This is our way."

She backed away from him. He retracted his wings to accommodate her. "I must return. There are many inside who need my help."

He forced his face to remain blank as his heart shattered. She turned on her heel and strode away without another word. Without even a look over her shoulder. As he'd feared, she was indifferent. Soul shredded, he rushed back to his teepee, fearing he had his answer and knowing he'd never be the same again.

# CHAPTER TWENTY-TWO

After the night meal where he'd hardly touched his food and could not bear to look in Maiara's direction, Alexander returned to his teepee, feeling completely dejected. He'd been wrong to share his feelings. He'd asked her to be his mate too soon. Tipped his hand. Made a fool out of himself. Ruined any hope of changing her opinion of him.

Grabbing his sketchbook, he brought charcoal to paper in a fury, outlining the crook of her nose, her angular cheekbones and square jaw, along with her hair that reminded him of the night spilling down to earth. He drew the stars in her eyes, captured the way the heavens seemed to peek out from inside her.

But when he sketched her mouth, all that would render on the paper was the tight line, the disappointment, the... Was it fear? He couldn't get the mouth right because he didn't understand her expression. Was she disgusted by what he was? Of course she was. He wasn't just another gender; he was another species.

Assessing his finished creation, he immediately hated it.

His lines were too heavy, too dark. He'd sullied her image with a layer of his angst. He folded the picture in half and tucked it in the back of the leather binding of his sketchbook, between the one of her naked in front of the mighty oak and the one of her hunched over the redcoat, healing him.

After storing it in his saddlebag, he prepared tea from dried mint that one of the women had given him. He hoped it would refresh him before his night's work. He hadn't had a full night's sleep since they'd arrived and, unlike his brothers, had been too busy obsessing over Maiara to make up the sleep during the day.

He'd finished half a mug full when Tobias slipped through the flap of the teepee followed by a flurry of blowing snow. "It's getting bad out there."

"I'll be all right once I shift," Alexander said, taking another large swig of tea. It was time to patrol the boundaries of the village.

"About that..." Tobias sat on the log he used as a stool and tapped his thumb against his thigh. "Gabriel decided to take the first shift tonight."

"Oh?"

Tobias rubbed the back of his neck. "I've been helping Maiara with her patients."

"And that has what bearing on the topic?" Alexander snapped.

"Tonight was the first night she requested you. It seems she needs help with a task beyond my abilities. A task only you can accomplish."

Alexander furrowed his brow. "You've been healing by her side for weeks. What could I possibly help her with that you could not?"

Tobias met his gaze and lowered his chin. "I couldn't

possibly say, but I did notice that she is alone in her dwelling tonight. She made sure I helped every patient home this afternoon before she made me promise to send you to her. Don't you find that unusual, Alexander?"

For a moment Alexander's brain tried to rearrange the words Tobias was saying to him to make sense, but no matter how he flipped and fiddled with the idea that Maiara needed his help, he couldn't make logical sense of it.

"Perhaps the healing she needs help with isn't the traditional kind," Tobias mumbled.

Alexander stilled as a current of electricity coursed from his fingertips to his toes. She didn't need help with healing; she needed him.

He sprang to his feet. "Can you—?" He could hardly form words, and the thought cut itself off abruptly in his throat.

"Protect the village tonight with Gabriel? Yes, for as long as you need, although I predict it won't be long at all." The corner of Tobias's mouth twitched.

Alexander pulled on his boots and gave his brother a devilish look. "Don't count on it." He burst out the flap and strode across the village with a singular determination. But when he reached her teepee, he wasn't sure what to do. Was it polite to walk in? Should he knock?

"Maiara?" he said in a loud clear voice. "Tobias told me to come. May I enter?"

The flap peeled back and her shadowed face appeared in the opening. "Yes. Come inside."

He stepped into her dwelling, the warmth and light of the fire enveloping him. Once his eyes had adjusted, he saw she wore nothing but a deerskin dress that reached to midthigh.

"Do you never grow cold?" she asked, looking at his

shirt, which was open at the neck. He hadn't bothered with his coat.

"No. Never." He smiled. "But I think you knew that." Her hair was loose around her shoulders, and the fire sent shadows dancing across her skin. He inhaled deeply her fresh spring scent. There was more to it tonight, a perfume. His eyes fell on a large silver bowl in the corner of the teepee with the same scent. She must have used it to bathe.

Her gaze locked with his, and she smoothed her hands down her dress until her fingers caught on the hem, then slowly lifted it over her head. Alexander inhaled sharply through his teeth. Maiara was perfection in human form. The light seemed to cling to her amber skin, her full, graceful breasts, each ending in dusky peaks. Her waist stretched long and trim below those glorious mounds with a shadowy oval navel he longed to explore. The rounded muscles of her hips and thighs teased pleasures unknown before his gaze fell on the dark patch at the juncture of her thighs. He feared his body's immediate reaction might tear his breeches.

"I am cold," she said. "Won't you lend me your warmth?"

He couldn't move. Pure joy cut through his flesh and pinned him in place. Part of him was afraid one wrong move might alter this blissful reality, wake him from this perfect dream. Bless the Mountain, his dragon rose to the occasion. Urged on by the beast within, he slowly spread his wings and, with one flap that made the fire dance, crossed to her and took her into his arms.

With one hand in the small of her back and the other threaded in the hair at the base of her skull, he brushed his mouth over hers. "I prayed you'd invite me in."

"I am afraid. Everyone I love dies, Alexander. I am a

*Midew*, gifted with the power of the Great Spirit to heal, but I could not save my mother or my father. I cannot heal my own heart." Her eyes glistened in the firelight.

"Then leave that to me." His lips met hers in a passionate kiss that traveled through his dragon, all the way to his soul.

MAIARA HAD NEVER FELT ANYTHING LIKE THIS KISS. He kissed her with a force and passion she hadn't thought existed in the real world. A rumble sounded deep in his chest, like the purr of a mountain cat, and she placed her hands upon his shirt and delighted in the vibration.

"The sound of you pleases me," she said.

"My mating trill. It comes with the wings."

Her fingers trailed to his breeches, tugging his shirttails out of their grip. "I want to feel it." She lifted the shirt over his head, over his wings. He kicked off his boots and helped her with the rest of his clothing.

The rumble came again, and a tingle of desire traveled the length of her skin. His manhood pressed long and thick into her lower belly. She tipped her hips and ground against him, longing for more. Aching for him and him alone.

She'd played with boys before. Not in the ways that invited babies, but in ways that brought pleasure. Alexander was far more impressive in every respect, and a thousand butterflies fluttered against the underside of her skin. She wanted him. She needed him.

His hands coasted down her back as his mouth explored hers with long, deep strokes that stole her breath but made her long to suffocate under such torture. He tasted of mint and smelled of smoke, fresh cut wood, and clover. She wanted to cover herself in that scent, roll in it like an animal frolicking in springtime grasses.

His hands moved lower, massaging her ribs, his thumbs brushing the underside of her breasts. She stroked down his chest and under his arms, along the inside of his wings. His body twitched against her and he closed his eyes, lowering his forehead to her shoulder.

"This feels good?" she whispered, and he nodded into the crook of her neck. She kept going, alternating between tickling the underside with her nails and stroking his wing with her palm. The rumbling purr increased in intensity.

His lips worked over her collarbone and trailed kisses lower until he suckled her right breast. Her nipple hardened and extended against his tongue, and lightning branched inside her. She'd never known this magic. He stirred music deep within her, a song to her heart and her head, like the sound of a breeze through the prairie grass. She needed more.

Taking his hand, she guided it between her legs and tipped her head back when his fingers began to move. Yes, that was it. It took friction to kindle fire. Her fingers dug in his hair and she kissed him on the mouth, long and hard, their tongues dancing to this savage beat. The music in her body grew louder, humming against his fingers, the fire he kindled racing through her blood.

And then magic burst through her, bowing her back and drawing a cry from deep within. He cradled her limp body through the surge of power. Magic. This was magic.

His hand hooked around her thigh and he lifted her, his wings spreading to keep his balance, filling the teepee. He pressed against her, spearing the pleasure forward. Arms braced on his shoulders, she worked her body around him, easing him inside her until he filled her completely.

"Say you are mine," he whispered in her ear.

"I am yours."

He thrust into her. "And I am yours." His beard and nose brushed the side of her face. His lips found her ear.

He made love to her for a small eternity, until her mind knew nothing but the feel of him, the sweat on her skin, the rhythm of their love dance. Until finally the magic rose within her once more. She rode him harder, moving her hips to that music once again. Building, building, like a mighty gale before the storm. The clouds broke. The rain poured down. His release echoed through her, found her own, and they galloped off together, hoofbeats thundering in her blood. Finally he sank to his knees on the furs and lowered her gently onto her back.

Once he'd helped her between the furs and tucked her into his side, he whispered to her, "*Ndukweyum.*" *My wife,* in her language.

She touched her forehead to his. "*DIneym, my husband.* I will ask the chief to bless this union when the sun rises."

He pressed his lips to her temple. "And what shall we do until the sun rises?" The smile he gave her shone in the darkness, lit only by the embers of the dying fire.

She trailed her fingers down the length of his body and showed him.

# CHAPTER TWENTY-THREE

The chief blessed their union the next morning, and from that day forward Alexander slept in Maiara's *nsoe'gen*. Gabriel and Tobias enjoyed the extra space and were happy for Alexander, although they never stopped teasing him about being owned by his human mate.

Indeed, Alexander denied Maiara nothing. If she wanted water, he fetched it. He brought her and the rest of the village elk and bison from the prairie below, as much as they could eat. And he watched over all of them every night, although he never saw the *wendigo*. He began to believe it had lost her scent along their journey and that the danger had passed.

Gabriel said the village had become Alexander's treasure. He could not argue with that. Maiara was more precious to him than an entire mountain of jewels.

One day the snow began to melt and purple crocuses popped their heads up through the earth to bask in the sun after a long winter's sleep. Bears woke from their slumber and were seen close to the village, and the chief said it was time to descend from the protection of the hills to the prairie and lake basin where they would join with other Potawatomi bands in their regular territory.

There was never any doubt that Alexander would stay with the tribe, stay with Maiara, but it soon became apparent that they'd tempted fate long enough and Tobias and Gabriel needed to move on. At Alexander's request, Maiara prayed to the Great Spirit for guidance.

While the three dragons prayed, she tossed a powder made from blood and herbs into their fire and studied the smoke as it rose and curled above their heads. That night, she had a dream that sent her tossing and turning in his arms. When she woke, she said she had the answer.

"You will be a *Midew*," Maiara said to Tobias. "A healer. You have the gift. All of the *Midewiwin* are gone. There is a great need. Another tribe lives at the mouth of the Checagou River. It is many miles from us, far enough I think to be safe for you, but your skills will be valued there."

Tobias raised an eyebrow but nodded slowly. "A healer. Yes, I think I'd like that. I've enjoyed learning from you, Maiara. We will rebuild the *Midewiwin* society, in time."

She smiled and gave him a curt nod. "The Great Spirit will guide you."

"And what of me?" Gabriel asked moodily. "Did the smoke show you what to do with the nonhealer?"

Maiara turned to face him head-on as she had always done with Gabriel. "A healer you are not, but I know where you belong. A warrior must go where a warrior is needed."

"And that is?"

"I have seen you far away in the place where the Great River empties into the sea. It is always warm in this place, and the land holds unmatched beauty. But it is also dangerous. Great beasts with sharp teeth and thick skin guard its gates. Most men will perish in its wilds, but you will not.

With your abilities, you will claim a land for yourself and find a place to exercise your magic."

"You see this?"

She nodded knowingly. "Magic will be extremely important to you one day, and this strange place will foster it in you."

Gabriel seemed to like the idea. He straightened and said, "Very well. Take me to this river. I will follow it to this land of beasts and magic."

And so, after a feast where the Potawatomi said their goodbyes and thanked them for their protection and their gifts of meat and healing, they loaded up their horses, and Maiara led them from the first real home they'd known in the New World.

They were on their third day of travel when they found the deer. It had been mauled almost beyond recognition, its flesh hanging in strips from its bones.

"Is this the work of the *wendigo*?" Tobias asked. Alexander held his breath, afraid if he spoke the name it would appear.

"A bear, I think," Maiara said, inspecting the carcass. "*Wendigo* would not leave so much flesh behind."

Still, as they progressed, Alexander was on high alert, barely sleeping at night and waking at the slightest sound. He was relieved when they reached the small band of Potawatomi people on the bank of the Checagou River. Once Maiara introduced herself, they welcomed them in and gave them a place to stay.

"This feels right," Tobias said, leaning back in his bed of furs. All of them had to share a single wigwam out of necessity, but it didn't matter. It was only for one night.

Beside Maiara, Alexander stared into the fire to the sound of his brothers' voices, speaking of hope and new dragon kingdoms. The fatigue from their travels weighed heavily on him, and their voices faded, sleep pulling him under until he sank into total blackness.

He woke to screams. Maiara pulled on his arm and yelled something in her language he couldn't understand. Not because he didn't know her language but because she spoke gibberish, parts of words and half thoughts from a panicked soul. She grabbed her knife and rushed from the wigwam. Alexander followed her, not bothering to dress or with shoes. Blood-curdling cries sliced through the night, urgent calls for help.

Gabriel was already outside. "The *wendigo*," he yelled, pointing to the place in the distance where a pale, lipless figure, more bone, teeth, and claws than flesh, held the body of one of the female elders. Who, he could not tell. The *wendigo* had eaten too much of her.

"We're surrounded. The Mohawk are here!" Maiara turned in a circle, raising her knife.

Gabriel's eyes flared red in the darkness. "I'll take the right flank. Tobias, the left. Alexander, the *wendigo* is yours."

"My pleasure." Alexander shifted quickly. His wings punched violently from his back, and his spine stretched and lengthened to a barbed tail. His turquoise heart cast a soft blue glow across the dirt. He glanced back at Maiara. She bared her teeth, then pointed her chin sharply at the *wendigo*.

*Ziiip.* An arrow coursed through the air and bounced off his scales. He swung his horned head in the direction of the sound and spotted his attacker, a Mohawk male with his bow still raised. With one mighty leap and a snap of his jaws, he tore the warrior's head off and sent it rolling toward the fire. Gabriel's dragon roared his approval. One dead, at least a hundred to go.

The *wendigo* dropped the body it was holding and roared. Alexander rushed the beast. The man-shaped thing was tall, maybe seven feet, and skeletal, but as Alexander attempted to bite it in two, its claws rose up and dug between his scales. He yelped, drew back. What was this creature? He'd never encountered anything in this world with this type of strength, agility, or with sharp enough claws to pierce a dragon's hide. But then the *wendigo* was supernatural, the spawn of demon magic.

Alexander's gaze caught on the blue orb shining from the beast's chest. It winked at him in the twilight as if it were alive, an all-seeing eye from the beyond. He could feel magic rolling off it. Was this the source of the *wendigo*'s power?

Again the monster attacked, spreading its jaws wide and swiping its claws toward Alexander. He snapped again. This time his teeth sank into the thing's shoulder, but the *wendigo* was unaffected. It buried its claws in Alexander's neck and tore itself free. Its flesh and bones knitted back together in an unnerving tangle of blood and gristle.

He shuffled away and spat the thing's blood from his mouth. His wounds would heal quickly enough, but if he couldn't tear it apart, how was he to kill it?

In Paragon, many creatures were immortal. Many had magic. But one universal weakness burdened them all. Aside from dragons, everything burned.

With a deep breath that ignited the flames inside him, he prepared to blast the *wendigo* with the hottest dragon fire he could produce. But the monster had other ideas. It raced into the woods. Alexander couldn't incinerate the thing without potentially starting the entire forest on fire. He had no other choice but to pursue it on foot. From the air, he might lose the trail.

At a full run, he weaved between the trees. The *wendigo* was fast and agile, leaping like some malformed stag over anything in its way. He poured on the speed, using his size and strength to plow through the foliage.

He gained on the monster from behind, stretching his neck and snapping within inches of the beast's gray flesh. That wouldn't do. He needed to use his fire. Coiling and striking, he drove the *wendigo* north to where the forest ended at a wall of sandstone, the side of one of the hills that bordered the area. The *wendigo* banked right, but the hesitation was enough to give Alexander a window of opportunity. With a deep breath, he showered the side of the mountain and the *wendigo* in dragon's fire.

A dragon's blast burned hotter than any earthly fire. It blew with an intensity that gouged the earth and scorched the stone. Still, the creature tried to run again for the shelter of the woods, its limbs ablaze. Alexander knocked it back against the stone with one mighty paw.

Its skin burned away and then muscle and connective tissue. When its skeleton collapsed in a heap, nothing but a steaming torso remained. Powered by some infernal force, it attempted to drag itself away from him with its one remaining arm, jaw working in a silent, burning scream.

He brought his foot down on its head and crushed its skull into a fine powder. Once it was clear the *wendigo* was no more, Alexander noticed again the wink of the blue orb through the bones and ash that had once been its ribs. A flood of memories came back to him.

He shifted into his human form and retrieved the orb from the remains. Now that it was in his hand, he knew for certain. This was Paragonian! It glowed intensely, brighter blue than it had been around the *wendigo*'s neck. He scowled. That was not a good sign.

Quickly he placed the orb on a flat rock at the base of the cliff and brought another stone down upon it with as much strength as he could muster. The crystal shattered and the blue light faded from its pieces. Definitely enchanted. But by whom and for what reason, he could only guess. If Brynhoff was behind this, they were in terrible danger.

Shifting back into his dragon form, Alexander took to the air and returned to the village. If the *wendigo* had a connection to Paragon, he had to warn Gabriel.

# CHAPTER TWENTY-FOUR

By the time Alexander returned to the village, his brothers' accomplishments could be measured by the dozens of steaming corpses to the north and south. The entire tribe had armed themselves, their best warriors circling the women and children. Gabriel and Tobias had kept them all safe.

While his brothers finished off the attackers on the perimeter, Alexander searched for any continued threat from the air. All seemed well. But where was Maiara?

He landed and shifted into his human form, striding toward the chief. He didn't bother to cover his nakedness. "Where is my wife?" he asked in their language.

The men and women of the tribe looked at each other, searching for Maiara among themselves. A growing panic formed in the pit of Alexander's belly. Why had the *wendigo* run? The soulless beast had sharp claws and teeth and an insatiable appetite. It did not know fear. He'd thought it was avoiding his dragon's fire, but now he wondered. Had it meant to draw him into the woods? Draw him out? Away from her?

"Where is my wife?" he bellowed. Frantically he searched their wigwam, then turned in a circle at the center of the village.

Gabriel's fierce roar drew his attention east. In the distance, he saw a Mohawk warrior racing into the shelter of the woods. There was someone in his arms, wrapped in a blanket. Maiara. He shifted so fast it was painful and rocketed to Gabriel's side, coasting over the woods and the trail where the Mohawk warrior rode his horse at breakneck speed.

The thick forest kept them from landing and intercepting the rider. If they muscled through the towering trees, the falling timber could kill her. Dropping low, their shadows loomed over the kidnapper. His horse was tiring. He'd have to stop soon, and when he did, Alexander would end him and take Maiara back.

The Indian galloped into a clearing on the side of the hill where two other Mohawk warriors waited. Alexander's heart clenched. Did he plan to hand her off to a new rider? Not on his life.

He overshot the Mohawk men and landed at the far end of the clearing. Although they shot arrows at him with expert aim, the weapons bounced harmlessly off his scales. Gabriel landed on the other end of the trail and made himself invisible. They had nowhere to go.

The warrior with the Maiara-sized blanket leaped down from his horse and unwrapped her, thrusting her in front of him like a human shield. She was alive. Afraid, but alive. Alexander closed in.

"Alexander," she said.

One of the warriors drew his dagger and held it to her throat. Alexander stopped moving. All three sets of eyes focused on him. Gabriel was close, coming up behind them.

He watched the depression of earth with each invisible step.

In one powerful snap, Gabriel tore two of the warriors in half. He couldn't take the third. If he did, he might injure Maiara. The last man screamed in terror at the sight of his fellow warriors being ripped apart by an invisible force. Alexander used the distraction to move in, shifting into his human form and liberating Maiara from the man's hold.

Gabriel struck, dragging the man back by the shoulder. But the warrior didn't go peacefully. He threw the dagger he'd held to Maiara's neck just before Gabriel tore him in two. Alexander never saw it coming. The blade landed in Maiara's back and she collapsed against him, her mouth open in a silent scream.

"No. No!" He caught her and withdrew the knife, tossing it aside. Its removal only served to make things worse. The wound bled and her breath whistled in her lungs. "Maiara, your amulet. Where's your amulet?" He searched her side for her otter skin pouch. It wasn't there.

"Tobias," she rasped.

He lifted her, sprouted wings, and flew, soaring back to the village as fast as he could fly, until the muscles in his back burned with the effort. He landed at the center of the village, yelling for Tobias before his feet hit the packed dirt.

Tobias arrived at his side, still naked from the shift. "What happened?"

"She's been stabbed. We need her amulet."

Tobias looked right, then left. "The wigwam!" His brother ran for the place they'd slept.

A gurgle rose from Maiara's throat, and Alexander pulled her close, his tears falling on her face.

"I love you," she whispered, more breath than words.

Nikan, who had been circling above them, landed on her chest in a flurry of feathers.

She stopped breathing.

"I love you too. No. No. Maiara, stay with me!" Alexander rested her on the ground and screamed for Tobias.

"Here!" Tobias yelled; he was beside her. "I have it." He placed the white shell in the hollow of her throat. Nikan folded her wings and lay quietly beside it. Maiara did not move. Alexander pressed the shell harder against her chest. Nothing.

"Maiara...," he begged. Hot tears raced down his face. "My wife! My mate! Why isn't it working?" He shook her gently. "Wake up. Come back to me."

Tobias placed two fingers on the side of her throat, his expression morphing into a mask of horror. "She... she's g-gone," he choked out. "We were too late."

Alexander's entire body began to tremble. "No... no."

"Alexander..." Gabriel placed a hand on his shoulder. How long had he been standing behind him?

Nudging Nikan off her, Alexander pulled Maiara into his arms again and rocked her. "It needs more time to work. Give it time."

He saw them now, the others. Every family in the tribe had surrounded them. Time became meaningless as he held her, whispered to her, pressed his lips to her forehead. She couldn't be dead. If she was, his soul would be torn in two and half of himself would go to the grave with her.

Her body cooled in his arms.

Several hours passed before he noticed the tribe was building something behind him. A pyre. An old woman came with gentle words, offering him food. He ignored her.

More time passed. Tobias came, rubbed his back, and pleaded with him to hand Maiara's body over. He refused.

He was covered in her dried blood.

And then Gabriel came. "Alexander, give me Maiara's body." There was no question in his words. When Gabriel spoke, he gave orders. Commands. His massive shoulders blocked out the afternoon sun, casting a shadow across Alexander's face. His older brother meant business.

"Always the prince," Alexander said through clenched teeth. "Fucking order everyone around like you're king of the world. All you are is a horse's ass, Gabriel. You were second best in Paragon and you are still second best, even now that Marius is dead." Anger rose in Alexander, burning in his chest, his ears, his cheeks. He liked the feel of it. As long as he was angry, the hurt felt dull in comparison.

"Give me her body," Gabriel ordered again. There was no more softness in his tone than the last time he gave the command.

"No."

Gabriel spread his wings. "Then I will fight you for her, but be aware, if I attack you and she's in your arms, I will not be responsible for any damage caused her."

Alexander's wings spread wide. "You will not lay a finger on her." He carefully rested her body on the ground behind him and stood to his full height. Raising his fists, he said, "Try it."

Gabriel's fist flew at his face. With an upward swing of his arm, he blocked the punch and returned a kick to the gut. Gabriel caught his foot and twisted. Spinning, Alexander spread his wings and yanked his foot away. It felt like a dance. But then each of these moves was rehearsed, practiced in a sparring pit in Paragon. Alexander needed more. He needed blood.

He swooped down on Gabriel, the talons on the ends of his wings hooking into his brother's as his fists flew. Face. Chest. Stomach. Face. Alexander lost himself in a hailstorm of flying fists. He tore his brother's cheek and reveled in the resulting splash of red. They were in the air, feet flying, then rolling on the ground, covered in dirt and dust. Gabriel blocked and kicked, but Alexander pounded relentlessly until his brother's blood coated his fists. Gabriel curled on his side, his arms crossed over his face.

It was the first and only time Alexander had ever beaten his brother in a fight. Oddly, seeing Gabriel huddled at his feet brought him no joy or peace. He stopped his foot before it connected with Gabriel's ribs. This wasn't the answer.

With his last ounce of energy, Alexander offered Gabriel his hand and helped him to his feet, but when he tried to pull away, his brother squeezed tighter and pulled him into a firm embrace.

"What are you doing?"

"It's okay, Alexander. It's going to be okay," Gabriel said softly.

"Hit me again. I want you to hit me." He struggled against his brother's hold and against the emotion that was welling inside him.

"No. That's done now. It's time for you to stop and say goodbye."

"I can't." Everything was wrong. Pressure built inside his body until it felt like his eyes would pop out of his skull and whatever was in his stomach would pour out his mouth. Instead, tears were all that came. A storm of them. They exited him in great angry sobs that Gabriel tried to soothe by holding him tighter. It didn't work.

"You have to say goodbye. You'll regret it if you don't." Abruptly Gabriel turned him around, and what he saw shattered his heart like glass. Maiara's people had taken her body and placed it on the pyre, her medicine bag positioned in her hands, the shell around her neck. The tribe circled her and chanted a song meant to usher her into the Land of Souls.

His anger died within the pressure of his brother's hug, but the emotion that replaced it was far worse.

The flames climbed.

"They're burning her." He sobbed.

"They have to. It's tradition with the *Midewiwin*. It will return her magic to the Great Spirit to be born again in another healer," Tobias explained. How long had he been there with his hand on his shoulder?

"I can't watch this." Alexander shook his head. Where had the day gone? How long had he hoarded her body against him? The sun sank toward the horizon, the sky painted violet and blue like a bruise; maybe even the Great Spirit felt the sting of Maiara's death.

"I'm sorry, Alexander." Tobias extended his arm around his shoulder, and Gabriel moved to the side to accommodate him. Soon they were holding him up. After some time, he became aware of a distant keening. The deep, tortured howl grew closer until he realized his mouth was open. The sound was coming from him. Only somehow it didn't seem big enough or loud enough to do justice for what he was feeling. This ache in his chest was crushing him from the inside out.

The fire claimed her. He could no longer see her through the flames. He had to go. He had to get out of there. His dragon lurched to the surface, his arms extending toward the dirt and shingling with scales.

"Alexander. Alexander, stop," Gabriel commanded.

It was too late to stop. He shifted into his dragon and

shrugged off his brothers. He couldn't be there. Couldn't breathe. And then he had an idea. He would find this Great Spirit and force it to return Maiara to him or else allow him to follow her into the Land of Souls.

With one last look at his brothers, he spread his wings and flew toward the setting sun. And he never returned.

# CHAPTER TWENTY-FIVE

2018
*Sedona, Arizona*

"That's how you ended up here?" Rowan wiped under her eyes, and her fingers came away wet. Alexander's story was tragically sad. Her heart broke for him all over again. "You kept flying toward the setting sun?"

Alexander wiped a tear from his own eye. "Eventually I gave up on that plan. Nikan and Willow followed me from the Potawatomi village. I could see I was exhausting them both. It takes a lot of work for a hawk to keep up with a dragon, and Willow had used magic to bring my things. He needed my energy to survive. By the time we'd reached Sedona, neither of them looked good. I was afraid I'd kill them both if I pushed any harder.

"Besides, Sedona called to me. I landed here, attracted by the energy, the heat. I thought it would be healing."

"What about the orb?" Nick asked. "Did you ever tell Gabriel that the *wendigo* had a connection to Paragon?"

"No." Alexander frowned. "Honestly, it was the last

thing on my mind after everything. But whoever gave it to the *wendigo*, as far as I know, nothing came of it. We all went our separate ways, and I never saw anything like it again."

His gaze fell on her hand, which had coupled with Nick's as Alexander's story unfolded. She exchanged glances with her mate, and they both let go at the same time. Rowan silently cursed. It must be painful for her brother to see them together.

"You don't have to pretend you aren't deliriously in love just because my life is a living hell."

Rowan sighed heavily, wishing there was some sort of psychological CPR she could do to bring Alexander back to life again. What had happened to him was too horrible. The darkness of it seemed to cling to her. "Is there anything I can do?"

Alexander leaned back in his chair and sipped his coffee. "Believe it or not, you already have. You were right."

"I was? About what?"

"It has helped to tell her story."

"Oh..." She didn't know what to say. She'd hoped it would help him, but there was so much sadness in the air she'd worried she'd made it worse.

"Maiara's people believe that the dead cross over to an otherworld, a Land of Souls. I hadn't thought about that in a long time, that her soul might still exist in another realm, another world. She used to talk to her ancestors when she'd heal someone. All this time, I rarely thought about that, rarely thought to talk to her, wherever she may be. I've been so focused on my own pain."

"You've been alone with this grief for a long time."

"I talked to her last night. Like she used to pray to her ancestors. I prayed to her. I prayed for her help to move on."

A lump formed in Rowan's throat. Her brother's expression was still one of pure agony as he stared out over the desert beyond the cave, but there was a hint of something more now in the creases around his eyes. If she hadn't known him since they were children, she might not have noticed, but she thought she saw the start of acceptance there, an understanding that his life had been better for knowing Maiara even if his mate was no longer with them.

"It's the beginning of a new day," Rowan said, then grimaced at how trite the phrase sounded once it had left her mouth. "I'm... sorry. That was..." She shook her head.

He gave her an exasperated look. "I need to be alone."

"Of course." She frowned.

"It's nothing personal. I just need time to create and to process everything."

She sighed. "You do realize Gabriel will kill me. We don't know when or where Eleanor will strike. None of us are supposed to be alone."

His head sagged forward on his shoulders. "I'll be here, Rowan. In my treasure cave, painting and recharging my batteries. There's no place safer for a dragon than this."

Rowan mulled that over. Nick looked tired, hungry, and like he needed some air. She supposed two days of discussing Maiara's death was hard on all of them. Reluctantly she nodded in agreement. "Okay. We'll go. I'll give you and Nyx a few days, and then I'm coming back for you. You'll text if you need anything?"

He nodded over the steam from his cup. "Deal."

IT TOOK THE BETTER PART OF THREE HOURS FOR ROWAN to relay everything she'd learned from Alexander to the others. They sat around the table in the small apartment Gabriel rented, picking at a meal of burritos and chips from a local dive.

"I remember the day she died," Tobias said. "Maiara was the reason I became a healer. I stayed with the Potawatomi and served as their *Midew* for a decade, until my presence became disruptive."

"Why was it disruptive?" Rowan asked.

"I wasn't aging. I had blond hair and looked like a white man. I started to garner a lot of questions, and as new *Midew* were named, they didn't want to associate with me. I thought it would be better for the tribe if I left. So I did. I ended up settling in what is now Chicago and never left."

Raven picked at her supper. "She had such an impact on all of you. She's the reason Gabriel ended up in New Orleans as well."

"There's something I still don't understand," Nick said. Rowan raised an eyebrow at him. Was there any question she hadn't answered? Her mate's inquisitive tendencies were beginning to give her heartburn. "Alexander left while the body was burning. He said Maiara's shell amulet was around her neck when the fire engulfed her remains. But a few days ago, Raven asked for that amulet so she could study Maiara's magic and Tobias admitted he had it. How did you get the amulet if she was burned with it?"

"I went back," Gabriel said. "In the middle of the night, after the fire burned itself out. I pulled it from her ashes."

Raven inhaled sharply, her hands resting on her swollen belly. "By the Mountain, Gabriel, you didn't even let the sun rise on her ashes before you stole her sacred healing amulet?"

Tobias rubbed the back of his neck. "Now you know why I was so surprised back in New Orleans in February when Gabriel told me he had it. Now you also understand why I wanted it. The tribe searched for the shell the next morning. They needed it. Everyone thought the Great Spirit had taken the amulet from them as some sort of punishment, along with their last and only healer. All those centuries... It wasn't until I helped you, Raven, that I learned Gabriel had it."

Gabriel growled. "I wasn't going to let them bury it with her ashes. It was too powerful. She was the last living *Midew*. No one else would have understood its magic."

Tobias growled. "You are truly ignorant if you believe that. You knew I'd been working side by side with her for months."

Rowan held up her hands as the temperature in the room rose, and the two dragons stared at each other as if they were thirty seconds away from re-creating a WWE *Smackdown* event. "Listen you two, I can see that there are all sorts of things ricocheting around those heads of yours. Gabriel, taking that amulet was just one more example of how you used to think the world revolved around you before Raven came along."

"Hey!" Gabriel folded his arms.

"And Tobias, you've known about this for several months now. This is not the time to get all pissy about it. There is only one person in this family whose anger is truly justified over this amulet thing, and that's Alexander. And the sad thing is, he doesn't even know about it yet. So both of you need to calm your dragons and shut the fuck up." She swung her pointed fingers like she was conducting a choir and then circled her hands into the universal "shut it" symbol.

Everyone stared at their plates in silence.

"Not to get involved in family business," Nick said after

Rowan sat back down, "but has anyone thought that Alexander might want it back? I mean, like the hawk, it was his wife's. Seems like he should have it... and that you should tell him."

Rowan stared at him, her shoulders tightening to the point of pain. Of course that should happen. But when?

"This is probably a good time for me to mention that I have had a chance to analyze the amulet's magic," Raven said, "and it's some of the strongest I've ever encountered. Now that I know the story of what she was, I'm sure I can find more about *Midew* magic, with or without the shell."

Rowan sighed. "I told Alex I'd come back for him in a few days. Maybe we should all present the amulet to him then. Nick's right. He deserves to have it back, and it might give him some closure."

"I'm not opposed to facing Alexander about what I did," Gabriel said, a rare repentant gleam in his eye. "Maybe it's time."

The storm of Rowan's emotions calmed into something far more hopeful. "If you approach this the right way, Gabriel, you could have him on the plane back to New Orleans in no time."

Raven stood and grabbed her purse.

"Where are you going?" Gabriel asked.

"To research *Midew* magic while I still have access to all that Sedona has to offer and the amulet. You heard the woman. I'm running out of time."

Gabriel ran his fingers through his hair. "Just be careful, Raven. Don't take any chances with the baby."

"When have I ever taken unnecessary risks?"

Everyone at the table stared at her accusingly.

"Please." Gabriel rolled his eyes toward the ceiling.

"Fine." She raised an eyebrow at Rowan. "You'd think I

didn't have a doctor, a healing amulet, and a dragon's tooth working in my favor."

Rowan gave her a crooked smile. "Boys." She hadn't known Raven long enough to peg her as a risk taker, but the way her brothers looked at her told a different story.

"He's right," Tobias said. "You need to be careful."

Nick glanced at Rowan and took a swig of his beer. "Can I just say I've never felt bored since I mated Rowan. You guys are an interesting bunch."

# CHAPTER TWENTY-SIX

"Thanks for coming," Raven said, staring down at the historical text she'd found in a pawnshop at the edge of town. She'd been drawn there by the store's name, Indigenous Relics. An ad on their website said they had the largest selection of healing herbs and crystals in Sedona.

But it was the collection of rare texts the owner had shown her in the back room she found particularly interesting. The man was a dark, shadowy figure, who sent goose bumps dancing up her arms every time he came within a foot of her, but he'd had the uncanny ability to show her exactly what she needed, and she'd texted Tobias immediately when she found it.

"Should I ask now or later why you called me in and not Rowan or Gabriel?" he asked.

"Because you worked as a healer with Maiara. You trained as a *Midew*. And what this says is too outrageous to share with anyone else unless I know for sure it's true."

His forehead wrinkled and he sidled up to her, looking over the page she was on. It was a reproduction of a text that was originally written on birch bark scrolls, and the content had blown her away.

"How are you even reading this? It's in Algonquian," Tobias asked.

"Translation spell." Raven rubbed her belly. It had felt tight since lunch, and she was kicking herself for overeating. "This says there were four levels of *Midew* magic."

Tobias nodded. "True. I had achieved level one."

"What level was Maiara?"

"I'm not sure, but after Rowan told that story today about her becoming one with the trees, I can only suspect she was at least a third level if not a fourth."

"Exactly. The ability to merge with other living things is very powerful magic. Only the most experienced shaman could do it."

"But she was young. How on earth could she have had that type of power so early on?" Tobias flipped the page and kept reading.

"Alexander said power ran in her family, and Willow had suspected she was a dryad, although Maiara herself said it was *Midew* magic. What if it was a little of both?" That was the part that sounded crazy, even to Raven, but she couldn't shake the thought it might be true.

"What are you saying?"

"This ancient text talks about a people in Algonquian legend called the *Pagwadjinini*, direct translation—forest people or people of the trees. From what we know, Maiara's entire family was killed, as was the rest of the *Midewiwin* society. We'll never know her biological origins. But what if there was some *Pagwadjinini*-like magic in her ancestry that allowed her to excel at her mystical abilities?"

"So what? She was a *Midew* prodigy. Why do we care?"

"Because according to this text, a level-three *Midew* can

temporarily join herself, body and soul, to the trees. Trees are stationary. Trees have a simple spiritual structure. It's all here."

"Okay." Tobias narrowed his eyes at her.

"A level-four *Midew* can join their soul to any other living creature."

"Come again?" Tobias allowed the page to drop from his fingers.

"A level-four *Midew*, according to this, was extremely rare, but he or she could cast their soul from their body and join it with another plant, animal, or even a person. Two souls in one body."

Leaning over the text, Tobias pressed a hand to his temple and began to read. "Not with anything. This says the *Midew* had to have had a close relationship with the living thing."

"And what living thing was closest to Maiara besides Nikan or Nyx as Alexander calls her? Nikan literally means *my friend* in Potawatomi. She told Alexander the hawk came to her when she became a healer and that the hawk was a bridge between the living and the dead. That's a real thing. I found it in the books. *Midew*s had an animal that helped them communicate with their ancestors. Nikan was hers."

"Are you saying what I think you're saying? Because this is big, Raven. You can't be wrong about this. If you are, it will tear him apart. He will never recover. Do you understand me?"

"I'm not wrong. I felt it the moment I held her. That hawk has magical energy. And it wasn't just because of a three-hundred-year-old spell that made it immortal."

"Don't say it. If you say it, we can't put the genie back in the bottle." Tobias squeezed his eyes closed.

"Maiara's soul is in that bird."

Tobias steadied himself on the desk. "All these years…"

"She knew she was dying and that you might not get to the amulet in time. So she put her soul into Nikan. Only no one understood what she was doing and there were no *Midew* left with the magic to put her back. Once they'd burned her, she had no body to put her back into!"

"We still don't have a body. Even if her soul is in the bird, what now?" Tobias asked. "We can't give Alexander false hope, Raven. It isn't fair to him."

She raised her eyes to his and smiled. "I think I can do it without a body. It won't be easy. As far as I know, no one has done anything like this before. But I found a spell, an ancient spell, and you know I can execute it."

"I was afraid you'd say that." Tobias rubbed the back of his neck. "Fuck, I can't decide if this is the best thing that could happen or the worst."

"It might be either. Let's wait to see if I can pull it off."

"Gabriel isn't going to like this."

Raven tucked the book under her arm and lifted the basket of crystals and other magical accoutrements she'd gathered from the floor near her feet. She headed for the owner, who was waiting in a pool of darkness behind the cash register. "Gabriel is my mate, not my prison warden. I'm doing this."

# CHAPTER TWENTY-SEVEN

"Willow, bring me more yellow," Alexander said, using his brush to tease the last of the color from his palette.

Willow appeared with a tube in his hand. "This is the last of it."

"Seriously?"

"I haven't ordered more in ages. You've preferred darker colors for some time."

Alexander added more of the sunny hue to his palette. "Well. Order more. I feel like trying something new." He blended the yellow with a bit of white and layered high-lights into his work.

"It's beautiful." Willow perused the painting from behind him. "The best you've done this year."

The picture was a self-portrait, Alexander as a dragon standing at the center of the Potawatomi winter village, a sunset behind the teepees, casting golden light over the snow. A glow came from the dwelling that had once been his and Maiara's. The happiest days of his life happened there, when he'd come back from patrolling the village and she'd be waiting for him beside the fire.

"For a long time, I was afraid to remember," Alexander said. "I thought it would hurt too much to think of her how she was, to talk to her spirit, and to open myself to whatever feelings came with it. I was wrong. Remembering this, it's helped me."

"You've done it justice. It is exactly as I remember it." Willow brought his pearlescent face closer to the canvas to appreciate the texture of the individual brushstrokes. Beside him, Nyx shifted on her perch and bobbed her head toward the painting. "Nyx likes it too."

When Alexander regarded his art, he felt—it wasn't exactly happy—but warm. For a second he forgot where he was and he was there again with her, in their home. He knew she was gone, and he was still sad about that. A piece of his soul would always be missing. But Rowan was right. Telling her story had made him lighter. Each word he'd spoken had been like moving a weight off himself and onto whoever was listening. It had become a shared burden with his telling it. He'd have to admit as much to Rowan when she returned. He owed her that.

"Do you think we should have a memorial for Maiara?" Alexander asked softly.

Willow's wings fluttered. "I think that is an excellent idea. What a wonderful way to honor her, and with your siblings here, they could also pay their respects. Tobias cared for her very much as a fellow healer, and Gabriel and Rowan knew her as well."

Alexander nodded his head. "I think you're right. She'd love it." He almost dropped his paintbrush when, in a flurry of flapping wings, Nyx flew from her perch and sailed out the mouth of the cave. "That's odd. She doesn't usually hunt this time of day," he said.

"It seems everyone in this family is changing." Willow smiled wistfully. "I'll bring you some tea and sandwiches, and we can make a plan for the memorial." He blinked out of sight.

A few minutes later, Alexander was putting the finishing touches on his painting when he heard footsteps behind him. "Just put it on the table, Willow."

"Alexander, it's me. Let me in," Rowan called through the wards.

He concentrated on his ring and flourished his hand in the air. "Come in, sister, and explain to me why you broke your promise. You told me three days, remember?" He grinned at her, happy to see her despite her early arrival.

"Wow," Rowan said as she neared his latest work. "This is stunning. Is that what it was like there?"

"I remember it like it was yesterday." He scratched his stubbled cheek. "I hadn't thought of it in a long time. I owe this one to you. You helped me remember. It feels good to remember."

"Where is Nikan? I mean Nyx?"

"Out hunting. She'll be back soon."

"Oh." Rowan fidgeted.

"You're early. What do have to tell me? Is Gabriel giving you a hard time?" He selected a different brush and dipped it into the black paint, adding his signature in the lower right corner of the painting.

"Uh, actually..."

He glimpsed her fidgeting out of the corner of his eye. "Out with it, sister. Where's Nick anyway?"

"He's with the others... right outside the cave." Rowan winced.

"What?" Alexander stood, paint from his brush dripping on the floor. "Why did you bring them here without my permission?"

"They have something to tell you, Alexander, and it's really important that you listen. Like, *really* important. Potentially life changing. You know I love you, and I would never invite them here if I didn't know in my heart that this was the best place for this conversation."

Alexander scowled. He did not like the sound of that. "And what is this life-changing thing?"

"I can't tell you. I can't, okay? I don't really understand it. Only Raven and Tobias do and you have to invite them in if you want them to tell you."

He shook his head. Maybe this was for the best. After they shared whatever so-called emergency that had brought them to his door, he could ask them for their help with the memorial. He went to the edge of the cave, past the barrier spell, and yelled down to the group gathered in the valley. "Come on up. Family reunion. I hope you brought snacks because Willow and I are running dangerously low on supplies."

He stepped back as Gabriel, carrying Raven, and Tobias, carrying Nick, landed on his ledge. They followed him inside. He motioned for them to find themselves a chair from the eclectic collection in his living room. Then he stared at Raven.

"Mountain help us, you look even more pregnant than two days ago."

"It just keeps growing," she said. She supported her back with both hands.

"My sister tells me you and Tobias are the only ones who can explain why you are here," he said to get the ball rolling. He couldn't take much more of this silent staring routine.

She nodded. "That's true."

"Then spill it. You're keeping me from my work." He gestured toward the painting.

Raven took a deep, fortifying breath. "When I held Nyx the first day we were here, something happened."

"Don't keep me in suspense." Alexander grabbed a clean towel and wiped the excess paint from his hands.

"A shock ran up my arm. It's the kind of thing that happens when I come in contact with a magical being."

He shrugged. "Nyx is an immortal hawk. Can't get much more magical than that." He wiped his brushes clean and dipped them in safflower oil before laying them out to dry.

Raven cleared her throat. "The power I felt wasn't from an enchanted animal. It was more a creature with true, inherent power. Like a witch or, or..."

Alexander turned back around, stared at her, and waited. What exactly was she trying to say?

Tobias nudged Raven's elbow, and the next words came out of her mouth in a flood of syllables. "I think Maiara's soul is in your hawk and with the help of this, we can bring her back." Alexander watched in horror as Raven pulled Maiara's healing amulet from her bag. He rushed toward her, taking the shell in his hand.

"Where did you get this?" he asked. His blood surged in his veins, and he swayed on his feet. Absently he noticed scales shingle up his arm.

"Deep breath, brother. Just listen to her." Tobias's hands were on his shoulders, and Gabriel moved between him and Raven, who took a healthy step back.

He closed his eyes and tried to settle the beast within.

"For fuck's sake, I'm not going to hurt her. I just want to know what she's doing with my wife's amulet."

Raven cleared her throat. "I believe that Nikan, Nyx as you call her, is a vessel for Maiara's soul. She transferred her soul into the bird before she died. With the amulet, the hawk, and a totem of Maiara, I believe I can bring her back."

Raven kept talking, but Alexander couldn't hear what she was saying. A buzzing started in his head, like a swarm of cicadas, low at first and then building to a deafening hum. Everything felt removed and disconnected, as if he were watching himself from outside his body. When was the last time he blinked? When was the last time he breathed? Had she really said what he thought she'd said?

A storm was brewing inside him. Anger, hurt, betrayal, fear, disbelief, and so many more emotions he couldn't even name swirled in his head and his heart. Torn in two was an apt analogy. He wanted to hug someone and hit someone all at the same time. "How sure are you?"

Rowan chewed her lip. He hadn't intended it, but there must have been menace in his voice because Rowan had moved in, shoulder to shoulder with Gabriel in front of Raven.

"Alexander, Raven is doing her best to help you," Rowan said. "Try to calm down."

He glared at her. "I'm not going to hurt Raven. But I think I deserve to know how sure she is about this. Is this a theory or a fact?"

Raven looked down at the floor of the cave. "A theory. This is all based on texts that are centuries old and written in an indigenous language. That said, I am 95 percent sure they are authentic and that this will work."

"How do you know?" He narrowed his eyes on her.

"It's how my magic works. I can absorb a spell off a page

and perform it perfectly the first time. I can touch a magical object and completely understand its power. I've touched your bird and I've touched the amulet. I can see the magic. I've seen this spell. I know what it feels like to perform it." She frowned. "No witch can guarantee the outcome of something like this, Alexander. It's never been done before, as far as I know, and there are so many variables. But I *feel* like I can do it."

"What the hell does that mean?" How could he put any hope or trust into a woman he'd known less than a week?

Raven sighed heavily. "It's like... like... seeing pieces of a puzzle that you know will fit before you try to put them together. I can see this, Alexander. The only thing I can't see is Maiara because I never knew her, but if you can show me her likeness, I know I can do it."

Mind racing, Alexander ran his thumb over the smooth white shell in his hand. A growl came from deep within his chest. "How is it that you even have her amulet? It was burned with her body."

"Oh shit, here we go," Nick mumbled and backed toward the kitchen.

Gabriel stepped forward. "I returned to the village and took it the night she died."

Alexander's wings punched out and he tackled Gabriel, rolling him backward. His fist connected with the dragon's jaw with a resounding crack that made everyone else gasp. It wasn't a premeditated thing. Old anger rushed to the surface and overflowed onto his brother.

To his surprise, Gabriel didn't block the punch or return it. Although far bigger and in peak physical condition, he allowed Alexander to sit on his chest and press a talon into the side of his throat. "You took my wife's *migiis* without permission? You fucking asshole. And you've had it the whole... this entire time! Why didn't you return it to me!" His talon dug in, and a bead of blood bubbled from Gabriel's neck.

"I didn't know where to find you until recently. You took off. You went into hiding, remember?" Gabriel's voice was matter-of-fact and surprisingly devoid of the aggression that seemed so at home in his disposition.

"Don't turn this on me." He hissed in Gabriel's face. "You never should have taken it."

"But it's a good thing I did, because it might just be the reason you're reunited with the one you love," Gabriel said. Although Alexander desperately wanted to channel the tangle of pain he was feeling into another blow, he took a deep breath instead.

"We're wasting time," Raven said. "Alexander, you can wail and fight this as long as you need to, but I'm pregnant and there will come a time, sooner rather than later, when I will have to leave this place. I have a flight Friday, in fact. And I don't know how long I'll be out of commission trying to bring this little beasty into the world. I can't make you any promises. Life isn't fair and magic isn't foolproof. But if you want me to try, you'd better decide now."

He shook his head. How, for the love of the Mountain, was someone supposed to decide something like this? Every step he took closer to accepting what Raven was saying as true was a step away from the small peace he'd finally found in letting Maiara go. He stood and backed away from Gabriel. "What are the risks?"

Raven nodded. "Good question. We don't have Maiara's body. Together, we can make her one. I have a spell for it. But it's possible she won't look exactly as you remember her."

"I don't care about that."

"She might not remember you."

That made his heart drop into his stomach.

"She's spent three hundred years inside a bird. I don't know how much of her consciousness has been in control. If it's been Nyx steering the ship, so to speak, I'm not sure what will be left of her mind."

Alexander shook his head. "She's in there."

Tobias raised an eyebrow. "How do you know?"

Folding his arms, he shook his head. "I just do. What else?" He pointed his chin at Raven.

"The spell, as written, is meant to be performed soon after the passing of a *Midew*. Maiara's soul has been separated from her body for centuries. She's effectively haunting the body of that bird. It's possible that after I free her, she'll choose to pass over to the Land of Souls rather than implant herself into the totem we make for her."

For a long stretch, Alexander said nothing. He stared across the red rock and contemplated what it would be like to go through all this only for it not to work. He had to be prepared for that possibility. And if Maiara's soul moved on, he knew intuitively that Nyx would move on as well. It was clear to him now that the only thing binding the hawk to him was Maiara. But his love deserved more than the half life she had now.

When he turned back toward them, his shoulders sagged. "Either way, this will be better for her. I can't imagine what she's endured these many years. If what you say is true, she deserves to m-move on." His voice cracked.

Rowan stepped forward and tried to hug him, but Alexander avoided her embrace. He loved his sister, but he just couldn't allow himself to crumble, and if she hugged him, he would crumble. "No. Rowan, not now." He focused on Raven. "Is there anything else?"

Raven's eyes shifted from side to side. "I'll need blood."

"Blood?"

"From you and Nyx. When I brought Gabriel back from the dead—"

"You resurrected Gabriel?"

She nodded. "I used my own blood because I'd swallowed his tooth. Maiara never had your tooth, just your bond. But Nyx has hosted her soul. Some of her blood and some of yours should be enough of a sacrifice for the magic to work."

Alexander scrubbed his face with his hands and rubbed his eyes. It felt like someone had drained all his blood and refilled his veins with concrete. Everything felt heavy.

"I need an answer, Alexander. Are we going to do this? Will you trust me to try?" Raven asked.

"What do you need me to do?"

There was a collective release of breath. "You're an artist. That should make this easier. I need to see exactly what she looked like. Paintings, sketches, all different angles. I need them all. The more real she seems in the art, the better. I will be rebuilding her using blood magic. If I can't see it in my mind, I have to fill in the gaps. I need every detail. Do you understand?"

Rowan piped up. "That shouldn't be a problem. You've probably painted ten thousand pictures of Maiara over the past twenty years alone."

Alexander narrowed his eyes on her. "I'll need a few hours to pull what I have together."

"Take all night. I need to rest and prepare." Raven rubbed her palms together in small circles. "I'll also need a totem, a physical object that represents Maiara. Perhaps a carving or a statue that you think she'd be attracted to."

That gave him pause. "I'll come up with something."

"This isn't an easy spell, but I'd like to start first thing in the morning. Can you have both things ready by then?"

Alexander bowed his head. "I'll do it."

All at once, his knees buckled. One moment he was fine, normal, facing Raven the same as any other time, and the next, a wave of blackness seemed to plow into him. The family rushed in. Rowan caught him by his left shoulder, Tobias his right. Gabriel helped them get him into a chair.

"We've got you." Gabriel tapped his cheeks with his hands. "You're going to make it through this."

The way Gabriel said it, Alexander wanted to believe it was true. But he wasn't sure. If this didn't work, if Raven failed and Maiara passed into the Land of Souls, Alexander didn't think he'd survive it. If what was left of his heart shattered again, he sure as hell wouldn't want to.

# CHAPTER TWENTY-EIGHT

D eep inside his treasure room in his secret sanctum, Alexander found the original sketchbook he'd brought to the New World. If Raven needed to see what Maiara really looked like, there was no better source than this. His sketchbook had been his comfort and constant companion up until her death.

After Maiara was killed and he fled to Sedona, Willow had brought him the sketchbook along with his other things, but he'd been too distraught to open it. For centuries it had remained undisturbed, the tied leather binder becoming stiff from lack of use.

Now he carefully untied the leather straps and opened the book. Although the edges of the pages had yellowed, his drawings were perfectly preserved. But which ones should he choose for the spell?

The sketch of Maiara standing defiantly in the door to the Owl's Roost showed her courage. He carefully turned the page and was back in the woods, watching her undress in front of a tree. This one captured her vulnerability. On the next page, she was leaning over the redcoat who'd been injured by the *wendigo*, compassion in her eyes. There was one of her in his arms and her hovering over him in his bed. And then there were dozens more of her, drinking from a stream, eating elk across the fire from him, holding a rabbit above her head that she'd shot with her bow.

So many memories. None of them alone adequately captured who she was. Every time he'd sketched or painted her image over the years, he'd done so with the intention of doing her justice. Only, no two-dimensional image could fully represent what it was like to be in her presence.

She was small in stature, but anyone who had been in her presence would hesitate to say so. She was formidable, flinty. She was a woman who'd lost everything but had survived through determination and perseverance. She was brave, strong, but vulnerable in a way that always reminded him she was human.

How could he show Raven how tall she seemed in person when her actual height in inches fell short of her personality? How could he represent how one look of her ebony eyes could bring a warrior to his knees? How her spine grew straight as a pine tree and her long limbs held the grace of a swan's neck? Her legs were sturdy as the mighty oaks she favored, and her skin was lit-from-within amber, darker than his but a color all its own. Could he even replicate it?

No painting or sketch could. He tossed the sketchbook down on his bed. Nyx, who'd arrived home after everyone else had left, swooped down on the bed and started tugging at the book with her beak and crumpling the pages with her talons. He heard an ominous rip.

"Stop that," Alexander said, shooing her away. She squawked at him and pecked the exposed page. A tight smile accompanied a prickle in his eyes as he perused the one she selected. On that night, Maiara had sat beside him by the fire. It was after they were bound to one another, when they rarely parted company. He hadn't spent much time looking at the picture before because it wasn't of Maiara but of her perspective that night, the chief standing before the central fire, telling the story of Moowis, the snow husband.

At the time, he'd thought it a silly legend, the type of story told around the fire to keep children in line. But now he remembered it with new eyes. In the story, a highly esteemed warrior courted a beautiful woman. At first she invited his attention, but when he desired her as his wife, she rudely and publicly humiliated him, saying she thought her astounding beauty could attract someone better than the warrior.

Angered by her narcissistic ways, the warrior beseeched his spirit guide for help teaching her a lesson. His guide bade him to create a man out of snow, bones, and rags. With the help of his spirit guide, the man sculpted a handsome suitor, whom he brought to life and named Moowis.

The warrior took Moowis back to the woman, who fell in love with him instantly. But the snow husband rejected her. Sick with love, the woman followed Moowis from the village and traveled far from her people, until one spring day, her love disappeared. The snow husband had melted into the earth.

The story was a warning about pride, but that wasn't the part that interested him. An idea came to him as he remembered the tale. Excitement made his breath quicken and his heart pound inside his chest. He straightened the page to get a better look, then narrowed his eyes on Nyx. "Are you really in there?"

The bird tilted her head and stared at him with soulful, amber eyes.

"Willow!" he called.

"Yes, my dragon?" The oread manifested beside him, his wings fluttering from whatever magical movement brought him there.

"I need clay. Lots of it."

"We have four boxes of Blick earthenware in storage, left over from that sculpture you did for the circle at Artist's Row."

"Bring it and get me more."

"I'll have to use magic. None of the stores are open this time of night."

"Do it. I'll need roughly three hundred pounds... and half-inch rebar. No, bring me quarter-inch instead; she was petite."

"That we have as well. I ordered in bulk last time." Willow dissolved, off to retrieve his supplies.

Alexander walked into the main room of the cave, still gripping the drawing like a security blanket, his creative gears turning in a way that made his head tingle. With the ease that accompanied his dragon strength, he threw the couch across the room as if it weighed nothing and pushed the rest of the furniture aside.

There wasn't enough light. Desperately he tore the shade off the floor lamp and tossed another log on the fire. It still wasn't enough. The rug would have to go. He rolled it and sent it in the direction of the couch.

Willow returned with what he'd asked for, looking a little gray. "Will that be all, sir?"

"Bring every lamp in the cave. I need light. Lots of light from every direction."

The oread nodded and retreated into the back rooms.

He returned with extension cords and a hodgepodge of light sources he set up around the room. Now he looked positively drained. Alexander took him into his arms and didn't let go until the color returned to his cheeks. "Thank you, my dragon."

"Rest. Recuperate. I'll handle this from here."

Willow bowed. "I hope whatever this is, it brings you peace." He faded away.

Alexander dug through the pieces of rebar and found what he was looking for, then drove one into the floor of the cave with his bare hands. About Maiara's hip-width apart and slightly back, he anchored a second piece. These would form the bones of her legs. Using his dragon strength, and fire when he needed it, he formed a frame for the clay, a steel skeleton. He gave her a spine, shoulders, neck, and a head. Too short. He added to the frame, making the waist longer. Perfect. This was perfect.

A human artist might take weeks on a project like this. Alexander didn't have weeks. What he had was superspeed, dragon fire, and nothing to lose. He formed her feet, remembering how his thumbs had once pressed into her graceful arches, then sculpted her ankles, long and narrow. They melded into muscular calves.

The hollow of the back of her knee was a place he'd kissed a thousand times. His hands smoothed along her thighs, his thumbs forming the folds between them. He'd known her body the way only a husband could. Wide, full hips narrowed to a muscular waist with a navel that had fascinated him, considering his kind did not naturally have one.

Two mounds of clay formed her buttocks. Along the rebar, he formed the muscles of her back, her shoulders, then filled in her breasts. One had been slightly larger than the other, and he concentrated on remembering every precious detail of their size and shape. Finally he formed her face, his thumbs sculpting her eyes, her nose with its slight hook at the end of the bridge, her jaw, her mouth. There she was. He saw her now in the clay. All he had to do was move the extra aside to reveal her. He formed her ears, the quirk of her cheek as she smiled.

At some point he noticed his hands were bleeding, his blood mixing with the red clay. Despite his dragon skin, his efforts had left them raw and they hurt now when he flexed his fingers. But once he'd sculpted her hair, using a comb to give it the texture he remembered, and glazed it and her eyes to ebony perfection, he walked around his creation and thought he couldn't possibly have fashioned a more accurate portrayal. This was Maiara, exactly as he remembered her.

Nyx flew to the fireplace mantel to get a better look. She cried her approval.

"It's her," Alexander said, then narrowed his eyes on the bird. "You."

The animal that stared back at him seemed no more human than before. Behind the hawk, the sun rose, its light warring with the lamps still glowing brightly around his work. He staggered from the room to his bed and collapsed facedown on the coverlet, his hands and body still covered in clay. He was asleep before he had a chance to doubt himself.

# CHAPTER TWENTY-NINE

R aven and Gabriel arrived at Alexander's cave just after nine and were thankful that Alexander had updated the wards to allow them to pass inside. After some discussion, they'd convinced the others to stay behind. The spell Raven would perform included complex and dark magic, and the chances it would be unintentionally disrupted, either from fear or distraction, increased with every observer.

Had Raven had her way, Gabriel would have stayed behind as well, but he'd refused, and she didn't have the strength to fight him. Still, she'd made him swear not to break her concentration for any reason.

"Holy goddess of the Mountain," Gabriel said.

Raven blinked to force her eyes to adjust to the dimmer light of the cave. Someone else was there, waiting for them. Only when her eyes regulated did she realize why Gabriel was so moved.

"It's her," he said. "Exactly her."

A clay likeness of Maiara stood in front of the fire. Raven had never met the woman, but the sculpture was more detailed than any she'd ever seen before. When the light from the fire flickered over the form, it almost looked like she was breathing, a woman covered in clay rather than made of it. "It's incredible. He must have stayed up all night sculpting this."

Gabriel pointed his chin toward the bed inside Alexander's treasure room. "He's still sleeping."

Gabriel's brother lay prone, covered in clay. For a second, Raven worried he was dead, but then his back rose and fell with his breath. Nyx slept on her perch beside him, her head tucked under her wing.

"Let him sleep for now. I have to prepare. Put the pack here." Raven pointed to a clear spot beside the clay woman. Gabriel lowered the duffel bag from his shoulder. She began to rummage through it.

"It feels like she's staring at me," Gabriel said.

"You can leave if it's too weird for you."

"Not a chance."

Raven placed a silver bowl at Maiara's feet and positioned a fresh orange, a silk handkerchief, and a lotus blossom inside it. This was an offering to try to keep the spirit on this plane until she could bind it to the totem.

She had expected to build Maiara's image out of magic and intention and that the totem would simply be an abstract starting point. With Maiara's likeness built for her, she'd have to adjust the spell slightly and pour her magic into the animation of it instead. Hypothetically, it should be easier. But this was all theory and conjecture. She had only her faith and her instincts to trust when it came to actual practice.

Digging in the bag, she found the salt she'd prepared for the ritual. Infused with fennel, peppermint, black pepper, and cinnamon, as well as snakeroot and rosary pea, it filled the room with a heady scent as she poured it. Carefully she formed three intertwining circles around the clay version of Maiara. Boundaries.

The magical energy she was about to pour out should ricochet around these circles, partially feeding her and the spell. When she was done, she stood back and admired her handiwork. The loops weren't perfectly round, but they were as good as they were going to get. She returned the salt to the bag and retrieved a pouch of powdered obsidian, using it to form three smaller circles, tangential to each of the rings. These would act as neutralizers in case there was an imbalance of power that was too much for her to handle.

She returned the pouch to the bag. One last touch. She'd brought four stones: howlite, for its ability to open a passageway to previous lives; moonstone, its dancing internal light irresistible to spirits; jasper, a source of spiritual energy; and turquoise, the stone that matched Alexander's ring and his dragon's heart.

She pressed the turquoise into the clay on the left side of the totem's chest. "I give you a heart, Maiara, made of the same material as Alexander's," she whispered. "Soon I hope to make it beat." She positioned the other three stones in the three circles around her.

"*Paramoni*," she whispered, waving her emerald ring over the work. The salt and stones hugged together and to the floor. Now they wouldn't be blown away, even by the strongest wind.

She inhaled deeply. She'd eaten too much again and her belly felt tight. Rubbing circles over it, she took a break, standing back to catch her breath. She could do this. If she successfully resurrected Maiara, Gabriel would have no trouble getting Alexander and his mate to return to New

Orleans where Raven's sophisticated network of wards could keep everyone safe and they could finally be a family.

Gabriel's wicked queen of a mother had stolen that from her mate for far too long, and she longed to do this, for him and for Rowan and Tobias. All she had to do was raise the dead. No big deal. She'd done it before.

"You're pale," Gabriel said.

"I'm fine," Raven lied. In fact, she felt a little queasy. *Just nerves*, she told herself. "And I'm ready. Can you wake Alexander?"

Gabriel flashed a mischievous grin. "My pleasure." Before Raven could say another word, Gabriel raced into the next room. His feet left the floor and landed on the bed next to Alexander, sending his body bouncing straight up. He belly flopped back on the mattress with an *oomph*.

"Gabriel, you're a foul beast regurgitated from the belly of Hades, do you know that?" Alexander rubbed his temples like his head ached.

"Yes. Straight from hell and no worse for wear," Gabriel quipped. "Time to rise, little brother. My beautiful wife is ready for you, and you should never keep a Tanglewood witch waiting. Trust me on that one."

Alexander slowly rolled over and sat up. "Tanglewood witch?"

"That was her maiden name. Tanglewood. She comes from a long line of witches, running all the way back to the goddess Circe herself. You're in good hands."

"Don't oversell me, Gabriel," Raven called, secretly enjoying the compliment. The truth was she'd never felt more in her skin than since she'd become a witch. Alexander rose and joined her in the main room in front of the fire.

"Is the totem acceptable?" he asked, one eyebrow betraying his confidence in his work.

"It's phenomenal." Raven reached for him and turned his blood-and-clay-coated palms up to get a better look. "What happened to your hands?"

"It's not as bad as it seems." Alexander pulled away and walked to the sink where he washed away the grime. Underneath it all, his skin had healed, but Raven understood what it took to even temporarily damage a dragon like that.

Raven followed him to the sink and watched red clay and what looked like dried blood swirl in the basin. "How did that happen?"

He gestured toward the sculpture. "I had to do it all by hand to get it right."

Raven grabbed a hand towel off the counter and dried his fingers. "You tore your skin making her likeness?"

He nodded. "It was necessary to get it right. That is exactly how I remember her."

"It's very good," Raven said. "More than I was expecting." In her head, she tried to calculate what effect his blood mixed in with the clay would have on the spell. She had no idea. Lost in thought, she held on to his hand for longer than necessary until Gabriel emitted a rumbling growl from behind her.

"That's it! Gabriel, you need to leave. Come back in three hours or when I text you."

"What? Why?"

"Because I don't need you making jealous or worried noises. Alexander, Nyx, and I have work to do, and I can't do it with you pulling the bonded dragon shit every time I look at him." Raven pointed at the cave entrance.

Sulking, Gabriel kissed her on the cheek. "I'll leave, but

GENEVIEVE JACK

I'm waiting at the bottom of the cliff. I'll be there if you need me."

She pulled him to her and gave him a proper kiss on the mouth. "Thank you." He nodded and flew from the cave.

Once he'd gone, she turned back to Alexander. "Are you ready to begin?"

After everything, she was not surprised when he began to tremble. "I think so."

"You're afraid," she said with nothing but kindness in her voice.

His dark blue eyes met hers. "Terrified. If this doesn't work..."

She squeezed his shoulders. "Let's cross that bridge if we come to it. I'd prefer not to come to it."

Once his shaking steadied, she asked him, "Do you need to eat or drink something before we get started?"

He shook his head. "I couldn't possibly keep anything down."

She let go and moved toward the symbol she'd drawn on the floor. "Bring Nikan." She used the name Maiara had given the hawk instead of Alexander's nickname of Nyx, but he didn't seem to mind. From this point forward, she was thinking of Maiara, of what it would take to lure her back into this world. He gathered the hawk into his arms and followed her to the three circles. "I need a sacrifice of her blood in the bowl at Maiara's feet."

Alexander gave the hawk an apologetic look and sprouted talons on his right hand. "Sorry, dear friend." He pierced the skin of her breast and held her over the bowl as the blood dripped over her earlier sacrifices. The hawk seemed resigned. She did not struggle or cry out.

"That's definitely not a normal bird," Raven murmured. "That should be enough. Now place her there." She

246

pointed toward the circle marked by the howlite. "I'll need a sacrifice of your blood also. In the bowl please."

Alexander sliced his forearm and watched the blood mix with Nikan's, coating the lotus blossom, the orange, and the silk.

"Good. That's enough." Raven pointed inside the circle marked with jasper. "Kneel there." He did as she asked. "And my sacrifice." She used her athame to prick the tip of her finger and allowed three drops of her blood to mingle with the rest. She pressed her thumb to the wound to stop the flow, then knelt in the circle with the moonstone.

The way she'd drawn the pattern, she and Alexander each faced one of the statue's hips. The bowl was between the totem's feet, and Nikan was in the circle behind it.

"What exactly am I supposed to do?" Alexander asked.

"Nothing yet. The purpose of this triquetra is to invite Maiara's spirit to leave Nikan. That's what the howlite is for. You and it are going to tempt her out. Our goal is to get her to inhabit this representation you've made. Don't be surprised if she doesn't jump right in. She'll be confused and might be distracted by her love for you or my power. But our circles are linked, so if we each hold our ground, she should eventually choose to inhabit this body."

"Should?"

"Yes."

Alexander sighed and gazed up at the statue of Maiara. "Okay. I'm ready when you are."

Raven raised her hands and began to chant. She didn't understand all the words that had been burned into the birch bark scrolls she studied, but she understood their meaning. She was praying to the Great Spirit and Maiara's own guardian spirit to draw her soul into the totem. She sang each memorized syllable from the heart, pouring herself into it. Her magic sparked across her skin. Her emerald ring glowed like the moon.

"Raven? Are the fireworks normal?" Alexander shouted over the hum of the magic.

"Call to her, Alexander. Call to Maiara." She resumed her chanting.

Alexander turned toward Nikan. "Maiara, if you're in there, come to me." He held his arms out to the hawk. "Come to me, my *Ndukweyum*."

Raven's magic crackled and snapped against her skin, catching on the edge of the circle and igniting it with purple light. Sweat formed at her hairline. *Burning hot today*. The pregnancy was like a supercharger. She chanted louder, pouring the extra energy into her voice.

Nikan flapped her wings wildly, her neck twisting until the top of her head pressed into the floor. She spun in place.

"You're killing her!" Alexander cried.

"Keep calling to her!" Raven demanded. Her voice reverberated through the room. She glanced at the tangential circle on her symbol. Purple light had begun to penetrate the obsidian. That wasn't supposed to happen yet. She tried to pull the reins back on her power. So much power. This wasn't just her pregnancy; this was the blood. The extra dragon's blood in the clay was meddling with the spell, running hotter than expected and creating a magical haze she could feel against her skin.

"Alexander, we need to do this now. Call to her like you mean it."

He straightened and tried again. "Maiara, come to me now!"

Nikan made a choking noise and opened her beak. A ball of light floated out of the bird and hovered in the center of the circle. The hawk flopped onto its side and lay perfectly still.

It was impossible not to see the heartbreak on Alexander's face at the bird's collapse, but he didn't lose his focus. "That's it. Come here." The light slammed into the side of the circle, and the curve of the symbol guided the bouncing soul toward the totem. To get to Alexander, it had to travel past the sacrificial bowl. Raven watched the blood, fruit, silk, and flowers boil into steam and rise as red vapor into the air.

Her blood was boiling as well. The magic neutralizer she'd built was now full of light, and the overflow spilled into Alexander's circle, into his safety zone. She was burning up. She needed to finish this spell or it would pull her apart.

The light neared the silver bowl and tumbled over the edge, coming to rest like a falling star in its belly at the totem's feet. The third neutralizer began to fill.

"Come on, Maiara. It's a good body. Take it!" she yelled, and her voice was not her own. The language was not her own.

Alexander's eyes widened. "Raven..." He stared at her belly.

She peered down and saw what he saw. Her entire abdomen was swelling and contracting with the magic, and her skin was as red as a flame. "I can't keep this up," she shouted.

Alexander stared at the light still resting in the bottom of the bowl. "Where is her amulet?"

Raven reached into her pocket and drew it out. "It won't help me. Not now."

"Put it around the totem's neck! It will show her where to go." He practically had to scream the words for her to hear them over the roar of the mounting magic. Purple wind blew like a hurricane through the cave, toppling the floor lamp and overturning the couch. On shaky legs, her hair whipping against her face, Raven stood and looped the amulet around the totem's neck. The last neutralizer filled.

Raven's abdomen contracted, and the pain was so intense she thought she might die. She grabbed her stomach and screamed. Someone had her. Strong arms swept her from the symbol and deposited her on a bed. The wind slowed, then stopped.

"Easy," Alexander said. He was hovering over her as the magic bled from her skin. "Close your eyes. Take deep breaths."

"But the spell—"

Alexander looked back at the sculpture and the remains of the spell. "I don't..." He shook his head. His eyes grew stormy.

Gabriel swooped into the cave and was by her side in an instant. "I heard screams."

"I'm fine," she said, tears welling. "It should have worked, Gabriel. The soul was right there."

Alexander left her side and approached the symbol, inspecting the silver receptacle. "It's empty. The sacrifice is gone. Does that mean she p-passed?"

Her heart broke for him, and she cursed inside her head. What had she done wrong? Gabriel squeezed her hand and stroked her sweat-soaked forehead.

A sharp crack echoed through the cave. "Oh dear goddess," Alexander muttered. "Mountain help me."

Raven made Gabriel help her to her feet, and together they staggered out of the bedroom to the boundaries of the ritual. Alexander stabbed a finger into the clay and pried away a chunk that shattered like terra cotta on the stone. Raven squinted. Was that what she thought it was?

Frantically Alexander chipped away at the sculpture. Raven didn't try to help. He needed to do this himself. But when she saw skin shift inside the totem, her heart leaped with hope. The rest of the clay shattered in an explosion that came from the inside out.

"It worked. It worked!" Raven yelled.

"Goddess of the Mountain, it's a miracle," Gabriel whispered.

Raven had to agree. A living, breathing Maiara stepped from the remains of the totem on shaky legs and collapsed into Alexander's arms.

# CHAPTER THIRTY

Darkness dug its claws into Maiara, trying to hold her inside its empty tomb. She fought to break its icy grip. On the edge of consciousness, she kicked and thrashed, fought toward the light. *Gasp.* Her lungs filled with air, and her lids fluttered against the bright glow of the world she was thrust into. The first thing she saw was a painting of herself and Nikan hanging on a wall of stone. The second was water.

She was still floating, but as her hands reached out, they slapped smooth white porcelain, a warm tub covered in a thin layer of bubbles. Behind her, someone was working a comb through her hair. She turned her head and made a high-pitched sound of excitement. Alexander. *Her* Alexander.

"Shh. Shh," he soothed as if she were a wild animal. "I won't hurt you."

Of course he wouldn't hurt her. But when she tried to tell him as much, all that came out was another squeak. Her voice wasn't working properly. In frustration, she grabbed his hand and squeezed.

"It's okay." His voice shook and his eyes filled with tears. "You may be disoriented. Raven tells me that's normal. Try to be patient."

She nodded. She wanted to ask him where they were, and *when* they were, but the inside of her throat felt raw and tight. She'd spent too long inside Nikan. At first she'd been an active participant in the bird's life, but as time wore on, she'd woken less and less frequently, and always, only, for Alexander's voice.

"Wha—?" Her lips rounded but she couldn't finish the word.

"You're in my bathtub, in the cave. Do you remember the cave from when you were in Nikan? And it's 2018."

She squinted her eyes as images of Alexander's cave home came back to her from a bird's-eye view. She could see herself landing on a perch, the treasure room, the kitchen. Flashes. Images. Sounds.

Her mind tripped over the year he'd given her. If it was 2018, she'd been inside Nikan for over three hundred leaf falls—years in his language. Her throat strained as she tried to ask him to say the year again. She slapped the water in frustration.

"Shh." He placed his hands on her arms, his soothing touch followed by equally comforting words. "Give it time." Carefully, he handed her a mug of something warm and hot from a tray beside him. She took a sip. Mint tea.

"It's been a long time, a really long time." Alexander knelt on the floor beside the tub and rubbed her shoulder. Tears filled his eyes and burned hot where they landed on her arm. She shifted the tea to the lip of the tub and reached for him, sweeping her thumb under his eye. The water from the bath left his cheek wet.

Flashes of memory came back to her. A cliff. A wire. Her gaze flicked down to his throat. Alexander had not been well. He'd not cared for himself while she was gone. She could see it now in the hollow of his cheeks and the ropey appearance of his arms. Tears came then, fat ones that plopped into the tub like bloated raindrops.

He chuckled darkly. "Not you too. Just tell me something, Maiara, do you remember me? Us together?"

She laughed. That she could do. She nodded enthusiastically, her mouth spreading into a smile.

He breathed a sigh of relief. "Praise the Mountain."

"Spi—" she said softly.

He responded with a grin that softened the gaunt lines of his face. The love shining through his eyes made him appear younger and reminded her of the early days of their relationship. Maybe that was appropriate. In some ways, they were starting over. "Sure. Praise the Great Spirit. I'll thank any damned deity in the universe for bringing you back to me."

She took another sip of tea, and this time, once she started she couldn't stop. An overwhelming thirst gripped her, followed by pangs of hunger of an intensity she'd rarely experienced. She handed him the empty cup and pointed inside it.

"Raven said you'd be hungry when you woke. Come on out and I'll have Willow make you something." He reached for a towel and helped her to stand. Her legs quivered like a newborn deer's, but he supported her weight as he wrapped the towel around her and lifted her out of the water. She shivered against his chest.

Tipping her head back to meet his dark blue gaze, she felt torn in two by the dichotomy between the sheer joy of being in his arms and the crushing memory of how she'd gotten there. Her head was a war zone of images. Three hundred years lost.

"Co—" she said, shivering violently.

Spreading his wings, he wrapped her inside them. "I can help with that."

Memories of all the times he'd kept her warm flooded her mind. She closed her eyes and leaned into him, taking comfort from his familiar smoky scent and the heat of his skin, already chasing the chill from her blood. She felt him press a kiss to the top of her head. As long as she had this, as long as she had him, everything else would fall into place.

THE BLACK T-SHIRT HE GAVE HER TO WEAR WAS MUCH too big on her, but Maiara didn't care. Alexander had propped her up in his bed under a pile of covers and told her how he planned to buy her all the modern clothes she wanted once they'd had time to take care of her immediate needs.

In no time, Willow arrived with a selection of meats, fruit, and cheeses and fresh baked bread that smelled like paradise. Alexander took it from him and sat beside her on the bed.

"I wasn't sure what you'd have a taste for," he said.

She pointed toward the bread. If she'd been strong enough, she would have snatched the entire loaf and brought it to her mouth. Instead, she waited patiently and trusted that Alexander would help her.

"Allow me." He sliced off a piece, hot steam rising from the soft white center, and slathered it with butter. When he

brought it to her lips, she closed her eyes as warm delicious-
ness melted in her mouth. She finished the piece in no time
at all and pointed to the rest of the loaf. Alexander did not
disappoint. He fed her the entire thing, bite by buttered
bite, and then all the strawberries and the cheese.

She paused and grabbed his wrist when he reached for a
piece of chicken. How could she tell him that it turned her
stomach? She licked her lips and tried to speak again.
"Mice," she said. The word was breathy but there.

His brows pinched over his nose. "Did you just say
*mice*? You don't want to eat mice, do you?"

She shook her head and laughed. Pointing at the meat,
she said it again, "Mice." How else could she explain that
the smell and texture of the chicken made her remember
life as a bird? Her shoulders slumped and she tapped her
forehead.

"Oh." Alexander narrowed his eyes. "Are you remembering eating mice when you were inside Nikan?"

She nodded and stuck out her tongue. Thank the Great
Spirit he seemed to understand.

"Okay. No chicken." He made a show of scraping it off
the tray and into the garbage.

She laughed and he stopped what he was doing to stare
at her. "I don't think there is anything I've missed more than
that sound."

She placed her hand on his thigh and tried to do for him
what he had done for her. She thought of all the happy
memories they'd shared together and poured them into her
expression and her touch. The words wouldn't come, not
yet, but she found a way to communicate. "Ba...ck," she
managed.

He nodded slowly. "Yes. You're back." He set the tray

aside and took her hand in his. "Somehow... Fuck... I'm just so grateful, Maiara."

With every ounce of strength she had, she pulled him into her arms.

# CHAPTER THIRTY-ONE

Only when she'd had her fill did Alexander help Maiara from the bedroom. It was her idea; she motioned that she wanted to stretch her legs. At first she leaned on him, testing her ability to walk on her own, but soon she took steps independently. Already she was stronger.

"That's it! You're doing great," he said as they slowly made their way into the main room. To his surprise, Raven and Gabriel were still there, huddled conspiratorially near the fire.

"I thought you two planned to head back to tell the others? It's been hours. Why are you still here?"

Raven frowned and lifted a small bundle near her feet into her arms. She cradled it like a baby. "I tried to save her, Alexander. I swear I did, but her body was never meant to live this long. It was Maiara's soul that kept her alive. Once we took her out..."

Alexander's chest tightened. He'd forgotten about Nyx, and the crushing guilt that came with that realization warred with the joy he'd been riding from Maiara's return. A lump formed in his throat. "She's dead?"

Maiara cried out and rushed forward on wobbling knees. She lifted the bundle into her arms and kissed the face of her hawk. "Ni...kan!" The name rasped in her tight throat, and tears raced down her face to the sound of her sobs. Alexander approached wearily, his own eyes burning.

"I'm so sorry," Raven said.

How could he blame the witch? This was the price of bringing his Maiara back. The truth was, some part of him expected this. He'd known when the bird fell on its side during the spell that its lifeless state might be permanent. He'd simply set the possibility aside to make room for what was happening with Maiara. Now though, the loss was real and it ached deep within his soul.

He held Maiara by the shoulders, the bird in her arms, and allowed himself to absorb the waves of grief that rolled into him. After all, no one was more familiar with grief than Alexander. This grief did not sting as much as what he'd suffered believing Maiara was gone, but it hurt. The hawk had been his constant companion for hundreds of years and was the reason his mate was here with him. Her loss was a brutal blow.

"I called her Nyx after the goddess of night." Alexander took her body from Maiara and nestled it in his arms. "I shouldn't have done that. Nikan was her name." He glanced at Raven. "It means *my friend* in Potawatomi," he explained. "She was my friend in every sense of the word, to the very end. She deserved better."

Gabriel placed a hand on his shoulder. "I realize I have only been here a few days, but I never saw you treat her with anything but kindness far surpassing how most treat their pets."

Raven agreed. "Alexander, truly, all of us thought you treated her like a partner. Do you remember how protective you were of her the first day I met you?"

He did. The guilt eased minutely as he thought of it. He'd heard it said that grief was just love with nowhere to go. Love previously given to the deceased bounced around inside a person until it finally came out in some way, usually as tears. Nikan was dead and Alexander had loved her, but this time his love had somewhere to go. It went straight into Maiara.

"Thank you, Nikan, for the sacrifice of your life to save my mate." Alexander stroked her feathers and hugged her swaddled body. Maiara stared up at him, her glossy eyes filled with pain. He handed the hawk back to her. The tightness in his chest eased again.

"She lived a long, full life," he said to her. "And I think she understood the sacrifice she would make. She loved you, Maiara."

His mate nodded, the corners of her mouth twitching as if she believed what he said. How could they not believe it when Nikan had participated in the spell to resurrect Maiara so willingly?

"We should give her a proper burial. A ceremony... Someplace nice," he said softly. Ironically, a day ago he had planned to have a memorial for Maiara. He couldn't help but feel some relief at the turn of events. Life was a series of hellos and goodbyes. This goodbye wouldn't be easy, but it was easier than the alternative.

Maiara nodded. "Please." The word came out clear, and he hoped her voice was returning.

Out of the corner of his eye, he saw Raven rub her hands over her belly. She looked exhausted and more than a little sad. "Let me prepare something. I can bring you a dress, and we can have a small ceremony. Maybe near one of the vortexes."

"You need rest," Gabriel said firmly.

"I'll be fine," Raven said, but Alexander thought she didn't look fine. She looked pale and gaunt. He didn't like the way her hands trembled on her abdomen.

"I have to agree with my brother on this one," Alexander said. "You need rest. There's no hurry. I'll take Maiara to get clothes and find the right spot. We'll bury Nikan tonight at sunset. She loved the sunset."

Maiara squeezed his hand in agreement.

Raven protested but Gabriel pulled her into his arms. "It's time to rest, little witch. You've done well."

Alexander watched her shoulders soften and her body collapse into Gabriel's embrace. His brother scooped her up, nodded in Alexander's direction, and flew off.

"Willow?"

The oread appeared beside him, hands folded. "Is there anything I can do?"

"Will you do me a favor and bring me that box we used for the gallery event?" Alexander's eyes flicked toward the bird.

Willow bowed. "I know just the one." He disappeared and returned almost immediately with an ornately painted wooden box.

"I found this at an estate sale. It reminded me of something you'd like. I've used it as a model in a few of my paintings." Alexander opened it for her. She ran her hand along the inside. It was a beautiful box made of bentwood cedar.

"Will this be okay?" He waited, watching her. She could carry Nikan's body around all day if she wished, if it would help her, but he could already see the truth in her eyes, a truth he had already accepted. The moment she'd put herself inside of Nikan, she'd known this would be the eventual outcome. A hawk was not meant to live forever.

She placed Nikan's body inside the box, a new wave of tears flooding her face. He closed the top and positioned it in a place of honor on the front table. Then he pulled her into his arms and kissed the top of her head.

Maiara wiped under her eyes. "What is... the name of the... witch who raised me?"

"Your voice is coming back!" He kissed her and hugged her to him. "Raven is her name. She is Gabriel's mate."

"She will have... baby soon."

"I'm not sure. I think she still has time."

Maiara shook her head. "Soon." She coughed into her hand as if the word strained her throat.

"Don't worry about that now. Come with me. We'll get you some clothes. Then I can show you a few spots that might be right for Nikan."

# CHAPTER THIRTY-TWO

"I'm fine, Gabriel. Really, is this necessary?" Raven allowed him to plump the pillow under her head and tuck the covers around her. Honestly, she was exhausted, and the attention was sweet, but she'd rather just be left alone to sleep.

"It is absolutely necessary. I'm going to get Tobias. He needs to examine you. You look pale."

She frowned but didn't argue. The pain she'd experienced during the spell to resurrect Maiara wasn't normal, and the truth was she still didn't feel well. Tobias was a talented doctor with centuries of experience, not to mention being a dragon himself. If anyone would know what was going on with a dragon/witch pregnancy, it would be him.

Gabriel kissed her on the forehead and closed the blinds on the windows. She must have fallen asleep before he made it out the door because the next thing she knew, Tobias was standing over her with his doctor's bag in hand.

"Gabriel said you were having some pain."

"Not anymore. Just when I was doing the spell— Did he tell you? We did it! Maiara's back."

He raised his eyebrows and gave a little nod. "I can't wait to see her again. She's the reason I'm able to help you today, the entire reason I became a healer and then a doctor." He pressed his fingers into her wrist, nonchalantly taking her pulse. "Can you tell me about the pain?"

"It felt like the baby was expanding and contracting with the flow of magic through my body. The muscles have felt tight before, but this was actually painful."

"What do you mean the muscles have felt tight before?"

"Oh, you know, like when we were at that occult shop and at the pharmacy. Anytime I'm on my feet too long, it just feels like a giant hand is squeezing me around the middle."

He scoffed. "And you didn't think this was something you needed to share with me?"

"There was a lot going on." Raven could tell by the way he widened his eyes that that was not the right answer. "It always went away, Tobias. I would have said something if it was really bothering me. Anyway, we're hopping on a plane tomorrow afternoon and going back to your fully equipped vampire-protected medical office in Chicago to bring this little guy into the world, right?"

Tobias rubbed the back of his head. "I need to examine you, Raven. Is that okay?" He reached into his bag and drew out a pair of rubber gloves.

"Of course," she said. It was awkward having your brother-in-law as your doctor, but he was her only hope of delivering a healthy baby. When she found out she was pregnant with a half dragon, half human, she'd been ecstatic. The pregnancy seemed like a miracle; she'd never thought children would be a possibility when she became Gabriel's mate.

But then Tobias, who had diagnosed her pregnancy

using an ultrasound, showed her what was developing inside her uterus. Dragons, it seemed, laid eggs not live young, and no one knew how this baby would be born because no human had ever carried an egg before, at least as far as any of them knew.

So it wasn't as if a human gynecologist could be her doctor. Tobias was her only hope of surviving this pregnancy and delivering a healthy baby. She stared at the ceiling while he quickly performed the exam she knew was necessary.

"Raven, I'm afraid tomorrow isn't soon enough. We need to get you on a plane today, preferably within the hour."

"What? Why?"

He snapped the gloves off into the garbage pail. "You're starting to dilate. A three, I'd say. That's early, but we don't know how fast this will go. It's too risky to fly commercially. We'll charter a plane and go straight to Chicago." He raised his phone to his ear and started rattling off instructions to someone she assumed must be his assistant.

Resting her hands on either side of her abdomen, she looked down at her protruding belly through the thin cotton of her T-shirt. "Are you saying the baby is coming?"

"Soon," he said, turning his mouth away from the phone to answer her before quickly continuing his dialogue. After a few minutes, he hung up and focused fully on her again. "She's on it. Don't worry. I'm going to take care of you."

"But... but I'm only four months pregnant. What if the baby isn't developed enough? What if the spell I did put me into premature labor?"

"We never expected you'd carry the egg for nine months. Dragons don't. This timing makes sense to me. Besides, we have all the equipment we need in Chicago to care for a preemie. Trust me, Raven. Let's get you back where it's safe, and I'll take care of everything."

"I need to pack." Raven started to sit up, but he caught her shoulder and pressed her back into the mattress.

"I have someone to do that for you." Tobias opened the door and Gabriel rushed in. "Pack her bags. I have my assistant chartering a plane. I'll let you know when we can take off." He grabbed his bag. "Now if you'll excuse me, I have my own bags to pack." He left the room with a practiced nod of reassurance.

"Gabriel, I—"

His hands balled into fists. "Do not even attempt to talk me out of getting you on that plane, Raven. You're going."

She sighed. "I know." The room turned wavy with her tears. "What I was going to say is I need help. I've been in these clothes all day. They stink of magic. Can you help me change?"

His shoulders drooped and he looked down at his hands. "Of course. I'm sorry I snapped at you."

"I understand. This is scary. Really scary."

He dug in a drawer and brought her one of her favorite maternity dresses. Kneeling in front of her, he helped her change clothes.

"You are a powerful witch, Raven, and my brother, for all his many annoyances, is a talented doctor. That's a heartening combination in and of itself, but add our immortal bond, and well, I understand you aren't *fragile*."

She rubbed her forehead. "I don't exactly feel strong at the moment."

"I know." He rested his palms on the stretchy material covering her thighs and stared up at her with an intensity that was pure dragon. "Both of us thought we'd have longer to prepare for this. And the truth is, there's no roadmap. No one has ever done what you're about to do." When she tried to look away, he cupped her jaw. "But I know you can do this."

The sincerity in his eyes made her breath catch in her throat. And as he spoke again, his voice was laced with grit. "The night I came for you in the hospital, the night we met, you were more dead than alive. I'd never seen anyone fight so hard for each scrap of life. I watched you battle your way back, not just physically but mentally and emotionally. You refused to be afraid, of anything.

"All that time, despite all my pretexts that I was your guardian, it was you who destroyed Crimson and resurrected me. You've never been helpless, Raven, or meek. You are the bravest, strongest witch I've ever known. And you can do this too."

She placed her hands on his face and touched her forehead to his. "Thank you. I needed to hear that today."

"Good. Now, just this once, allow me to treat you like you're made of glass even if we both know it isn't true."

She pressed her lips to his. "Just this once."

# CHAPTER THIRTY-THREE

Aborella's plan was finally coming to fruition. It had taken time and patience, but the amulet she'd given Avery had served its purpose. Raven had divulged her location. And although Avery proved to be a tough nut to crack, crack she did. Despite the young woman's strong mind and resilience to milkwood, Aborella had managed fleeting moments of influence over her. Enough to get them both here.

"I'm not sure about this, Charlotte," Avery said to her as she pulled into the Church of New Horizons. "Raven doesn't like surprises, and visiting her on her honeymoon feels intrusive." She stopped the car in the middle of the parking lot and shook her head. "What are we doing here? How has this gone this far? This is wrong. I'm turning around."

Aborella reached across the front seat and placed her hand on Avery's shoulder, sending a pulse of persuasive magic through the woman. The marble-sized crystal around her neck glowed brighter. "Park the car. We're going to see your sister. You want to see her, don't you? You have to introduce me to her."

Avery blinked, her lashes fluttering like the wings of a dying fly. "Of course. What was I thinking? You need to meet Raven." To Aborella's delight, she parked the car.

Unfortunately, as soon as she removed her hand, Avery's own thoughts broke through again. "Why isn't Dad here? Shouldn't he introduce his fiancée to his daughter?"

"He'd only slow us down, darling. This is just about us girls." Aborella continued to explain how absolutely normal it was to visit Raven and watched Avery's expression blank at the lull of her voice. Whatever protective enchantment Raven had placed on her sister, it was a strong one. Keeping the woman under control was costing her massive amounts of energy.

Together, they walked toward the central courtyard. Aborella had dressed in a lightweight gray suit, her red hair coiled along the back of her head. She'd developed this look for Charlotte because it had proved to be the most effective with these humans. Men were often attracted to her, and women intimidated.

Avery, on the other hand, wore a simple white sundress that made her appear young, innocent, and naive. Deceptive. The human was far stronger, smarter, and more intuitive than most. Aborella knew better than to underestimate her.

Now to find her sister, the witch. An apartment building stretched across the grounds to their right, a dated structure with maybe fifty rooms. Ahead of them was a newer, mostly glass building, and to their left, a meticulously landscaped area marked with a sign that read YOGA STUDIO.

"There's the welcome center," Avery said, pointing to

the glass building. "Raven didn't tell me what room she was in, but I'm sure they'd know."

"No." Aborella studied the pulsing orb around her neck. The light shifted toward the apartments. "She's there."

"But we don't know the unit. It's the middle of the afternoon. She could be anywhere." Avery shook her head. "Why don't I text her and ask?"

Aborella seized her wrist before she could reach for her phone. "And ruin the surprise?" she said through her teeth.

"You're hurting me!" Avery attempted to yank her hand away.

Cursing, Aborella gave her another shot of influence and groaned with the effort. She didn't stop until Avery's facial muscles drooped. There. With that amount of fairy magic coursing through her blood, Avery should finally obey. For how long, she wasn't sure. She needed to hurry.

"Excuse me!" An Asian man in a red-and-yellow robe with two long braids waved his hands at them. Aborella swore again under her breath. He was too close to convincingly pretend she didn't hear him.

"Can I help you?" she said through a tight smile.

The man laughed and extended his hand. "Actually, I was wondering if *I* could help *you*. I am Master Gu. I run New Horizons."

Aborella pumped his hand, and he gave her a pronounced frown.

"Have you recently lost someone precious to you?" He lowered his voice. "A child perhaps."

"No. Why?" Aborella answered in an annoyed tone, although she followed it up with a smile befitting her identity as Charlotte.

"Your aura is dark. Very dark." He turned to shake Avery's hand and smiled brightly in her direction. "Yours, however, is the most brilliant gold and white. I've only ever seen one other person with that aura. Actually, she looks a little like you, but more... well, pregnant."

"That's my sister," Avery said, her eyelashes fluttering. "That's who we're here to see."

He folded his hands. "I'm sorry to say her husband called down earlier to tell me they were checking out this afternoon. You may be too late."

Aborella glanced between Avery and Gu and decided to cut her losses. Pivoting, she ran for the stairs of the apartment building, leaving Avery and the protesting Master Gu behind. She rushed to the second floor, drawn forward by the scent of dragon and the tingle of power on her skin. Lucky her. She was close.

Touching each door with the tips of her fingers, she narrowed her eyes and concentrated. The tingle grew more intense until she reached a door that was already cracked. It swung open for her, as easy as brushing aside a spider's web, and what she saw inside gave her a wicked thrill.

"Did you get the car loaded?" Raven asked, her back to Aborella as she bent over a suitcase open on the bed. Surprise, surprise, the witch's pregnancy had advanced. Her stomach was the size of a beach ball, and Aborella could sense the unique magic of the infant inside her.

"I've come a long way for you," Aborella crooned.

Raven whirled. "Charlotte? What are you doing here?"

In the mirror above the dresser, Aborella glimpsed Gabriel on the concrete walkway. As he neared, she saw exactly when he caught her scent. His casual walk turned into a run.

In a flash, Aborella spun behind Raven, grabbed her about the shoulders—careful not to touch her skin directly —and brought the razor-sharp edge of a blade to the witch's throat. "Easy, Gabriel. Don't give me a reason to spill her blood. The empress will take her either dead or alive."

It was a lie but a good one. The empress wanted all of them brought back alive, Raven and the baby she was carrying most of all, but Gabriel didn't need to know that.

"What the fucking hell!" Avery yelled from the doorway. "Charlotte, put down the knife!"

"The empress?" Raven's hands reached for her.

Not this time. Quickly, Aborella whispered a paralysis spell in her ear and watched the witch's arms drop limp to her sides. "Don't you dare touch me, witch. I'll curse you hard enough to make you wet yourself."

"Charlotte." Avery stepped around Gabriel and into the room. "Give me the knife."

"Avery," Gabriel commanded. "Go get my brother Tobias. Room 10."

"Stay right where you are, Avery. I might need you," Aborella said.

Avery stopped, although the sweat on her upper lip suggested Aborella's hold over her would soon give out.

Gabriel growled. "Let her go, *Aborella*."

She laughed. So the heir did know who she was. "I'm flattered you remember me. What gave me away, *my prince?*"

Gabriel sniffed the air like an animal. His voice was barely more than a hiss when he answered her. "You don't forget the stink of fairy."

"I missed you too." Aborella dropped her illusion. Avery started to scream. Raven's eyes widened in terror, and she struggled against her paralyzed limbs. No doubt the witch would love to touch her and drain her power, but Aborella wouldn't make the same mistake twice. She zapped Raven with another dose of magic and had to hold her up as she went limp.

"Where are the heirs?" Aborella asked Gabriel. She shifted Raven's weight to one arm to reach into her pocket and wrap her fingers around the Paragonian *immurcador* there. The weapon had the power to cage and transport all of them back to Paragon. She would have liked to catch Tobias and Rowan too, but Raven and Gabriel would do for a start. Aborella could return for the others.

"Let her go and we can talk," Gabriel said.

Inside her pocket, Aborella's thumb stretched to activate the device.

"Go to the funeral," Raven blurted. Aborella didn't know what that meant, but she wasn't taking any chances. She drew the trap. Too late. Raven dissolved into a column of smoke before it engaged. Aborella's knife passed harmlessly through the dark fog she'd become before she disappeared entirely.

Aborella cursed. Raven was far more powerful than she remembered, and she could not return to Paragon with Gabriel alone. She deactivated the *immurcador* and returned it to her pocket just as Gabriel's talons sank into her gut. Pain radiated through her, sharp and intense. The symbols in her skin twisted and spiraled, magic meant to keep her alive.

"Die, bitch," Gabriel seethed into her face.

Using the last of her power, she teleported to the safety of the nearest plant life, surprised to find herself among the landscaping of the outdoor yoga studio. At first she could do nothing but lie still in the dirt, but with time her fingers twitched, then crawled to the base of the nearest tree. As the breeze rattled the leaves above her, she watched them turn from green to yellow to brown as she healed and her illusion snapped back into place. Cloaked again in her power, she stood and swaggered from between the trees, a shadow blowing through New Horizons.

In Raven's condition, she wouldn't make it far. All Aborella had to do was wait for the heirs to take the bait, and she'd have what she wanted in no time.

# CHAPTER THIRTY-FOUR

Maiara held the box containing the precious remains of her Nikan and sang the song of her ancestors as well as she could. The song was meant to guide the bird to the Land of Souls. Although she'd recovered her voice well enough to sing, when she attempted the high notes, it turned into a breathy rasp and she had to clear her throat before continuing.

After exploring sites with Alexander, she'd chosen this particular crag to bury Nikan because it was close to Alexander's cave but only reachable through flight. Nikan would be at peace here, alone with her kind, her body resting between the roots of a desert willow. She couldn't think of a more peaceful place.

Once she'd sung the last note, she placed the box inside the hole Alexander had dug. He covered it with earth. Although Raven and Gabriel had wanted to be there, they'd contacted Alexander on his phone, a device she wasn't at all comfortable with, to let them know Raven's health would not allow it. It seemed Maiara's instincts about her pregnancy were correct. She was close to delivery and had to leave Sedona immediately.

"May your flight to the next world be smooth and effortless, my friend," Alexander said toward the small grave.

Maiara leaned into his side and said, "She will rest now."

He kissed her temple.

A piercing scream echoed in the valley below, and they both peered over the side of the red rock in the direction of the sound. "Who is that?" Maiara asked. All she could make out was a silhouette rushing into the cave.

"There's trouble. We have to go." Alexander swept her into his arms, spread his wings, and swooped down. Maiara's heart quickened with the drop, but her stomach clenched once she was close enough to make out the identity of their visitor. Something was very wrong. Raven lay just inside the entrance to the cave, her hair slick with sweat. There was blood between her legs.

Alexander cursed. He set Maiara down and swept Raven into his arms.

"Take her to the bed," she said to Alexander. "I'll examine her."

He was already there, lowering her gently to the mattress. "What happened, Raven? Where's Gabriel? He told me you were leaving for Chicago tonight." Alexander held her hand while Maiara wet a towel and put it across her forehead. The poor woman was burning up.

"Aborella is h-here," Raven stuttered, and Maiara watched Alexander recoil. Whoever this Aborella was, her mate feared her. "She tried to take me. I couldn't let her. This was the only place nearby I knew she couldn't trace me, but getting here required a teleportation spell. I think I'm in labor."

"Yes, the baby is coming," Maiara confirmed, palpating her abdomen. The muscles constricted under her palms, a strong contraction. As a healer, Maiara knew the signs, and she started mentally preparing a list of the things she'd need.

"You have to call Tobias. He's the only one who can deliver this baby." Raven gripped Alexander's arm until her fingers turned white.

Maiara placed a comforting hand on her shoulder. "I have delivered many babies. I am a healer. I will take care of you."

Raven shook her head and screamed as another contraction racked her body. "This isn't an ordinary baby. It's an egg. A dragon's egg! Do you understand?"

Maiara shook her head. She did not understand, but it was clear this was no ordinary pregnancy. Raven's skin rippled with light, and it was all Maiara could do to remain calm for Raven's sake.

Alexander fired off a text. "They're on their way. Gabriel says he got your message. When did you have time to send Gabriel a message?"

"I told him to come to the funeral. Nikan's funeral. It was the only location I could think of that Gabriel would know but Aborella wouldn't, and it was close to the cave. I'm sorry to put you in this position, Alexander, but your home is the only place warded against Aborella. I had no choice but to come here."

"I am happy you came to me. This is where you should be, Raven. I'll keep you safe," Alexander said, taking her hand in his.

Maiara flashed back to the night Alexander had promised to keep *her* safe. He'd barely known her then. From the first moment they'd met, he'd put her needs

GENEVIEVE JACK

above his own. He'd always been empathetic and fiercely loyal.

At the same time, his relationship with Gabriel seemed strained. For so much of their early relationship, she'd observed her mate's struggle with finding his own identity in the shadow of his brother, which made this act all the more meaningful. The protection he offered Raven was genuine and unconditional. He held back no affection from his brother's mate.

Her chest felt tight. Jealousy. She recognized the feeling but not the source. She didn't feel threatened romantically by Raven, but the discomfort she was feeling had no other name. And then it came to her. Alexander had something she'd never had: a family. Brothers, sisters, and their mates. She squared her jaw. How foolish of her not to see. This witch was the reason Maiara was alive and here with Alexander. What was that but the action of family?

Maiara decided then that she would do whatever it took to help Raven, not out of any sense of obligation but because she was well and truly her kin now. She closed her eyes and centered herself. It had been a long time since she'd called on her *Midewiwin* magic, but it was still there, waiting for her. Like her ability to speak, it had atrophied but remained with her.

"Where is my medicine bag?" she asked Alexander, forming each word with effort.

"It burned with you. All we have is your *migiis*." Alexander hastened into the main room and returned with the white shell amulet. He handed it to her.

"This will not help with pain. Only to heal." Maiara slipped it into the pocket of her dress, knowing she would likely need to use its healing properties before the night was through.

"What do you need to help with pain?" Alexander asked.

"Nothing." Maiara took Raven's hands between her own and prayed to the Great Spirit to allow her to share the woman's pain. The results were immediate and excruciating, but she clamped her jaw and refused to scream. Instead, she took joy in watching Raven's face soften and her breath flow into her lungs evenly. She could do this. She would do this.

"Oh, that's better." Raven released a shaky breath. "I think the contraction is over."

Maiara closed her eyes and rolled with the agony. "Almost." Alexander met her gaze and held it, his eyes wide when he realized what she was doing. The contraction abated, and Maiara released Raven's hands.

"Alexander," Gabriel called from outside the cave.

With a gesture of her mate's hand, three people rushed into the room, Gabriel, Tobias, and a woman who looked remarkably like Raven.

"Avery, thank God you're safe," Raven said. Maiara watched the dark-haired woman cross to Raven's side. "Maiara, this is my sister, Avery."

Gabriel rushed to his mate and kissed her forehead. "I had her, Raven. My claws were in her flesh, but Aborella escaped. I would have chased after her, but I knew you'd need Tobias."

For his part, Tobias was already taking Raven's pulse and observing her as only a doctor could. "Rowan and Nick stayed behind to keep watch and act as a distraction."

"I didn't know about Charlotte. I mean Aborella. She's been manipulating me since your wedding," Avery said. "Gabriel told me everything. My God, Raven, my head is spinning with it all. It feels like I'm in a dream... or a nightmare. I have so many questions. Please believe me. I'm so sorry. So incredibly sorry."

Maiara could see the guilt roll off the woman called Avery, smell her tears. She seemed to vibrate with remorse. Then she noticed the blue crystal orb the size of a marble around her neck.

"Where did you get that?" Maiara asked, visions of the *wendigo* coming back to her like a nightmare.

"It's powerful," Raven added before another contraction rolled through her and stole her breath. Maiara took her hand and helped her through it.

"This?" Avery lifted it off her chest and fluttered her lashes at it. "It was a gift from..." Her eyes widened and she tore it from her neck as if it burned.

"Alexander!" Maiara cried his name through the pain. He knew what to do.

He snatched the amulet from Avery's hand, placed it on the stones near his feet, and smashed it with the base of the heavy cast-iron lamp beside the bed. It shattered. The blue light bled from its pieces.

"What was that, brother?" Gabriel's pupils burned with apprehension.

"Nothing good." Alexander explained how he'd found the same thing around the *wendigo*'s neck when he'd killed the beast centuries ago.

Maiara's blood ran cold, and the base of her skull prickled with the chill it gave her. So many years. So far away, and still the beast was breathing down her neck, threatening the ones she loved.

"Charlotte gave it to me." Avery's hand pressed into her chest. "I mean Aborella. Oh my God, was she controlling me with that thing?"

"And likely using it to spy on you and subsequently the rest of us," Tobias said. "If that was enchanted by Aborella, you didn't stand a chance once she had it around your neck."

Avery covered her mouth with her hands. "That's how she knew to come here."

"Does she know where we are?" Maiara asked. She did not know who this Aborella was, but if she'd been in league with the *wendigo*, she could only imagine she was a demon.

Silence weighed heavily in the room, and the men exchanged worried glances. Maiara had personally witnessed Gabriel, Tobias, and Alexander protecting her village. Their dragons were things of nightmares. If the brothers, together, feared Aborella, she must be powerful indeed. Maiara gritted her teeth. She refused to let the demon woman hurt anyone else she loved.

"At the moment, Aborella is the least of our worries." Tobias turned his attention back to Raven. The witch flushed as another contraction gripped her, and a moan parted her lips.

"Tobias?" Gabriel dragged out the word and turned toward his brother with pleading eyes. "Can you stop this? Long enough for us to transport her to a surgical center. I'll take a plane by force if I have to."

"I don't know. I need to examine her again. Can everyone leave the room?"

Gabriel grumbled. "I don't see why that's necessary."

Panting, Raven pointed toward the door. "Gabriel, just go! Please."

Gabriel hesitated but Alexander ushered him and Avery out. "Come on, big guy. Let's give the healers some room to work."

285

Before Maiara could follow them from the room, Tobias stopped her with a hand on her upper arm. "I'll need your assistance. If you're willing."

Maiara gave him a quick nod. "Yes. I will help you."

Tobias beamed a brilliant white smile down on her. "Just like old times."

Maiara wasn't sure about that. In her time, a woman would not be giving birth to a dragon egg.

Retrieving a pair of gloves from his bag, Tobias snapped them on. "Raven, just lean back. I'm going to check you again."

Maiara already knew what he would find. "She is ready, Tobias. The baby is coming."

Raven squeezed her hand, her eyes frantic. "Is that true? How do you know?"

After a quick exam, Tobias blew out a deep breath. "I'm sorry, Raven, but Maiara is right. It's time."

Another contraction hit Raven and she cried out. Maiara drained off some of the pain. She muffled a gasp.

"You're helping her?" Tobias whispered to Maiara as he dug in his bag.

Speech was impossible, but she nodded, her knuckles paling as they gripped Raven's hands. Finally the contraction abated, and she let her go.

"They're getting stronger," Raven said, voice trembling. Her tone was one Maiara had heard many times before. Every mother reached this point. As powerful a witch as Raven was, giving birth meant letting go. What was about to happen was out of her control, bigger than anything that had ever happened to her before.

"Trust." Maiara clutched her fingers and rode the next wave of pain with her. "You are in the hands of the Great Spirit."

As soon as it had eased, Tobias jabbed a needle into Raven's thigh and pressed the plunger. "This will take the edge off."

"What is that?" Maiara asked.

"A medicine to dull the pain. Better than willow bark."

"Oh." The tools and new medicines in Tobias's arsenal fascinated Maiara. When they had more time, she hoped Tobias would teach her modern healing the way she had taught him her ways.

Raven's body went limp and then her eyes closed. Maiara took the opportunity to whisper to Tobias. "The little one is..." Maiara motioned with her hands.

"Correct. It's too big," Tobias confirmed. "We have to take it out cesarean."

Maiara shook her head, not understanding the word. Tobias made the motion for cutting open the womb. She raised her hand to her mouth. She had seen it done once, but the mother did not survive.

Raven moaned but didn't open her eyes.

"The medication has taken effect. Good." Tobias dug in his bag again and removed a soft roll full of narrow, sharp knives and other metal tools. "We need to do this now before things get complicated."

"What could be more complicated than this?" Maiara couldn't imagine anything more difficult than cutting open a woman to remove what was inside her.

Tobias helped her into a pair of gloves. "If the baby doesn't want to come willingly."

Maiara shot him a horrified look. "What type of baby doesn't want to be born?"

Tobias frowned. "Dragons are an interesting species. A dragon mother is fireproof, and her eggs are born burning.

Raven is not fireproof. Let's just hope this baby is more witch than it is dragon. Do you have your amulet?"

"Yes."

"Good. Then call Gabriel. We're going to need him to hold her down."

# CHAPTER THIRTY-FIVE

R aven drifted in and out of sleep. Whatever Tobias had given her had made her incredibly drowsy, and she floated off whenever the pain lessened. Then a contraction would come and rip her from her slumber before the drug washed her under again.

This time when she woke, Gabriel was standing over her, and he wasn't smiling. "Tobias has to get the baby out, Raven. It's going to hurt."

"How? They can't do it here," Raven mumbled. She didn't even have an IV.

"They have to." His dark eyes burned.

Raven finally understood through the haze of the drugs and the pain. Tobias needed to perform the cesarean, here and now. Without anesthesia. Fear knocked on her heart, but she refused to open the door.

The moment she'd learned she was pregnant with Gabriel's child, she'd known this wouldn't be easy. Tobias had tried to convince her to end the pregnancy there and then. He'd told her it would most likely kill her. Legend warned the child of a witch and a dragon would be a monster.

But Raven had faced death before and she loved a man others thought was a monster. She loved this child. Through gritted teeth, she said, "Do it."

Gabriel nodded toward Tobias and then circled her wrists with his hands. She locked her eyes on him.

"Hold her," Tobias said. A cold, searing pain sliced under her belly button.

She tried not to scream, but in the end, she failed. Tipping to the side, she heaved and heard Gabriel curse as she threw up over the side of the bed.

"I said hold her, Gabriel! By the Mountain, man!" Tobias snapped. Raven did not fight Gabriel as he held her shoulders down. "Now, Maiara. This is the hard part."

Maiara grabbed one of Raven's hands and the pain lessened considerably. The healer's lips moved in silent prayer. She was taking some of the pain. Raven would have to thank her for that later.

Dimly, Raven risked a glance at what Tobias was doing. The egg was halfway out of her abdomen, its outer shell like a coiled string of pearls. Surreal. Was the haze in the room drug induced or from the blur of her tears? Either way, the egg was beautiful, and it pulsed peacock blue at the center. Her baby's heart. Tobias cut away at some type of biological web that kept him from removing it.

Beside her, Maiara groaned. "Tobias, quickly!"

Desperate to get the baby out, he wrapped an arm around the egg and attempted to tear it free. Crackling magic stirred in the air around them. If she'd been able to speak, she would have warned them all to get back—she knew this magic—but she was too weak. Purple lightning ignited from the shell and across her skin, sending Gabriel, Maiara, and Tobias flying. The egg stayed where it was.

Raven wailed as the full magnitude of the pain slammed into her. Every nerve ending burned like she was on fire. Tobias attempted to get to his feet to help her and fell down again, his legs trembling. Maiara reached for her, no doubt to help with the pain, but she'd been thrown too far away and her legs, like Tobias's, failed her.

And through it all, Raven could feel the echo of an emotion coming from the egg. All that purple magic was something she could sense, absorb, as she did with every other kind of magic. And in it, she saw the truth.

Her baby was scared.

With her last ounce of strength, she reached for the egg, her teeth chattering from an unexpected wave of cold that overwhelmed her flesh. Her fingers dug into the bumpy exterior, wet with her own blood. Grunting with the effort, she heaved. Using her muscles but also her witch's connection to the elements, she willed her child into existence with a spell that came from nowhere else but the depths of her soul.

The pain was unfathomable. Her flesh tore and her blood spilled, but her child gave way. She collapsed against the bed with the egg tucked into the crook of her elbow.

All at once, her body went rigid, muscles locking. Then everything went dark.

THE LIGHTS CAME BACK ON FOR RAVEN AND ALL THE pain was gone. She stood beside herself as absolute chaos broke loose in the room. Gabriel was howling as if his heart was being pried from his chest with a dull spoon. He hovered over a corpse holding a giant pearl.

That couldn't be her, could it? The body was too pale to be human, and all the light had gone from the blue eyes, the pupils nothing more than pinpricks. The abdomen was torn open from hip to rib in an ugly mess that might as well be called a disembowelment.

Maiara placed her healing amulet on the body's neck, the skin of the corpse barely darker than the white shell. Again, Raven resisted the idea that it was her lying there. She couldn't accept it. She was right here, warm and safe, watching it all.

Tobias tried to replace all her abdominal parts, fumbling with bloody innards and clamps and strings. Raven had a sudden comical vision of Humpty Dumpty. She'd had a great fall. *You'll never put all the pieces back together, Tobias. Never.*

Gabriel pounded on her chest. *Be careful,* she thought. *You'll hurt the baby.* The egg after all was still nestled in the crook of her arm in all its pearlescent glory. It was all about the child now, she realized. That was the important thing.

"You're a mess," a woman's voice said.

Raven jumped at the sound. A dark-haired goddess appeared at her side. There was no doubt she was a goddess. She wore a white gown that draped around her perfect olive skin in a way no human could pull off, its color brighter than any she'd seen before. Her eyes were the color of liquid gold. Being in her presence was like standing in the sun.

"Who are you?" Raven asked.

"You don't recognize me, granddaughter? I suppose I should insert a number of greats before grand, but the gods and goddesses put little stock in measuring time. I wouldn't know how many greats, and I would be hard-pressed to name your entire lineage. Surely when you look upon me, you must see some part of yourself."

"Circe." She said the name with reverence.

The goddess bowed her head. "Yes, it is I."

"I can't believe you're here." Dark realization traveled through her soul. "Am I dead?"

"Yes," Circe said. "Whether you stay that way is still to be known."

The stuff she was made of turned to cold lace like her soul was nothing more than a delicate frost on stone. She'd read the Greek gods were easily offended. Raven lowered her eyes, trying to find the right words. "I have so much to thank you for, Circe. My magic. My mate. Please, goddess, I beg you for one more favor. I want to know my child. If there is anything you can do, please help me live."

Unmoved, Circe raised a hand. "We have little time together, Raven, and there is something I must tell you. A message you must hear and remember."

Raven didn't understand, but she hoped the message was for the living and not the underworld.

"A long time ago, your ancestor and her two sisters discovered a book of spells called the *Golden Grimoire*. The grimoire belonged to Hera herself, a gift from Zeus containing the secrets of the immortals. Anyone capable of wielding the spells inside can harness the power of the gods. Afraid of the grimoire falling into the wrong hands, Hera convinced Hades to secure it for her in the underworld. There it stayed for centuries until the three sisters conjured it."

"What does that have to do with me?"

"When Hera discovered their insurrection, the three sisters took refuge in the five kingdoms, one of the few realms beyond Hera's control. Can you imagine what happened next, Raven?"

"Hera tried to get it back?"

Circe nodded. "As soon as Hera discovered the book's location, she demanded that the goddess of the Mountain return it to her. But like me, the Mountain is a descendant of a titan. Zeus and Hera have little power over her. Rejected, Hera poisoned the ears of the king and queen of Paragon, making them ravenous for power. It is because of her that your mate is here.

"Everything happening in Paragon is fueled by Hera's jealousy and her desire to get that book back. And she is merciless. She has always hated my creation and will burn Paragon down to pluck the book from its ashes if unchecked."

"Your creation. That's right, you created dragon shifters."

Circe nodded.

"I don't understand. She's Hera, the queen of the gods. If she wanted to burn Paragon down, why hasn't she already? Why not snap her fingers and call the book to her?"

"Even gods and goddesses have rules and limitations," Circe said. "Paragon is under my protection as well as the Mountain's, and we have friends among the gods. We've succeeded at keeping Hera in check, but she has weakened our hold from the inside. The dark magic keeping Eleanor and Brynhoff on the throne is also corrupting the Mountain. She is vulnerable, and if the Mountain falls, Paragon falls."

"Why are you telling me this?"

"Mark me, Raven, only when the treasure of Paragon sits upon the throne and the *Golden Grimoire* is returned to

Hera will their world or this one be safe. I will help you along the way when I can."

Raven's head spun. How could she possibly process everything she'd been told? "But... what do you expect me to do?"

The goddess stared down at the egg, still pulsing in the crook of her body's arm. "Don't you know, granddaughter? The truth is in front of you."

She didn't know, and she had no idea what the goddess wanted from her. "But I'm dead!" She pointed at her body and the people she loved working diligently over it.

The goddess's gaze burned into hers, and the smile she gave her washed over her like the light from a star. "Don't underestimate yourself, granddaughter. The three sisters are the most powerful magical beings in any universe. Reunite them. Use the magic you were born to yield. Save Paragon."

"But... but..."

"Remember." The goddess leaned over and whispered a poem in her ear that rooted in her mind. "It's time, Raven. Breathe." Circe grabbed her by the shoulders and pressed her mouth to Raven's in a kiss that ignited her lips and seared her throat. Light branched to her hips and elbows. It blazed in her fingers and toes. Circe's kiss was like drinking sunlight, and when that liquid fire had filled every part of her, she crashed back into her broken body. Breath flowed into her lungs and pain followed, branching through her body once again.

Eyes wide, Raven clawed at the amulet around her neck and held it in her fist. She was a witch who could absorb magic, and she did so now, drawing healing power into herself from the shell, from Maiara, from the dragon tooth that still dwelled in her stomach.

"For the love of the goddess," Tobias whispered. He dropped the needle he was using to try to stitch her abdomen and backed away. Maiara cried out and pulled her hand away, and Gabriel stopped beating against her heart.

Inch by ravaged inch, Raven's body mended itself, everything back in place, the muscles rejoining, the skin adhering itself in layers. The stitches Tobias had finished fell from her newly formed skin, digested and spit out by her healed body.

Everything hurt and her limbs trembled despite being whole again. She needed water. Nourishment. Only then did she realize her arms were empty.

Tongue like leather, she struggled to speak, but when she did, her voice reverberated through the room. "Where's my baby?"

# CHAPTER THIRTY-SIX

For most of Raven's life, motherhood was an abstract concept that lurked in the periphery of her experiences. Only in her wildest imagination had she dreamed of being a mother at all, and nowhere in those dreams had a pearl shell come into play. But Raven lived in a world of magic now, and her child did too.

"Am I awake? Because this feels like a dream. Is this a dream?" Avery leaned back in the plush leather couch and stared at the egg nestled among the burning logs in the fireplace.

"You're not dreaming." Raven sipped tea in the seat beside her. "And you haven't lost your mind." Gabriel had carried her out there a few minutes ago and propped her up in a nest of pillows. With Willow's help, he'd made a tray of food and drink for her as well. Although weak and sore, Raven felt in amazing shape, considering she'd been dead less than an hour ago.

"Is it okay for it to be in the fire? Burning like that?" Avery asked. Her tone was equal parts wonder and skepticism.

297

Gabriel refilled Raven's tea and fed her a finger sandwich from the tray as if she were a child. Raven loved the attention of her mate and kissed his fingers between bites. While she was chewing, he answered for her.

"Not only is it okay, it is good for the whelp. In Paragon, dragon mothers place their eggs beside a stream of lava in the mountain to incubate. See how the shell glows? The heat fuels the magic. If you touch it, you'll find the shell itself is barely hot." Gabriel never took his eyes off Raven as he spoke.

"I'll take your word for it," Avery said.

Raven's newborn was the size of a small watermelon with a bumpy shell that reminded her of a Fabergé egg decorated with hundreds of large pearls. A one-inch ribbon of smooth white broke the otherwise uniform exterior in a spiral from tip to base. It was through this thin strip that she viewed a silhouette. Raven smiled when the dark outline of five fingers pressed against the inside of the shell. Her baby's tiny hand.

The rest of the shell glowed from within, either blue or green depending on what angle she looked at it. It was as bizarre as it was beautiful.

"Have you thought about names?" Avery asked. She seemed as entranced by the egg as Raven was.

Gabriel fed Raven a bite of pasta. She chewed and swallowed before answering. "Not yet."

Avery gave a low, breathy laugh. "Is he going to feed you the entire time?"

Raven grinned at her sister. "Maybe. Does it bother you?"

"Bothered is a strong word. I've just never experienced intimacy like this before. I can't imagine anyone feeding me from their fingers." Her wistful gaze latched onto Gabriel as he stroked Raven's hair.

Gabriel smirked, his dark eyes leveling on her sister. "Maybe you need to date a different sort of man."

It was intimate, but more than that, it was their bond. Raven sympathized. Alexander and Maiara were cuddled together in a chair made for one, painted into their own world. She and Gabriel were connecting over a meal. And although Tobias wasn't currently in the room, he had a similar bond with Sabrina.

As a human, Avery would likely never experience the same. When dragons mated, they mated for life. She hoped her sister would know love one day, but even if she did, it would likely be different than hers and Gabriel's.

Tobias came out of the bathroom, rubbing a towel against his wet head. He'd been so covered in Raven's blood he'd needed to shower. Thankfully, Willow had insisted on cleaning up the bedroom. Her heart warmed with gratefulness for the oread.

"So, is anyone going to talk about the fact that the most powerful fairy in all of Paragon is out there, in Sedona, hunting us?" Tobias asked. "And that she might already know where we are?"

Gabriel made a low, grumbling sound. "Not yet. Give Raven time to catch her breath and enjoy the child. Come, Tobias. Look for yourself. It is small as dragon eggs go but healthy. It has taken to the fire as expected."

"Oh, I think your child is far more exceptional than you give it credit for, considering it almost knocked the three of us unconscious."

Although Tobias said it in an almost ominous tone, Gabriel's reaction expressed nothing short of pride. "He will be a strong little dragon with his mother's power."

"And we will all arm ourselves with defensive magic when she reaches the terrible twos. It could be a girl, you know." Tobias poured himself a cup of tea.

"I'd welcome a girl," Gabriel said. "She will be fierce and all the other dragons will fear her."

Raven raised an eyebrow at him.

"I still think we need to talk about Aborella sooner rather than later," Tobias said. "We can't hide in here forever."

Gabriel held up his phone. "Rowan and Nick have been patrolling New Horizons. Aborella hasn't returned to the vehicle or to the room. There is no place safer than this cave. Alexander has so many layers of magic around this thing, I'm surprised Rowan was able to find it at all."

"She used Nick," Alexander said. "That human is worthy of her."

Tobias sighed heavily, his frustration evident. "I need to call Sabrina and let her know what's going on. She was expecting me home tonight."

"Where is your wife, Tobias?" Avery asked.

"Sabrina is in Chicago running the coven," he said.

Avery's eyebrows shot up. "Your wife is a witch too?"

He shook his head. "No. A vampire."

"There are vampires!" Avery slapped the arm of the sofa. "Am I the only human left in the world?"

"I am human," Maiara said, then frowned. "At least I was. I am unsure now. My *Midew* powers were divine but not immortal." She touched her face lightly. "I am not sure what I am now."

"You should feed her your tooth, Alexander, to be safe," Gabriel suggested.

Alexander nodded and asked Maiara in a whisper if she'd be willing.

"Your tooth..." Avery said. "You swallow each other's teeth?"

They all looked at her like she had two heads. "Of course not," Gabriel said. "We don't randomly swallow each other's teeth. Dragons only have so many."

Raven came to her rescue with an explanation. "Dragons are magical creatures, and if they want to bind a mortal to them, either for love or for employment, they feed them their tooth, and it imbues the mortal with the dragon's immortality. Unless I am killed by violent means, I will live as long as Gabriel does."

"Is that how you became a witch?" Avery whispered the word *witch* like she still couldn't believe it was true.

"Kind of."

"Oh! That must be how you survived your cancer." Avery's jaw dropped as she put it all together. "He fed you his tooth and turned you into a witch."

"Not really. I... was always a witch. The tooth enhances what's already there," Raven said.

"How could it already be there?" Avery asked with a snort. "We grew up together. It's not as if it could be hereditary. Did you sell your soul to the devil or something?"

Raven froze. Her blue eyes held Avery's as the entire room fell silent aside from the crackling fire. Why had she never considered this before? Raven was a Tanglewood witch, descended from Circe. Avery shared the same heritage. Was it possible her sister was a witch as well, her abilities sleeping latent somewhere inside her? Maybe.

But this was not the time or the place to discuss this, not without extensive research. It would be wrong to worry Avery when she had no reason to suspect her sister had any power.

301

"Raven? How did you become a witch?" Avery pressed again.

She rubbed her face and leaned back against the sofa. "I'm... I'm sorry, Avery. I'm exhausted and probably not making sense."

Concerned, Gabriel turned to his brother. "Where?"

"Take the second bedroom," Alexander said. "Down the passageway. There's a fireplace. We can move the baby in there. Avery can take the couch. I'll have Willow find a mat for Tobias."

Tobias shook his head. "Don't bother. I'll shift and go deeper into the cave."

"Shift?" Avery scratched the side of her head as if all the new information was making it itch.

"Into my dragon form," Tobias explained.

"Of course, because it couldn't just be the wings and everything," Avery mumbled. "You all actually turn into dragons?"

The three siblings nodded in unison.

"Avery, are you going to be all right?" Raven squeezed her hand. "Maybe you should eat something. Have the rest of what Gabriel made me." She pointed at the remaining food on the tray.

"Okay. Um. I'll be okay. I just really need to sleep. It's a lot, Rave. Just a lot. And I... Part of me wishes I'd known sooner so that maybe I could have suspected there was something going on with Charlotte, I mean Aborella. But I'm not sure I'd have believed it—"

"I know," Raven said. "It's okay. I forgive you for any part you played bringing her here, and I'm sorry, genuinely, that I didn't tell you earlier. I should have."

"Do you think we should warn Dad?"

Gabriel shook his head. "He's not in any danger, Avery.

Now that Aborella knows where we are, she'll hunt for us here. He's safe in New Orleans."

After they exchanged good-nights, Raven allowed Gabriel to carry her to bed. Her mind raced. Her sister was part of this now. Everything would need to change, and she wasn't sure Avery was ready for any of it.

As soon as Gabriel laid her on the bed in the back room and placed their child in the fire Willow had started in the fireplace, Raven reached for him. "I have to tell you something."

"What is it? Are you having pain again? I can get Tobias."

"No. Listen to me. Avery is my sister."

"I know."

"I am a witch because I descended from Circe. That means Avery—"

"Also descended from Circe, yes. But that doesn't mean she's a witch. Remember, even before I fed you my tooth, you had psychic abilities. That's how I found you. She may not have inherited the magic." Gabriel stretched out beside her and covered both of them in a fluffy black comforter.

"True." Raven frowned. "But maybe she did."

"Why didn't you tell her of the possibility when she asked?"

"She's been through too much today. I just couldn't add one more thing." She sighed heavily.

He pulled her onto his chest. "Rest, Raven. After everything, the only one you should be worried about is you." He groaned. "Tobias thought you'd... died. I... thought you died."

She cuddled into his side. "I think... maybe I did."

He raised his head to look at her.

"It felt like I was standing there, watching it all. I had the strangest dream that I saw my ancestor, the goddess Circe."

"You dreamed about Circe?" he asked, gently stroking her hair.

She nodded, her eyelids heavy. She gave up fighting the exhaustion and just closed them. "She was strange and wonderful. Her eyes were like molten gold. Do you think that's because she's the daughter of Helios?"

"What did she say to you?"

"She said Hera was behind what happened in Paragon. Her *Golden Grimoire* was stolen and hidden on your world. She said Hera corrupted Eleanor and Brynhoff. She wanted to overthrow the kingdom to weaken Paragon's goddess of the Mountain. Circe is helping to protect Paragon, but she said if the mountain falls, your world will fall. Something about gods having limits and rules. I don't fully understand."

It sounded ridiculous now. Goddesses at war. Hidden grimoires. Raven needed sleep to sort it all out.

"Gods are strengthened by belief and ritual. Eleanor has cast aside the old ways." Gabriel trailed his fingers along her arm. "What else did she say?"

She yawned. "She said I should find the three sisters. Isn't that weird? Like the name of my mom's bar. She said the three sisters were the most powerful beings in the universe and could wield magic strong enough to save Paragon. Only when the treasure of Paragon sits upon the throne and the *Golden Grimoire* is returned to Hera will Paragon be safe and at peace." Raven shook her head. "It sounds so crazy now."

"Did Circe think you should go back to Paragon?"

"Hmmm. I think so. She whispered a little poem in my ear:

*Three sisters the way will make*
*the book, the tree, the throne to take.*
*One will read it, one will slay, one will sing death away.*
*The treasure then will rise again,*
*complete the crown in the dragon's den*
*A ring of jewels that number nine*
*must use their hearts to return what's thine.*
*With the heirs upon the throne,*
*the queen shall fall an aged crone.*
*Only then will goddess sleep*
*her deadly fire at last appeased*
*And wrong undone peace doth reign*
*never war to come again.*"

"What does it mean?" Gabriel whispered.

Raven sighed, her mind close to sleep. "I don't know. Maybe it was just a dream. Maybe it doesn't mean anything. But she was beautiful. My brain is so weird."

"Hmm." He tucked the blankets around her. "Sleep now, Raven. There will be time tomorrow to face all these things."

With her ear pressed to his heart and enveloped in his warmth, she drifted off in the safety of his arms.

# CHAPTER THIRTY-SEVEN

Maiara snuggled into Alexander's side in his bed beside a mountain of treasure the likes of which she'd never known. The gems reflected the candlelight and color, and shadows danced across his bare chest. This was his way.

Strange, all their time together before had been spent living her way among her people. He had never complained of this, although it must have been far different from what he was used to. Treasure, dragon eggs, wings to fly, a kingdom in a faraway land—he'd told her about all these things before, but it was different now, seeing them for what they were.

Willow had lit candles around the room, and a warm glow filled their section of the cave. It brought peace to her heart. It reminded her of their teepee when they were first mated.

"Are you tired? Do you want me to blow out the candles?" Alexander asked.

"No." There was much to be said, and she'd only recently found her voice.

"You saw something today you'll never see again. A dragon egg born to a witch, a former human. Who would have ever thought such a thing was possible?"

"She died," Maiara said.

"Hmm?"

"She came back, but she was gone. I feared I would have to tell her mate that his wife had taken my place in the Land of Souls."

"Oh hell." Alexander rubbed his eyes.

"How long until the egg will hatch?"

"No one knows. In dragons, the gestation is about a year. Half inside the mother, half outside. But with the mother being a human witch, no one understands for sure what we're dealing with."

There were many things Maiara didn't understand. Her mind jumped to Avery and the amulet they'd destroyed. "Why do you think Avery had the same amulet as the *wendigo*?"

Alexander threaded his fingers behind his head. "I never had a chance to speak with you after I killed the *wendigo*. The orb was Paragonian. It was from my world."

Maiara dragged breath through her teeth. "How would something from your world end up around the neck of the *wendigo*?"

"That, I don't know. In Paragon, enchanted orbs like that were used to spy on our enemies. They were made by Aborella."

"Who is this Aborella?"

"She's a fairy sorceress who works for my mother Eleanor. I told you once that dragons could perform some magic."

She nodded. It had been a long time ago, but she remembered.

THE DRAGON OF SEDONA

"We are magical beings, and some magic spells will work for us, but our magic is not as powerful as that of a witch or a fairy. Witches draw their power from the elements. Fairies draw from living things. Aborella can literally drain the life out of a plant she touches and turn that life force into magic."

"She is a demon," Maiara said.

"I can't argue with that. But in our world, we call her a fairy."

"My people told stories of the *wendigo*. It was said that they were once warriors who sold their souls to the devil in exchange for power. Do you think this Aborella had the power to change a man into the monster you killed?"

Alexander rubbed his chin. "It's possible."

"Why did Avery not change into a monster?"

One of his dark eyebrows lifted. "Avery wouldn't have asked for power in exchange for wearing the orb. She was wearing it because Aborella had posed as her father's girl-friend and given it to her."

Maiara brought her fists to her forehead. "But why?" Her voice cracked. "Why would this fairy sorceress do such a thing as to create the monster that would kill my family if she is not even from this world?"

Alexander's eyes narrowed, his fingers trailing absently along her arm. "That's a very good question. After King Brynhoff murdered my brother, our mother transported us to this realm. Once we arrived here, we found a message she'd prerecorded in an enchanted crystal. Her last words to us were that we must stay apart or Brynhoff would find us and kill us. Our collective magical signature would give away our location if we stayed together in one place for too long. We thought she'd saved us."

"But she was lying," Maiara said. She'd gleaned that much from his brothers.

"Yes, she was. I've only recently learned that my mother was in on the coup. She sent us here to get us out of the way so we wouldn't challenge her for the throne. And her warning to stay apart was only to keep us weak. Together we might figure out what she was doing and retaliate; apart we would be too busy surviving to be much of a threat. I suppose there was some compassion in it, her not wanting to slaughter us all. I have no idea how she explained our absence to the people of Paragon."

He shook his head. "In any case, in light of what I know now, Aborella must have created the *wendigo* to ensure we either followed our mother's edict or paid with our lives. She's a powerful seer. If her visions had shown her we would eventually travel to the New World..." He looked her in the eye. "You said the *wendigo* attacked the *Midewiwin* at a ceremony when they were all together."

"Yes," she said softly.

"When their magical signature was strongest."

"Yes."

"And then it came after us when we were all together."

"Yes." Their gazes met and locked.

"Why didn't it follow us to the winter camp?" Alexander asked.

Maiara's head ached, and she closed her eyes and rubbed her temples. Why? Why? Why? It came to her in a long-lost memory, the symbols she'd noticed when they'd ridden into the Potawatomi village. "Keme. The *Midew* of that tribe was very powerful. He once shared with me that he did a spell of protection over that place so his people would never be attacked in their vulnerable winter village.

The *wendigo* didn't attack us there because it couldn't find us."

Alexander growled. "And then when we left, it found us again."

She placed her hands over her face, anger coiling like a snake within her. She could hear its warning rattle in her ears. She hated this Aborella, this creature she'd never met, to the core of her being, to the marrow of her bones.

"I am sorry I brought this pain upon you," Alexander rasped. "In searching for me and my siblings, Aborella created the thing that destroyed your family. I can never make this right. Maiara, you must know how sorry I am."

When she looked at him again, his expression broke her heart. Nothing short of devastation darkened his eyes.

"I swear to you, had I known—"

"This is not your fault, Alexander." She ground her teeth. "One day we will kill her and have our revenge."

He brushed her hair back from her face, his eyes becoming dark pits. "I promise you."

She turned on her back and stared at the rough ceiling of the cave. "Aborella is deadly. It will be dangerous to kill her."

"True."

"You tried to take your own life while I was in Nikan."

He frowned but he didn't deny it. After a long moment, he said, "I didn't know you were inside her. I wanted to join you in the Land of Souls."

"And that is the thing we must talk about." She stared at him through eyes narrowed to slits. "I cannot be your entire reason for living. No person can or should hold that honor. The honor of life-giver can only be given to one like the Great Spirit." She pointed at the ceiling. "Or your goddess of the Mountain. I am not forever. I cannot be your beginning and your end."

He shook his head, a smile playing at the corners of his mouth. "We will change all that. I will give you my tooth, and we will be bound together, your life to mine."

She shook her head. "This is not the *Midewiwin* way."

He sat up, hugging his knees to his chest. His dark blue eyes turned purple from the fire burning within them. "Considering you put your soul into a hawk to survive, I think the *Midewiwin* way must be more accepting of immortality than you're suggesting."

She shook her head. "Aborella will come and we will fight her. If it is the will of the Great Spirit that we once again be parted—"

He shook his head vehemently. "No, I won't allow it."

She sat up then too and squared her shoulders. "We do not have a say over where the wind blows or how fast the water flows or how tall the grasses grow. We decide only to turn our face to it, sink our toes under it, and trail our hands through it."

"Losing you was like losing half of myself."

"What if something happens to you? You have told me dragons can be killed. Your brother Marius was killed."

"In rare cases, yes, we can." He scowled.

"And if that happens, do you expect me to leap onto your funeral pyre and die with you?"

"No, of course not." A muscle in his jaw twitched.

"What would you want for me if Aborella killed you?"

"I'd want you..." His brow furrowed. "Well, I'd want you to remember me, but I'd want you to carry on. The world needs healers. My brothers would take care of you." He licked his lips. "I'd want you to find happiness again."

There it was, the light of understanding flickering in his eyes. "The world needs artists too."

Their eyes locked and held.

She took his hands in hers. "Pain is an evil taskmaster, a monster who sometimes lives inside us and makes us do things to appease it. I love you, Alexander, and accept all that you are and all that you've done. All I ask is that you make peace now with the Great Spirit. Banish the darkness from your soul.

"And know that if I ever do pass into the next world without you, I will still be with you, here." She touched the space over his heart. "I don't want the sacrifice of your death to the pain monster. I want the victory of your joy over it. That is how you will honor me."

"Then promise, here and now, that should anything happen to either of us in the future, the one who remains will carry on," Alexander said with conviction.

She took his hand in hers. "I promise."

"I promise too." A muscle in his jaw twitched. "Now, enough about dying. When we face Aborella, I plan to win." He rolled onto his back and stared at the ceiling again. The candlelight played along his chest, his stiffly held shoulders. She refused to leave things like this between them.

She rose onto her knees. At first, his mind remained in some faraway place. She waited. Eventually his gaze shifted to her. Slowly she lifted her sleeping gown over her head, allowing the cool air of the cave to caress her skin.

Without warning, he sprang from the bed, took her in his arms, and rolled her onto her back, nothing but long, lean muscle caging her in his embrace. A high-pitched noise escaped her throat as her back hit the mattress. His gaze swept over her face.

Kneeling, he seized her legs and slid her to him until she

straddled his hips, with her back on the mattress. His wings rose, strong and fierce behind him, his gaze darkly hungry. What a sight to behold. There was her hunter. There was the man who had stood for her against the white men in the tavern, against her own people before the chief, against her enemies.

"Won't you share your heat with me, *dIneym*?"

"Always."

He leaned over her, nestled between her thighs, and met her mouth with his. The memory of their love dance came back to her with the first stroke of his tongue. His fingers threaded into her hair, and he massaged her neck in time with the rhythm of his kiss. And although he might have started the kiss, she took control, kindling a deep and desperate fire. His hand worked between them, stroking along the outer curve of her breast.

"You made this body from clay?" she said, suddenly realizing that his fingers had, in fact, touched every part of her. It was easy to forget. She felt like herself.

His lips tickled her ear. "I sculpted the totem, which transformed into you. You are flesh, not clay. But yes, I did sculpt you."

She placed her hand over his as he cupped her breast. "You never thought to change anything?" she said mischievously. "Make these bigger?" She moved his hand down her side to caress her bottom. "This rounder?"

He rose and lifted her with him until he knelt on the bed with her straddling his lap. He shot her a boyish grin. "There is no improving on perfection."

"You are a wise *dIneym*. Your wisdom will be rewarded."

She rose onto her knees and worked his shorts down beneath her. He helped her remove them. His manhood stood proud and thick between them. She wrapped her hand around it and enjoyed the resulting purr of his mating trill. "Maiara, oh goddess..."

"There is one thing," she said, watching his eyelids droop and his head tip back.

"What's that?"

"We should make sure this new body works like the old one."

"An important goal, I agree." He stroked up her thighs, ran his thumbs along the tangle of nerves at her center. She licked her lips and moaned. "That's a good sign." He lowered her until she rested on the mattress in front of him again, then ran his nose along her jaw and down her neck, placing a kiss between her breasts. "You smell like Maiara."

"What does Maiara smell like?" She laughed.

"Like fresh air, pine trees, birch bark." She stopped laughing and inhaled his smoky scent as he flicked his tongue under her nipple. He kneaded her breasts, toying with the hard nubs at their tips, then trailing his fingers feather soft across her torso and down to her hips. "You feel like Maiara."

Her back arched against his caress, and her knees drifted farther apart. His lips brushed along her inner thigh. "Alexander, you tease me." She sighed.

"That sounds like Maiara. Let's see if you pass the taste test." His hot breath drifted lower, warming the delicate flesh between her legs. And then his tongue darted up her center and circled her most sensitive flesh. He remembered exactly how to touch her and she moaned, raising her hips and begging for more.

Alexander did not disappoint. She watched his wings work above her as he nibbled and sucked until her entire body felt like a single raw nerve. The jewels beside her glowed brighter, the light dancing like stars above her. With the touch of his fingers, she was floating among those stars, careening into the light like she was one with the sun itself.

"Oh yes, you taste like Maiara," he whispered. He slid over her, entering her just as she was coming down from her flight. The pressure made the lightning inside her strike again. He rolled her over until she was on top of him, riding him toward the moon once more. Wild and free, she was back in her skin, his heat warming her, sweat breaking out across her chest.

Finally she felt him buck under her. With his head tipped back, she thought her heart might burst from the sight of him letting go. She'd never known a man more worthy of her love. Lightning struck again inside her, and she gave herself over to the blinding light, folding herself against him. Heart-to-heart, face-to-face.

He wrapped his wings around her and stroked her hair down the length of her back. "In my professional opinion, this is your true body. You are Maiara. My Maiara." He kissed her on the temple.

Limbs still tangled, she had to agree. She finally felt like herself again. Which made her realize something. For over three hundred years, Alexander had remained true to her.

"How long would you have waited for me, Alexander?"

"Until death grew tired of me and either took me in or gave you up."

Just as she thought.

# CHAPTER THIRTY-EIGHT

After a long night of complex magic, Aborella arrived at Shaman's Cave and regarded the rocky red landscape. She longed to rest, longed for home, but now was not the time. The heirs were close. She could feel it. The empress would reward her perseverance.

She'd used the enchanted orb to trail Avery almost all the way here until the pulse of magic was cut off abruptly. All was not lost, however. There was another trail, a weaker trail. It took her time and energy to sort it like a single thread from a twist of yarn, but she'd done it.

It all came down to common sense. Alexander, like all dragons, would be drawn to a mountain cave, high enough to be safe from human trespassers and in a place like this where the natural energy made her skin tingle. She'd been Eleanor's seer for long enough to understand the predilections of her kind.

As the sun edged over the horizon, she flew in the direction her instinct and the faint scent of dragon encouraged her to go. Fairies couldn't make themselves invisible, but they were experts at illusion. She camouflaged herself to match the natural surroundings. Not that she cared if a human saw her. With any luck, she wouldn't be in this realm long enough to suffer the consequences. Escaping notice would save her time and energy though, and she was already drained from her work to get there.

A tingle passed along her neck. She was close. Very close. She inhaled deeply and caught the scent of smoke and silver. A dragon's treasure trove. She landed in front of a tall mesa and stared up the red rock. It was there, somewhere, concealed. What she needed was the help of a human.

"Avery," she sang toward the rock, not in her own voice but in Avery's father's. Although she'd pumped the girl full of milkwood root and persuasive enchantments, Avery had been painfully resistant to both. If magic wouldn't work, she'd have to use illusion. "Avery. Aaaavery."

A rock skipped down the side of the cliff. *That's it. Take the bait, girl. A little closer.*

Aborella raced toward the face that peeked over the edge of a lip in the side of the mountain. Avery's black hair floated on the morning breeze, her bare toes curled over the rocky crag. She was shocked when Avery sensed her presence. Impossibly, despite her camouflage, Avery looked right at her. The woman's eyes grew wide and she turned, running toward the side of the mountain.

"Stop!" Aborella commanded, but her hold over the woman failed again, leaving her only one option. A curse flew from Aborella's fingertips like a lit match and buried itself in the back of Avery's head, a worm in an apple, just before Avery disappeared. A smile spread the fairy's lips.

"Found you. Time to come out and play."

# CHAPTER THIRTY-NINE

Maiara woke to the sound of a scream. She rolled from the bed and landed on her feet, pulling on the clothes she'd worn the night before at record speed. But when she reached for the door, Alexander's hand landed on hers. He brought a finger to his lips.

Wings spread, he leaned his ear against the door.

"Help!" Avery cried, in a strangled, muffled voice that sent a chill through Maiara.

Alexander opened the door and they both rushed into the main room. Avery lay on the floor in front of his protective ward, holding her head. Tobias was already there, examining her.

"What's going on?" Alexander asked.

"Aborella," Avery whimpered.

Tobias pointed at the entrance to the cave. At first he couldn't see what Tobias did, but then the fairy-shaped outline against the sky became more evident.

"Aborella, show yourself!" he demanded.

Her illusion melted away. Like something out of his

worst nightmares, the dark purple fairy loomed outside the barrier, her pointed teeth filling an exaggerated grin.

Maiara's heart flooded with rage as she looked upon the fairy. This was the demon responsible for the *wendigo*, the one she'd vowed to kill. Alexander's wings extended and his talons sprouted from his knuckles.

All that rage needed somewhere to go. Maiara raced to the block of knives on the kitchen counter, drew the largest one, and threw. There was a gasp as the sharp steel coasted over Avery's head, past Tobias's cheek and lodged in Aborella's gut. A buzzing had started in her head that sounded like a swarm of bees but could have been the voices of all those who had died by the fairy's hand, calling to her from the Land of Lost Souls.

The block was in her hands. She hurled one blade after another, her limbs moving at a speed she'd never thought possible. Each landed in the fairy, who cursed and flailed, backing toward the edge. But when the block was empty and Maiara cast it aside, the fairy stood taller and pulled the largest one from her bleeding purple gut.

"You know better." Aborella launched the knife back at Maiara, who ducked, only to see the blade dissolve in the wards at the cave entrance.

"Steel can't hurt her," Alexander said.

"What can?"

"Holy Hades. She's found us." Gabriel arrived behind them, still rubbing the sleep from his eyes.

"My head!" Avery pressed the heels of her palms against her temples. Raven emerged from the second bedroom with the egg in her arms and whispered to Tobias, who was desperately trying to soothe her sister.

"What kills fairies?" Maiara asked louder.

Gabriel answered in a whisper. "The books say iron, but I have never tested the theory."

"Careful, brother," Alexander murmured. "She can't see us or reach us, but she can hear us."

Maiara searched the cave for something—anything—made of iron. Her eyes fell on the fireplace poker. Was it iron? It looked as if it was.

Avery's screams echoed through the cave.

"Tobias, what's wrong with her?" Raven asked.

"She's crushing me. She's hurting me!" Blood fell in fat drops from her nose and splattered on the stone.

"Tobias?" Raven asked.

"I don't know," Tobias said. "This isn't medical, it's—"

"Please, oh God, please make it stop," Avery begged. Blood was flowing from her ears now.

Maiara placed her hands on Avery's head and reached out with her *Midew* powers. "This is dark magic."

Gabriel stepped to the barrier and positioned himself across from Aborella. "Release her, or I will tear your heart from your chest, you filthy, scum-sucking *insect*."

Aborella's wings flapped as rapidly as a hummingbird's, and she rose until she was hovering above him. "Invite me inside and we can talk about it."

"The only invitation you'll get from me is to hell, you evil parasite."

"Oh, Gabriel, you always did have a way of buttering me up with your sweet words. How I've missed our witty banter. But save your breath. When I return you to your mother's side, you'll need it."

Avery fell forward onto her belly, howling in a pool of her own blood.

"The mind is a terrible thing to waste, don't you think?" Aborella seethed. "If you don't give me what I want, my curse will crush Avery's skull. You know I can do it." She landed and paced outside the barrier. "Invite me in or prepare to watch her head explode."

Avery screamed again and kept screaming, drawing everyone's attention to her. Everyone but Maiara, whose gaze stayed locked on Aborella. The fairy stared straight at Avery, despite the barrier. She wasn't blinking.

Maiara could stand no more. She drew the poker from the rack as if it were a sword. With a warrior's cry, she bolted toward the mouth of the cave, sprang off Alexander's chair, and launched herself into the air and through the wards. Shock filled Aborella's eyes as Maiara descended from above and drove the iron straight through the fairy's heart. Both of them toppled over the side of the cliff.

PEOPLE OFTEN SAID THEIR LIFE FLASHED BEFORE THEIR eyes in extreme circumstances. For Raven, nothing flashed. On the contrary, time seemed to slow and show her the world in a series of snapshots.

Maiara leaped into the air in a feat of athleticism that shocked Raven, passed through the magical wards, and landed a blow to Aborella's heart with an iron poker that Raven hadn't even realized the healer was holding.

Aborella shuffled backward under the weight of the tiny but fierce woman who drove the iron through up to her fists. Raven cried out in horror as both Maiara and Aborella toppled over the side of the cliff.

Before Raven could even think of a levitation spell, Alexander was over the edge, folding his wings and diving out of sight. She held her breath. Seconds ticked by. And then a cheer broke her lips when Alexander shot into the sky with Maiara, bloody iron still gripped in her clutches, in his arms.

Avery started coughing like she had something caught in her throat. "Avery?" Raven searched her brain for a spell that would counter the curse, but without knowing specifically which curse Aborella had used, she wasn't sure how to help her sister.

With a gut-wrenching heave, a spark flew from Avery's mouth.

"Raven!" Tobias exclaimed.

"*Excindo!*" Raven stomped on it. The spark dissipated into dust. She placed a hand on Avery's shoulder. "Are you okay?"

Avery's terrified gaze met hers. The bleeding had abated, but her eyes were wild. "The pain is gone." She stared at her bloody hands. "Oh God, Raven, what's happening?"

Tobias glared at Gabriel. "Are you ready to finish this?"

Gabriel's lips peeled back from his teeth. "Now while she's weak."

Raven stepped toward Gabriel, cradling the egg. "Don't you dare do anything stupid. Your wife and your baby need you."

"I wouldn't think of it." Gabriel placed a kiss upon her forehead. The two men stripped as they spoke, scales already shingling up their arms.

"If something happens to me, tell Sabrina I love her," Tobias said.

Raven prayed to every god she'd ever believed in that she wouldn't need to make that call.

The wet crack of bones accompanied a brief, deep slurping like drawing slime through a straw and then the snap of an overstretched rubber band. Gabriel's black dragon, tinged in green with a vicious-looking barb on his tail followed Tobias's silver-blue one out the mouth of the cave.

"Be careful," Raven pleaded. A moment later they'd joined Maiara and Alexander in the fray.

Beyond the wards, the three dragons tumbled through the air with Aborella in a flurry of talons, wings, and crackling magic. The iron hadn't slowed her down. Black lightning flew from Aborella's hand and knocked Tobias out of the sky. Raven frowned. Aborella was too strong. Too powerful.

Turning back toward Avery, Raven shook her sister by her shoulder. Avery's terrified, tear-filled gaze locked on hers. "Listen to me. I promise you that after this is over, you can crumble. You can cry all day, eat ice cream until you puke, and watch Netflix until your eyes bleed. But right now I need to see the Avery Tanglewood who was strong enough to stare into the face of my cancer and still show up every day. I need the Avery who kept Mom alive when Dad left her."

Avery stopped crying. It was like she'd flipped a switch. Her blue eyes turned cold and hard as ice. Her voice was even when she said, "What do you need me to do?"

"I'm going to need you to babysit."

# CHAPTER FORTY

C rossing to the fireplace, Raven heaped wood inside in the shape of a cradle and placed the egg within it. With a snap of her fingers and a whispered incantation, she ignited the logs. Flames enveloped her precious child, and she watched the shell glow bright within its heat.

"What do you want me to do?" Avery had washed the blood from her face and looked ready for anything.

Raven kissed her on the cheek. "Keep the fire burning. And..." She handed her the phone from her pocket. "Gabriel's sister's name is Rowan Valor. If I'm not back in twenty minutes, call her and tell her we need her help."

She nodded. "I love you, Raven. Whatever you're going to do, please be careful."

Raven pulled her into a hug. "I will."

She left her sister's side and walked through the wards to the lip of the cave. Below her was a scene that didn't look real. Aborella's dark purple form stood among the desert brush, looking like a flower among the red soil and green foliage. Her fingers crackled with dark energy. She didn't have a weapon. She didn't need one.

Two dragons circled above her. The emerald heart of Gabriel blazed across the sky from Tobias's sapphire one. They'd become a yin and yang, spiraling dark and light, the fire in their lungs building. On the ground, Alexander, turquoise with scales lined in bronze, prowled toward her, Maiara straddling his back with the fireplace iron in her fist. The two were closing in.

One of Aborella's purple hands weaseled into a bag on her hip and removed a glowing blue marble. Another orb, slightly bigger than the one that had been around her sister's neck. A Paragonian grenade! Raven had intimate experience with the weapon. Scoria had used one on her in Chicago. If Aborella cracked it open, the magic inside would cripple the nervous system of anything it touched. All their muscles would seize until they couldn't even draw breath.

"Not on my watch," she whispered. Calling on a spell she'd absorbed in New Orleans, she spread her arms wide and recited the incantation. *"Turbinis vasti scorpum compriment. Turbinis vasti scorpium compriment."* The words tumbled from her lips in rapid succession.

The clicking came from far and wide, winds sweeping toward her, carrying hundreds of scorpions to the base of the mesa. Bringing her hands together quickly, she gathered them all into a whirlwind of death, her arms shaking from the effort. Forming a triangle with her thumb and forefingers, she made sure the tornado had the size and strength to reach her target. Thrusting forward with all the physical and mental strength she could muster, she pushed the spell toward Aborella.

The dusty cyclone sped across the desert and rammed into Aborella just as she attempted to drop the grenade. But the orb was caught by the wind as the scorpions attacked. The fairy howled and swatted as hundreds of claws and stingers dug into her flesh.

Raven twisted her shoulders and teleported to the scene below just as the whirlwind died. She caught the grenade in her hand before it could reach the ground. Aborella seethed, tearing the scorpions off her flesh and crushing them in her fists.

"You fucking witch. I'll fry you until your eyes pop out of your skull." Aborella raised her hands and blasted black lightning from her fingers.

"*Cogitatio!*" Raven crossed her arms before the lightning hit her, the reflection spell forming a shield around her body. Raven smelled the ends of her hair burning as it blew beyond the shield's boundaries, but it worked. Aborella flew back as her own lightning plowed into her.

Panting, Raven dropped the shield. Gabriel landed behind her, Tobias to her right. Alexander closed in. The great turquoise dragon snapped and tore Aborella in two, throwing her head and arms in one direction with the flick of his massive head and letting her legs fall where she'd stood, her purple blood soaking into the earth.

Maiara raised the bloody iron poker into the air and whooped a warrior's howl that seemed too loud and deep to come from her small-statured frame. But Alexander's dragon began to cough, then spit bursts of fire, then trembled from head to tail.

"Maiara, get down. There's something wrong." Raven gestured to her. The dark-haired woman leaped from her seat, landing in a squat.

Alexander's dragon heaved once more. Purple poison sprayed between his razor-sharp teeth while his body seized and shook. The two women watched in horror as he transformed into his human form and curled on his side, shivering.

"Alexander!" Maiara rushed to him. "He's sick. Her blood is poison. Help me move him."

Raven took his legs and helped Maiara carry him to the base of a nearby tree, away from the blood. "Do you have your amulet?"

"Always. It is the *Midew* way." She pulled it from a pouch at her waist and put it around Alexander's neck.

Raven turned back toward Aborella and the two dragons who were watching the fairy's remains warily. She didn't blame them for being cautious. After seeing what Aborella's blood had done to Alexander, she didn't want Gabriel anywhere near it.

Like something out of her worst nightmares, Aborella's head rose off the stone, and her arms and wings moved. Raven's stomach clenched. The land around Aborella was dying. Every plant turned brown and curled in on itself. Even the nearby trees and bushes succumbed to the blight. It spread like a dark brown plague from her remains outward. She was draining the life, feeding herself. Raven's stomach turned. It looked like... yes, her legs were moving toward her torso, as did the purple innards Alexander had purged.

"She's pulling herself back together," Raven said. "She's draining the life around her and using the power to heal herself. I have to stop her."

"Why don't they burn her?" Maiara asked, her eyes darting toward the dragons.

Alexander's eyes fluttered. "She's immune to dragon fire. A gift from my mother."

Raven frowned. "I have to drain her. I did it before

when I was in Paragon. If I can touch her, she can be killed."

"Hurry," Maiara said. "Before she becomes whole again."

Raven agreed. With a twist of her shoulders, she teleported to Aborella's side. The fairy's legs had reached her torso, and purple ribbons of magic were winding between the two halves, rejoining them. Raven reached out and grabbed Aborella's upper arm, feeling her fruity magic absorb through her fingers. Her purple skin faded to lavender.

"You should know, witch, to never underestimate a full-grown fairy." Aborella had used her free hand to reach into her bag and produce a glowing blue disk. Gabriel roared from behind her, and Raven reached for the weapon whose function she did not know. But it was too late. Aborella hurled the disk to the ground between her, Gabriel, and Tobias.

A net of purple lightning wrapped around them, and the world started to spin. Raven felt her reality rip like a delicate piece of tissue paper. She was a marble tipped from a cup.

The next moment, her legs collapsed and her elbows slapped a polished obsidian floor. All the wind squeezed from her lungs. She drew air in tiny sips and had to fight to lift her head. Gabriel was there. He blinked rapidly in the dim light, then crawled to her. Together, they helped each other up. A polished black floor. Roughhewn walls. Aborella was gone. Where the hell were they?

"Fucking fairy," a voice rasped behind her.

"Tobias!" Raven ran to him. He was in his human form as well. Together, she and Gabriel helped him to his feet.

"Are we where I think we are?" Tobias asked.

Raven took a good look around. There was only one door and it was barred.

Gabriel placed his hands gently on her shoulders. "We're in the dungeons of Paragon."

# CHAPTER FORTY-ONE

It took all her will and power for Maiara to drag Alexander out of the tree. He was naked from shifting, as was she—her clothing was shredded from entering the tree without undressing—and the sun beat down upon their exposed skin. Underneath her, the rocks dug into her knees as she gathered his head in her lap.

When she'd watched Aborella pull the disk from her pocket, she felt like she was in the woods again, running from the *wendigo*, her hand in her father's. The function of the object was a mystery to her, but Aborella's nature wasn't. The fairy was evil and the disk had to be dangerous. She saw her escape, but this time she refused to leave the one she loved behind. Despite the promise she'd made to Alexander the night before, she wasn't willing to live without him.

It had been centuries since she'd used her magic and even then, she'd had more consistent results with oak trees than any other type. But her power had grown since then. She'd felt it inside her, swelling like a frog's throat. She'd prayed to the Great Spirit, wrapped her arms around

Alexander, and willed them both into the trunk of the strange desert tree beside them.

Getting him inside the bark with her was only the beginning. She'd held him there as long as she dared, as the strange purple net captured his siblings and fell ineffectually around them. Could he breathe through the branches the way she could? By the gasping breaths he took now, she assumed she'd been right not to wait a moment longer before coming out.

"They are gone," she said. "Aborella took them."

Alexander clambered onto his knees, still drawing deep breaths into his lungs. "We were inside the tree?"

"Yes. I hid you."

He cradled her face and landed a kiss on her lips. "By the Mountain, Maiara, you are the bravest woman I've ever known." She took the compliment with a soft smile and a raised chin. "Did you see what happened to my brothers and Raven?"

She explained about the device Aborella had used.

"That's a Paragonian *immurcador*. It's like a net of pure energy." He cursed. Overhead, he saw Rowan fly by with Nick in her arms and land on the lip of the cave. "Someone called my sister. Good, we're going to need her." He stood and held his hand out to her. Maiara allowed him to sweep her into his arms.

ROWAN WAITED WITH NICK OUTSIDE THE BARRIER, HER heart racing. "Oh, thank the goddess! Alexander, Maiara, what's going on? Where's Raven? She texted that it was an emergency."

"Come inside and we'll explain." Alexander waved his

hand and let her through the ward where Avery was waiting for them, Raven's phone in her hand.

"*I* texted you," Avery said. Rowan hadn't seen the woman since Raven's wedding, but there was no forgetting Raven's sister. They looked remarkably alike. "Raven told me to. I didn't know what else to do." She stared out at the place where Aborella and her sister had once been as if she could will them back there.

Rowan watched Alexander sweep Maiara into his room, noticing they were both naked. Alexander's lack of dress, she could explain. Maiara's was a mystery. Beside her, Nick looked as agitated as she felt.

She focused on Avery. "Tell me what happened to my brothers and Raven."

"They're gone. That purple... fairy thing used some sort of disk. There was a... net of magic." Avery shook her head. "One second they were there, the next they were gone."

"Fuck. Fuck. Fuck!" Rowan grabbed her head. "That's an *immurcador*. She's got them. They're probably in the dungeons of Paragon by now."

Avery's face paled to the point it was almost gray.

"Avery, I think you should sit down." Rowan helped her to the couch. "I know this is a lot, but stay strong. We'll figure out what to do." She had no idea what they would do, but she didn't need the added trouble of Avery hitting her head when she passed out.

"It's just..." Avery rubbed her palms on her thighs, her gaze locked on the fireplace.

Slowly Rowan turned her head. There, nestled among the logs, a dragon egg glowed and pulsed within the flames.

"Is that Raven's?" Rowan's voice held a note of panic. Maiara and Alexander, now dressed, arrived by her side and stared into the fireplace, similarly horrified.

"Yes. That's my niece or nephew." Avery blew out a heavy breath. "In a shell... in the flames. She told me to keep the fire going."

"Fuck." Rowan's knees gave out and she landed on the sofa on the other side of Avery.

"Fuck," Avery repeated.

"What does this word *fuck* mean?" Maiara asked. She and Alexander seemed to be holding each other up.

"It means this is terrible," Rowan explained. "We're in an unpleasant situation where life has wronged us."

Maiara nodded. "Fuck."

"Rowan, what do we do?" Alexander asked, slumping in the chair next to the fire and pulling Maiara into his lap.

"Why are you asking me?" Rowan snapped. "I don't know anything about dragon eggs!"

"You're a girl and you were going to be queen," Alexander protested. "Didn't anyone teach you anything about raising whelps?"

Rowan rolled her eyes. Typical male. "Yes." She tapped her foot in annoyance.

"Well?"

"All we need to do is find a volcano and leave the egg at its heart, and it will hatch in six months," she said, layering on the sarcasm. "Oh wait, that doesn't apply to this situation at all because this thing is half witch and we don't have a volcano!" Rowan crossed her arms over her chest and glared at him. "There. That's the extent of my knowledge."

"How are we supposed to care for that thing until we find Raven and the others?" Avery's voice rose in pitch, infused with panic and anxiety. "I told her I'd keep the fire going while she helped fight the battle. I didn't know she wouldn't be coming back."

"Fuck!" Maiara said again.

Alexander raised an eyebrow at his mate.

"Did I use it incorrectly?"

He shook his head. "Oh no. This is exactly the type of situation that warrants that particular word." His eyes drifted back toward the pearl among the flames.

"How do we get them back?" Avery asked. "Is there even a way to go to Paragon?"

Rowan's mouth worked uselessly until she found her voice. "Technically, yes. Either Alexander or I can open a portal using our rings. But..."

"But what?" Avery spread her hands, completely exasperated. "We need to get my sister back so she can be with her baby."

Alexander shook his head. "It would be a suicide mission. Aborella works for the empress. The palace is protected by an army of dragons. It would take more power than all of us have together to get them out, even under perfect circumstances."

"Then what do we do? We can't just leave them there. From what Gabriel told me, they would be political prisoners. Will they be tortured? Killed? What about the egg?" Avery leaned forward and rested her head in her hands.

"It doesn't help if we're all killed too," Rowan said softly. "Action is needed, certainly, but we have to be smart about it."

Tears gathered in Avery's eyes. "I feel like this is my fault. Aborella used me to get to you."

Rowan rubbed Avery's back with her hand. "Aborella has worked for our mother for centuries. She's an extremely powerful and wicked fairy. Believe me, there was nothing you could do."

Nick massaged Rowan's shoulders from behind the

couch. "As the other human here, I concur. You can't blame yourself, Avery."

"Guilt isn't going to bring our family back," Alexander said.

Nick's hands paused on her shoulders. "No. It won't. Only one thing will."

Rowan turned her head to look at him. "Nick?"

"An army. We need an army. When I wanted you back from the vampires, Rowan, I found your brothers, and they helped me bust you out. I'm going out on a limb here and saying that the way to get Gabriel, Raven, and Tobias home is to find your other siblings. They know the palace, just like you do. If we work together—"

"We haven't seen them in hundreds of years, Nick. I wouldn't even know where to start looking." Rowan threw up her hands.

Alexander agreed. "Not a clue where they could be."

Nick squinted at Rowan. "What if we use Harriet?"

"Who's Harriet?" Avery asked.

"My best friend," said Rowan. "She's psychic, but her powers do have limitations." Still, Rowan was sure Harriet could help them, perhaps not with an exact location, but she could get them close.

Nick tipped his head. "She's done a bang-up job finding things in the past, and Tobias's mate Sabrina seems awful good at making things happen. If all else fails, you're mated to a detective." He winked at Rowan over a crooked grin. "I have resources. If Harriet and Sabrina get us close, given a description, I might be able to track them down."

Alexander rubbed his hands together. "It could work."

Rowan sighed. "Before we go any further, we need to tell Sabrina what's going on. She deserves to know her mate has been kidnapped."

Avery blinked. "Can you also ask her if she knows what to do with that?" She pointed back at the fireplace.

The room plunged into silence. Rowan frowned. She'd almost forgotten about the egg as they'd discussed their plans to get Raven back. "It needs to stay hot," she said. "Someone needs to make sure it stays hot."

Everyone in the room stared at her. She stood from the couch and approached the fire. Squatting down, she watched the pulsing blue beat of the baby's heart. "Gabriel, you are so going to owe me for this until the day you die."

The silhouette shifted, and a tiny hand pressed against the inside of the shell. She could see it clearly through the smooth ribbon of white that wrapped around the otherwise bumpy exterior. Five fingers like a human hand. A living hand.

Nick appeared beside her. "Just until we can get Raven and Gabriel back, right? How hard could it be?"

She looked up at him and shrugged. "I have no idea."

She reached into the flames to get a better look, but she'd barely gathered the young one into her arms before purple lightning sparked across the shell. "Ah!" The shock ran through her, and the egg flew from her hands despite her best efforts.

Avery dove forward, catching the giant pearl an inch from the floor.

Maiara stood. "That happened before, when we delivered the egg. Tobias said it was the witch blood. Only Raven was able to touch it."

Rowan stared at Avery, who was having no problem handling her sister's young.

"Gabriel was right, the shell is cool to the touch, despite being in the flames." The wonder in her voice was palpable.

"Completely fireproof," Rowan said. "It won't retain the heat. That's why you have to keep it warm."

Avery smiled at the egg, cradling it gently in her arms. "I must look enough like Raven. Or maybe it's because we share the same blood. This little guy isn't afraid of me." She placed her hand over the silhouette of fingers inside the shell. "I'm your Aunt Avery. I'm going to take care of you."

Rowan threaded her fingers with Nick's and moved closer. "Avery?"

Avery lifted her face and smiled. "I'll do it. I'll care for my niece or nephew. I owe it to my sister. I promised her."

No one uttered a single word of protest.

# CHAPTER FORTY-TWO

"A private jet. By the Mountain, being head of a vampire coven does have its advantages." Alexander climbed the stairs and boarded the shiny black Cessna behind Maiara. Rowan, Nick, and Avery were already on board.

"It's a loaner," Rowan said, slamming the door on an overhead bin. "Sabrina said the owner owed her a favor."

"Who's the owner?" Alexander helped Maiara find a place for her bag and showed her how to buckle in. He could tell she was nervous. It was her first time on an airplane, and if there was one thing she wasn't comfortable with yet about 2018, it was the technology.

"She told me it was better if I didn't know." Rowan shrugged.

Alexander moved past Avery, who was carefully stowing the egg under her seat. The portable incubator that housed her niece or nephew was Nick's brainchild. He'd read about an inventor who had patented one to use in third-world countries and created his own version. It was basically a dog crate lined with an electric blanket and powered by a battery pack.

"Hey, it fits," Nick said from his seat beside Rowan.

"Simple but ingenious," she said.

Alexander turned his full attention on his mate. Maiara shifted in her seat beside him and tightened her seat belt.

"You say we will fly in this?"

He threaded his fingers into hers. "People do it all the time now. You must have seen airplanes before while you were inside Nikan."

"From a distance."

"But you saw them fly, so you know it's possible." Alexander kissed her temple. "I wouldn't think someone who had lived as a bird would be afraid to fly."

Maiara's brow furrowed. "It's different when they are your own wings."

"Now you'll have to trust in mine." Alexander gestured toward his back and the wings she knew were there. He'd never let her fall, and in her heart he was sure she realized that.

Still, she squinted skeptically out the window at the wing.

"So, where exactly are we off to?" Avery asked.

Rowan answered. "Oxford. There's a professor of history there who specializes in myth and folklore and agreed to assess a seventeenth-century manuscript my gallery recently acquired. It seems he has a special interest in dragons. Harriet thought he'd be a good place to start."

"As good as any," Maiara said. Her palm was sweaty inside his own.

"You know," Alexander said to her, "you dove off a cliff with a homicidal fairy and didn't even blink."

"Yes. That is true."

"But this scares you."

"It is very heavy, and I don't understand how the wings work." The corners of her mouth sagged.

He was distracted when the pilot, a sophisticated woman in a blue uniform, exited the cockpit, raised the stairs, and sealed the door. She wore her dark hair coiled at the back of her head, and she faced away from them, but Alexander thought there was something acutely familiar about her. He couldn't quite place where he'd seen her before, and he narrowed his eyes, willing her to turn around.

Finally his wish was granted. She finished with the stairs and approached them, a bright, practiced smile spreading her lips. Alexander started. She was stunning, with skin that seemed lit from within and eyes the color of molten gold. Those had to be contacts. No one had eyes that color. It was like looking into the face of the sun itself. Alexander darted a glance at Rowan, who widened her eyes and shrugged.

"You'll have to excuse the lack of service on this flight. Your host made it clear that the confidentiality of your travels requires we limit your crew to pilot and copilot. Please help yourself to the snacks and drinks at the back of the plane if you need anything," the pilot said, then turned and looked directly at Avery.

Alexander's breath hitched. That was where he'd seen her before. Aside from the gold eyes and the general glow, the pilot resembled Raven and Avery. Not exactly, but in the way of a distant relative. "Do you need anything?"

Avery swallowed. "No. I'm fine."

"Very well. I'm Captain Dawn. We should have you in London in approximately twelve hours with one stop to refuel along the way."

She turned toward Maiara, who was still gripping Alexander's hand for dear life.

"I promise you," Captain Dawn said. "You are in good hands. I'll take you exactly where you need to be."

The pilot turned and retreated to the cockpit. The engine roared to life.

Moments later, the plane barreled down the runway and lifted into the star-filled Arizona sky. Once the plane leveled out, Maiara's grip loosened. "Better?" Alexander asked.

She raised her chin. "The pilot lied."

"About what?"

"She said she would take me where I need to be. I am already where I need to be." Maiara kissed him tenderly and leaned her head against his shoulder.

He wrapped an arm around her, beyond grateful for whatever life would bring now that they were together. "I couldn't agree more."

I HOPE YOU'VE ENJOYED THE DRAGON OF SEDONA. While Raven, Gabriel, and Tobias remain imprisoned in Paragon, the others are on their way to London to look for their missing siblings. Only Nathaniel doesn't want to be found, not by them or his ex-lover, an American pop star named Clarissa who needs his help solving a sudden problem with her voice. Order THE DRAGON OF CECIL COURT now, or turn the page to read a free excerpt!

# SNEAK PEEK OF THE DRAGON OF CECIL COURT

## THE TREASURE OF PARAGON BOOK 5

**Old flames still burn hot.**

*He's only ever had one weakness.*

Nathaniel Clarke has a secret. Before he became the owner of an occult bookshop on Bookseller's Row, he was a prince of the kingdom of Paragon. Now the dragon shifter is the high priest of the Order of the Dragon, a society of the most powerful supernatural beings in London. He's only ever had one weakness, and he hasn't seen her in a decade.

*She's only ever been good at one thing.*

American pop singer Clarissa Black survived by singing on street corners before Nathaniel came into her life and unlocked the latent magic inside her. Despite their passionate affair, she refused Nathaniel's proposal to pursue her music career. Her multi-platinum albums have made her a star but one with few people she can trust.

*It only takes one spark to change two lives forever.*

When Clarissa's voice fails her during a show in London, it's an excuse to reconnect with the man who remains her deepest regret. Nathaniel is reluctant to open old wounds but can't refuse Clarissa's plea for help or the passion her nearness awakens in him. But as he closes in on breaking the curse, Nathaniel learns the cause of what ails her is tangled with the deadly past he left behind.

# THE
# DRAGON
## OF
# CECIL COURT

THE TREASURE OF PARAGON BOOK 5

USA TODAY BESTSELLING AUTHOR
# GENEVIEVE JACK

# THE DRAGON OF CECIL COURT

## London

Nathaniel Clarke lingered outside Relics and Runes occult bookstore, his pipe nestled in his palm. Not so long ago, he'd have fired the Turkish tobacco, loosely tamped within its bent rosewood bowl, in the comfort of his office, but smoking indoors was illegal these days in London. Bad for humans. He supposed when your lifespan was a mere hundred years or less, cutting it short by a decade or more for the sake of a smoke was reckless.

As an immortal dragon, Nathaniel couldn't get cancer or any other human disease, and considering he could breathe fire, a little smoke was completely harmless to his composition. Humans, however, were important to Nathaniel, making up the majority of the occult book market. Plus he enjoyed the company of a few of them. He'd prefer to keep them alive.

No matter—it was early and Cecil Court had yet to suffer the tread of visitors' footsteps, which gave him an opportunity to both enjoy his favorite smoke and make use of the enchanting properties of this particular tobacco blend. Specially developed by a friend—a warlock and master tobacconist—the heady smoke served a number of purposes. For one, it alerted him of imminent danger. This morning though, his use for it was far more mundane, to render his storefront irresistible to shoppers.

He flipped the top of his butane lighter and circled the flame over the tobacco, then let it burn out. A good false light. Ah yes, the scent was heavenly. He lit it again and took a ceremonious puff. The thick smoke curled along his tongue before he blew it out in a perfect, cloudlike ring that floated toward the summer sky.

"Honestly, Clarke, are you still flushing good money away on that dreadful habit?" Mr. Greene, owner of the neighboring bookshop, appeared beside him, broom in hand, and raised his bushy gray eyebrows. He stared pointedly at Nathaniel's pipe. "You're going to blow an artery if you keep that up."

"Not everyone can be the picture of health as you are, Greene." Nathaniel pointed a knuckle at the man and winked. "I'm of the mind to enjoy what years I have with a good smoke."

"Because you're a young chap. Wait until you're old like me and regret comes to roost." He straightened his sweater vest over his overlarge paunch.

"I daresay, I predict you'll outlive us all."

The elderly man chuckled. "From your lips to God's ears." He gave his doorstep a few half-hearted sweeps. "Speaking of regrets of the past and all that, have you heard the news this morning?"

"I haven't had the pleasure." Nathaniel puffed his pipe and blew a smoke ring over Greene's head. Actually, he took no pleasure in current events. The world was in a constant state of wearying political angst. After three hundred years, he'd seen empires rise and fall. It didn't matter to him which blowhard was in office or who was seen hobnobbing with whom. Nathaniel existed above it all. And if he didn't like something, all he had to do was wait. Everything ended eventually, aside from him.

Greene wagged his finger. "Oh dear. I would have thought you'd be the first to know."

"Hmm? What's that?" He sent a tiny smoke ring through the center of a bigger one. The enchantment was taking hold. Already the brass around his door appeared shinier and the red paint that coated its wood gleamed as if he'd painted it yesterday.

"That fling of yours from a few years ago, the songbird from the States. You know, the pretty one."

Nathaniel released his smoke in an uncontrolled and unattractive exhale. "You don't mean..."

"The fish that got away, Clarke. You know the one. The woman. Ahh, I've lost my head." Greene tapped the heel of his palm against his temple. "Can't think of it. Something... Clarissa! That's it."

"Clarissa is in London?" An uninvited tingle radiated from the back of Nathaniel's neck, down his arms, and made his hands go numb. For the love of the Mountain, he did not need to hear Clarissa was in town today.

"She is! But that's not why everyone's talking about her. It seems she was performing for a corporate audience, the people who make those home gadgets. Tanaka Corp. Anyhow, her voice gave out completely in the middle of her performance. She had to be escorted from the stage. The Tanaka people were royally cheesed off over it. And, well, there are all sorts of rumors now going round about why.

GENEVIEVE JACK

Drugs or whatnot. People are suggesting she might have to cancel her concert at the O2 later this month."

"Hmm." Nathaniel ground his teeth. Clarissa was a witch, a powerful one, and if her voice had given out, there was a dark reason for it. He stared down into his pipe. Today might be a good day to close up shop and take a holiday. Bora-Bora sounded like a nice diversion.

"So you hadn't heard. You two don't keep in touch then?"

Nathaniel sighed. "No. It was a fleeting affair. She has her career, and I have..." He gestured vaguely in the direction of Relics and Runes.

"Righto! Dodged a bullet, I'd say. Bad luck to have a woman that beautiful, if you don't mind my saying so. My Minerva, rest her soul, wasn't a looker, but boy could she cook. That's the type of woman you can rely on. Good cook. Loyal soul."

"If only there were more Minervas out there." Nathaniel pictured the heavyset woman with wild gray hair who'd passed away a few years ago and carefully kept his expression reverential.

"God broke the mold when he made her." Greene wiped a tear from his eye and glanced at his watch. "Is that the time? Oh dear. We'll be opening soon. I'd better ready the shop. Good day, Clarke."

"Good day." Returning the man's little wave, Nathaniel watched him disappear inside his shop, then leaned against the doorframe and closed his eyes. So Clarissa was in town. It didn't mean anything. And her voice giving out could have a number of causes, perhaps a virus of the throat or a nodule on the vocal cords. She was probably visiting a doctor even now. With any luck, she'd be on a plane back to America in no time.

He opened his eyes. Bringing his pipe to his lips, he allowed the thick smoke to linger on his tongue before slowly and deliberately blowing a perfect ring... that morphed into a crimson heart as it floated toward the clear blue sky.

"Fuck."

He whirled and fumbled with the door, setting his pipe on the counter and mumbling incoherently as he passed the books on witchcraft, Jungian theory, the tarot cards, the crystals, the grimoires and the yoga magazines, to the small greenhouse of magical herbs at the back. He plucked two potted rosemary plants from the sill and hurried back to place them on either side of the front door.

"Rosemary by the garden gate...," he mumbled. Where were his cards? He needed to read his cards.

The bell above the door rang.

"Jesus, Nathaniel, rosemary? It only protects you against those who would do you harm. When have I ever wanted to hurt you?"

Clarissa stepped across his threshold as if she'd been summoned by his earlier use of her name, like the devil or a demon. A real possibility now that he thought of it. Her blond hair was covered in a rose-colored scarf, and large dark glasses hid her blue eyes. But there was no mistaking her lithe figure and catlike grace. Or her scent. The floral and earthy notes of lilies and moss hit his nose.

She reached up and removed her glasses. "I think I'm being followed."

"Then you'd better be on your way. Where's your security?"

"Everyone wants to know what happened last night." Her gaze roved over his face. His suit. "You look exactly the same. I mean, I knew you didn't age, but my God. Is that the pocket square I bought you?"

"I hear footsteps in the alley. You should go before the paparazzi arrive."

She shuffled closer to him. "Hide me. Please!"

The door opened. Cursing his own stupidity, he curled her into his arms and cloaked both of them in invisibility. He pressed a finger to his lips, although she of all people knew to remain silent.

Two men entered the store, one tall and suave, the other looking like he'd slept on the floor of a pub the night before. Both had cameras ready. They swept through the rooms, searched behind the counter.

"I know she came in here. I saw her," the taller one said. He eyed the still-smoking pipe. "Hello?" he called. "Anyone here?"

The slovenly one squinted his eyes. "There's a lower level." The two jogged down the stairs to where Nathaniel shelved the books on fairies and druids among other things.

Nathaniel lowered his finger from his mouth, but not the invisibility that cloaked them both.

"You've got a lot of nerve coming back here after all this time," he whispered to her.

"I need your help." Her lips were red. He had a strong desire to smear her lipstick.

"No."

"Believe me, if I had any other choice, I would have made it. You're the only one who can help me."

"No." It was out of the question really. Not after how they'd left things.

The two men jogged back up the stairs, visibly baffled. "Gone. Just gone," the tall man said. "Into thin air."

"Are you sure it was her?"

Tall Man rubbed his chin. "Could've been a decoy, I suppose. It was odd she had no security."

"There's a back door," the short man said, pointing with his chin.

They rushed into the courtyard. Nathaniel waited until he could no longer hear their footsteps or their voices before he dropped the invisibility.

"Next time I'll let them find you." He dusted off his hands as if holding her had filthied them.

"That hurts, Nate. It really does. After all we've meant to each other."

"Ancient history."

"But a pleasant one. As pasts go, I'm happy with ours."

"Speak for yourself." He smoothed the sleeve of his jacket and moved behind the counter. Better. He'd prefer a lead wall between them, but the counter would have to do. "Enjoy the pleasant weather." He gestured toward the door.

"There's something wrong with my voice."

"See a doctor."

"It's not that type of problem," she whispered.

The bell above the door dinged and the first customer of the day strolled in. Nathaniel greeted the man, who beelined straight to the section on witchcraft.

He shrugged. "I don't know anything about vocal performance. But best of luck to you." He gestured toward the door again.

She took a deep breath and blew it out slowly, then approached the counter. "Please... Nathaniel... If you ever cared for me... If what we had ever meant anything to you... I need your help."

He narrowed his eyes on her. "You can do it yourself."

Slowly she shook her head. "No. I. Can't."

Realization dawned and he leaned forward to sniff her

throat. As usual, she smelled of lilies and moss, but the magical tang that always accompanied her scent was missing. Clarissa's magical Bunsen burner was on the fritz. Interesting. Not interesting enough for him to feed his heart into a meat grinder by allowing her back into his life, but interesting.

Still, it was impossible not to remember the good times what with her standing right in front of him. He met her gaze and held it.

"Nathaniel?" she pleaded.

"No," he said again. And he meant it.

THANK YOU FOR READING THIS EXCERPT OF THE DRAGON OF CECIL COURT. Pick up your copy wherever you buy books,

## MEET GENEVIEVE JACK

Award winning and USA Today bestselling author Genevieve Jack writes wild, witty, and wicked-hot paranormal romance and fantasy. Coffee and wine are her biofuel, the love lives of witches, shifters, and vampires her favorite topic of conversation. She harbors a passion for old cemeteries and ghost tours, thanks to her years attending a high school rumored to be haunted. Her perfect day involves a heavy dose of nature and one crazy dog. Learn more at GenevieveJack.com.

**Do you know Jack?** Keep in touch to stay in the know about new releases, sales, and giveaways.

Join my VIP reader group
Sign up for my newsletter

facebook.com/AuthorGenevieveJack

twitter.com/genevieve_jack

instagram.com/authorgenevievejack

bookbub.com/authors/genevieve-jack

# MORE FROM GENEVIEVE JACK!

## The Treasure of Paragon

The Dragon of New Orleans, Book 1

Windy City Dragon, Book 2,

Manhattan Dragon, Book 3

The Dragon of Sedona, Book 4

The Dragon of Cecil Court, Book 5

Highland Dragon, Book 6

Hidden Dragon, Book 7

The Dragons of Paragon, Book 8

The Last Dragon, Book 9

## The Three Sisters

The Tanglewood Witches

Tanglewood Magic

Tanglewood Legacy

## Knight Games Series

The Ghost and The Graveyard, Book 1

Kick the Candle, Book 2

Queen of the Hill, Book 3

Mother May I, Book 4

Logan, Book 5

# ACKNOWLEDGMENTS

The Dragon of Sedona was a challenging novel to write. There isn't a long history of romance novels that begin with the heroine already dead, and telling this story between past and present proved challenging from a research perspective as well as a plotting and pacing one. But the creative energy that I call my muse insisted that this was the way this story must be told. As hard as it was to write, I am happy with the results and want to thank a few people who helped me bring DOS to fruition.

This novel wouldn't be possible without the continued support of members of the High Tea Society and Heart & Scroll. You know who you are. Thank you for helping me bring this one into the world.

Also, thank you to Tina Winograd and Anne at Victory Editing for bringing out the best in this story, to Deranged Doctor for the cover art that perfectly captured Alexander, and finally, to my family for their love and encouragement.

To the fans of this series, thank you for reading my dragons to life.

Made in the USA
Middletown, DE
04 August 2021